DECKED, WRECKED AND PUCKED

LEA ROSE

Copyright © 2025 by Lea Rose

All rights reserved.

No portion of this book may be reproduced in any form without written permission from the publisher or author, except as permitted by U.S. copyright law.

The story, all names, characters, and incidents portrayed in this production are fictitious. No identification with actual persons (living or deceased), places, buildings, and products is intended or should be inferred.

No generative artificial intelligence (AI) was used in the creation of this work. The author explicitly prohibits the use of this publication, in whole or in part, for training or developing AI technologies, including but not limited to systems capable of producing text in the same style, voice, or genre as this book. All rights to license this work for AI training or machine learning purposes are expressly reserved by the author.

Editing by Steph White (Kat's literary Services)

Proofreading by Vanessa Esquibel (Kat's literary Services)

 Formatted with Vellum

PLAYLIST

Back To December - Taylor Swift
When I Dream Of You - Reed Wonder & Aurora Olivias
Lovely - Billie Eilish
Holly Jolly Christmas - Michael Bublé
Sight Of You - Tulisa
Back To Friends - Sombr
Sailor Song - Gigi Perez
White Christmas - Bing Crosby
The First Time - Damiano David
Chasing Cars - Tommee Profitt
Hurts So Good - Astrid S
We Can't Be Friends - Ariana Grande
Still Falling For You - Ellie Goulding
All I Want For Christmas Is You - Mariah Carey

INTRODUCTION

I was today years old when I learned the difference between spice and smut.
This is smut, my loves.
All-the-dicks-in-all-the-holes smut.
You're welcome.
Enjoy.
Love, Lea

If your only questions are who's coming next and how many mouths it takes, you're exactly where you belong.

Enjoy the filth. Stay for the love.

PROLOGUE
ROMAN

THEN

Lips drag across my throat, the rough, unfamiliar scrape of stubble leaving a trail of heat along my skin. There's nothing soft about the way they're touching me, nothing gentle. Just raw friction lighting me up in ways I've never let myself admit I wanted.

It makes me question everything.

Who the hell I am.

Why I shoved this part of myself so far down.

Why I never allowed myself to feel this before.

But Zeke and Jasper... they see me.

I don't even know how I ended up here.

I was out running in the storm, trying to shut my brain up, but somewhere between the first drop of rain and the third mile, I stopped lying to myself. I called bullshit on every excuse I'd been clinging to and found myself sprinting through the downpour straight to their door.

There I was, soaked to the skin, lungs burning, heart racing for reasons that had nothing to do with cardio and everything to do with *them*.

When Jasper opened the door barefoot and bare-chested, he didn't need to ask why I was there. He just knew.

He's been testing my boundaries since the day I found him and Zeke together, daring me to react to him, and Jesus, I wanted to. But I kept telling myself it was nothing. I forced myself to pretend I didn't feel the floor drop out beneath me every time we were out on the ice and they'd drift just a little closer.

Clearly, I failed spectacularly because now I'm here, pinned between them, being touched in ways I've never experienced before.

Zeke's hands are everywhere, mapping me like he's learning me by touch. His palms slide over my chest, lingering at my collarbone before drifting down my stomach and skimming the hard edge of muscle. Jasper's touch is bolder, more demanding, his hand already finding the waistband of my sweats.

"Is this okay, Captain?" Jasper murmurs against my jaw.

I nod, my breath catching in my throat.

"Roman, we need your words."

Instead of answering Zeke, I grip the back of his neck and slam our mouths together—tongues colliding and fighting for dominance—neither of us willing to give an inch.

"I think that's pretty clear, baby," Jasper says, sliding my sweatpants down over my hips.

I don't stop him. I strip my underwear right along with them, baring myself completely in front of another man for the first time outside a locker room.

Except this isn't just one man, it's two.

Two teammates.

Two friends.

Two people I never thought I'd want like this.

But fuck the rules.

Fuck the implications.

Fuck what's supposed to happen, or what comes after.

Because this pull has got its hands around my throat, and I don't ever want it to let go.

"I want both of you out of those clothes," I growl, feeling needy as hell.

Clothes hit the floor in a blur, and suddenly we're all naked—skin pressed to skin, cocks hard and leaking, bodies humming with what's about to happen. I'm already so close to the edge I could lose it before anything even starts.

The last time I felt like this was when I was with—*No. Can't go there. That door stays shut.*

I'm kissing Jasper while Zeke grinds our cocks together until I'm seeing stars.

"Holy shit," I groan, rutting against him, "Why does your dick feel so fucking good against mine?"

Zeke's lips graze my neck. "Because it's us. Because it's you. And fuck, I want to hear the sounds you make when you come for us."

"I wanna watch you pound Zeke's ass," Jasper pants into my mouth.

"What do you say, Rome? You wanna sink that thick cock in me?"

"Fuck me..." Jasper groans, falling back against the pillows while his hand works his length. "I'd give my right nut to watch that."

I've done this before with girls, never with guys. But ass is ass. Flesh and heat and the same tightness, no matter who it belongs to.

I know this should feel like a bigger step than it does, but it doesn't. Not with them. Not when the need to feel both of them wipes out every other thought until giving in is the only thing I can do.

"On your back," I order, and Zeke stretches out across the mattress.

Jasper leans in and kisses him, and I can't look away. The wet slide of their mouths and the whimpers they can't hold back—it all goes straight through me, making my mouth water and my pulse race.

Fuck, I want this.

I want them.

Before I can overthink it, I'm on Zeke, dragging my tongue along the thick vein running up his cock. I swallow him down, and the pure masculine taste of him is nothing like I expected but everything I've been craving. I wrap my fist around the base, stroking what I can't take while I suck hard around the head, hollowing my cheeks and letting him feel every bit of it.

"Fuck, Rome," Zeke groans, his hips bucking up.

Okay. He's into it. Good to know.

"Show me what else he likes," I rasp as I release him and look over at Jasper. He just grins, and the two of us settle between Zeke's thighs like we've done this a hundred times before.

Jasper grabs the back of my neck and pulls me into a kiss, groaning the second he tastes Zeke on my tongue.

That's when it really hits me—not all at once, but slowly, in the unhurried stroke of Jasper's tongue against mine.

The trust.

The heat.

The fucking rightness of it.

When he finally pulls back, he reaches for the lube and squeezes it over his fingers, handing it to me without a word. I follow his lead, hands a little shaky as I slick my fingers and trail them down between Zeke's cheeks. When Jasper sinks the first finger in, Zeke moans, rolling his hips up to meet him.

"Fuck yes. Give me more."

I press a finger in alongside Jasper's, our knuckles brushing as we scissor him open together.

"Get inside me, Roman," Zeke begs, breathless, his head thrown back as a sheen of sweat coats his chest.

I freeze, my heart pounding in my throat. "Please tell me you've got condoms. I'm pretty sure my dick will never forgive either of you if you don't."

"We don't fuck around," Jasper says, and suddenly his hand is under my jaw, tilting my face until I have no choice but to meet his molten-brown eyes. "It's just us. If you're good, we're good."

"I'm good."

Jasper's grin curls across his lips as he leans in, his breath warm against my mouth. "I can't wait to watch you lose control, Captain."

I slip a hand beneath Zeke's thigh, lifting and spreading him wide, exposing every inch of him as I line my cock up at his entrance. I press in slow, inch by inch, until I'm buried to the hilt, hips flush against his ass, my cock throbbing inside him.

"Holy shit," I gasp, my head falling forward. "I can't believe I'm inside you."

Zeke's eyes find mine, his pupils blown wide. "You feel so good... but I need you to move, baby."

Baby.

That word does something to me that I know I'm not coming back from.

I start to thrust, slow at first, because I need to see this. I need to hear every sound he makes and burn this memory into my brain.

"I swear to God, this is the hottest fucking thing I've ever seen—you two like this," Jasper groans from where he's sprawled beside Zeke on the bed.

"Fuck, you feel unreal." My fingers dig into Zeke's hips as I drive in deeper. "So damn tight."

The control I thought I had is slipping fast, sliding into something desperate as I start pounding harder, faster, chasing the sensation of his body squeezing the hell out of me.

"Get over here," Zeke growls, and Jasper straddles his chest so he's facing me.

Zeke spits on his fingers and slowly pushes inside Jasper, and the sight nearly finishes me.

"Jesus Christ, I'm close," I pant, hips thrusting harder, faster.

Zeke arches beneath us, every muscle gone tight, shuddering as he comes without a single hand on him—just me and the relentless way I'm fucking him. His ass clamps down around my cock, squeezing so hard it's like he's ripping my orgasm out of me, taking everything I have and then some.

"Fuck—fuck, fuck," I roar, my body snapping tight as I come, emptying myself inside him until I'm shaking with it.

Jasper follows, cursing as he spills all over Zeke's stomach.

The sudden intrusive thought hits me like a brick:

I want to taste it.

All of it.

Them.

Me.

I don't care.

I want to ruin myself on it, because I already know one taste won't be enough.

One hit, and I'll be addicted.

"Do it," Jasper says, like he's in my head and already knows exactly where my thoughts just went.

I ease out of Zeke with a shudder and lower myself to him. My tongue licks across the mess smeared over his skin—Jasper's release, Zeke's release. It's warm, salty, and deliciously male, and the moment it hits my tongue, I know I'm fucked.

"I want more of this," I rasp, collapsing back onto the mattress between them, sweat-slick and utterly wrecked. "Unless..."

"Unless what?" Jasper asks.

"Unless this isn't what you want. I don't know what you two are."

"What we are is crazy about each other. And what we just did with you is something we both wanted. If you want more, then you're ours, and we're yours."

"I want..."

Zeke pushes up on one elbow and presses a kiss to my shoulder like he's testing the waters now that I'm coming down from the high. When he leans in and brushes a lighter kiss over my lips, I don't flinch.

"You don't have to decide tonight," Zeke whispers, his forehead resting against mine. "Just know that you're wanted here by both of us."

"Can we go slow?"

Jasper lets out a low laugh, shaking his head. "You call that slow?"

"Now that..." I blow out a shaky breath. "That—I'm all in, and we can go as fast as you want. But the relationship part? That's harder for me. I don't open up easily."

"You think we don't already know that? You're a fucking fortress, Captain. You've been one as long as we've known you. But you're going to feel safe with us. I promise you that."

Call it instinct, but I already know this thing between us isn't casual. Not the way they touch me, not the way they look at me like I'm something they've been waiting for.

This is trust.

This is history.

This is a connection that's been under my skin for longer than I ever let myself see, and now that I feel it, I know it's going to be something special.

CHAPTER ONE
ZEKE

The stadium erupts into chaos as Roman weaves past two defenders before sending the puck clean into the top corner of the net, slamming home the championship-winning goal.

Their goalie didn't even move.

The red light flashes behind the net, the buzzer blares, and the arena explodes. My teammates flood the ice in celebration, sticks flying, gloves scattered around like confetti, with screams echoing through the rafters. But Roman and Jasper? They gravitate toward each other first. They throw their arms around each other, and I reach them seconds later, pulled into their orbit like I always am.

There's no kiss, not here. But the way Roman buries his face into my shoulder, while Jasper's hand finds mine and squeezes tight, says everything we can't. It's all the affection we can risk, but for now, it's enough.

I glance up to see Coach getting tossed around like a rag doll, laughing his ass off with tears in his eyes as we all celebrate. The crowd roars, and there's a wall of sound and flashing lights, but for just a second, all I can hear is our heartbeats syncing up.

When we finally break apart, my eyes scan the crowd,

searching for the other piece of me that sets my soul ablaze. And when I find her seat, the one she sits in for every game, there she is. Navy blue eyes collide with mine, hitting me with the force of a body check. They pierce straight through me, reaching places only Roman and Jasper have claim to, but I'd carve out a new space for her.

Addison Hope has been living in my head rent-free since she sat down beside me in the one class we shared. Her beautiful eyes and shy smile knocked me on my ass, and I was gone before she even said a word.

"My daughter, Addison, will be helping out with team management this season. She asked to get involved, and I'm trusting that you boys don't need to be reminded about the rules."

Just like that, she went from potentially attainable to completely untouchable. Off-limits in every way that matters. The kind of forbidden that makes you ache just thinking about it, because everyone knows the golden rule of hockey: You don't fuck around with the coach's daughter. No matter how bad you want to.

We settled for friendship instead, and it's beautiful in its own right. We have a connection I'd fight to protect, but god, the number of times I've caught myself wondering what it would be like to kiss her. And it's not just me—I've seen the way Roman still watches her when she comes to practices, and how Jasper's whole body tenses up whenever she laughs at one of his jokes.

We've all got our own Addison Hope-shaped complications, carefully tucked away where Coach can't see them.

"We fucking did it, baby," Jasper whispers against my ear, pulling me into what, from the outside, probably looks like the most platonic bro hug imaginable.

No one would ever guess that only a few hours ago, he had one hand twisted in my hair and the other braced against the locker while he fucked my mouth. Not exactly my smartest move, but

Jasper's a reckless little fucker with a hard-on for risk and zero fear of consequences. The number of times we've almost been caught is honestly ridiculous. The back of the equipment room, the showers, and even in the damn trainer's office.

He gets off on the danger.

I get off on him.

Now he's smiling like butter wouldn't melt, with his arm slung casually around my shoulder, while I can still taste him in the back of my throat.

"We're getting drafted together. I can feel it," I say as the three of us—Roman, Jasper, and me—stand shoulder to shoulder, soaking in the thunder of the crowd.

"It's all three of us or nothing. The scouts just need to understand we're lethal on the ice together, and we don't fucking split." Roman's deep voice is firm, not giving an inch.

"Damn right we are," Jasper adds, before his elbow finds my ribs. "Well, well, look who's here." I follow his gaze to find Addie in the crowd again, beaming with her friends.

"Come on, you knew she'd be here," Roman says, brushing it off like he always does when Addie comes up.

"She's here for her dad," I say, but there's something in the way she looks at me sometimes—at all of us—that makes me wonder if maybe...

But no, Coach made it crystal clear: *hands off his daughter.*

Not that Roman ever listened. He and Addie have a history that predates the little three-way we found ourselves in. He has his own special brand of torture when it comes to her, which runs deeper than Jasper's or mine. What happened between them left scars that have yet to fully heal.

"Well, she certainly isn't here for you, Rome," Jasper teases.

Even though he's poking the bear, he always knows exactly when Roman needs the distraction.

"Fuck you." Roman laughs, shoving Jasper playfully before flipping him off and skating away. But even as the team celebrates around him, I see the way his eyes keep drifting back to the stands.

For three bi guys who've sworn off everyone else, Addie's always been our exception.

We don't sleep around.

No drunk mistakes.

No meaningless shit.

Just us three, locked tight.

Unbreakable.

But Addison Hope has always been the wild card—the one who could break every rule we've made and somehow still be exactly what we need.

You'd have to be an idiot not to see how beautiful she is, but that's not what hooked me. What got me was the friendship we built over time and the way she let me see every version of her.

I got the real, unfiltered Addison, and that's when the attraction really took hold.

Jasper's been caught in her orbit too. I catch him making her laugh and see how she leans into him as if he's the safe place where she can breathe a little easier.

Jasper has this way about him—one I've felt myself since the day we met—where he can take your worst day and turn it into your best without even trying. Just pure Jasper magic.

The three of us walk into the party like we just won the fucking world.

Because we kind of did.

State champs.

There's music, sweat, and the buzz of a hundred bodies celebrating us, but none of it matters when I see Addison in the corner of the living room, half lit by the shitty string lights, standing way too close to Mikey King. She's laughing, sipping something from a plastic cup, and her head is tilted slightly to the side in a way that makes her long blonde hair cascade over her shoulder.

Mikey's our goalie. He used to be great, but now he's just a lazy fuck, coasting on the scraps of whatever talent he had left. He's overrated as hell and a walking ego with a dick for a brain.

But Addie knows exactly what kind of asshole he is, which makes it even more infuriating to watch her feed his ego with that smile—the one that makes her eyes crinkle in the corners and should be aimed at anyone but him.

"Nope, fuck that." Jasper's gone before I can stop him, stalking over to where Addie's cornered, and in one smooth motion, he hoists her over his shoulder.

"What the fuck, Hastings?" Mikey's voice cracks with anger as Jasper strolls deeper into the house Mikey shares with his twin, Mitch.

Pretty sure their parents were high as fuck when they picked those names.

"You think something's gonna happen there?" Roman watches Jasper and Addie disappear into the crowd.

"Like it hasn't been almost happening for a long time now?"

"What I wouldn't give to watch," Roman mutters, and there's enough heat in his voice to make my skin prickle.

"Ever thought about telling her about us?"

"Nope." Roman's answer comes fast. "Me and her—we're never crossing that line again, but I see how she looks at you both." His voice drops lower, rougher. "It's up to you guys what you do, but I'm not getting pushed out for anyone."

I've seen the way she still looks at him when she thinks no

one's watching. If he gave her the word, she'd fall right back into him, no questions asked.

He starts to step toward the house, but I catch his wrist.

My Roman.

Captain of our team and the strongest guy I know, but he's an emotional fortress. His walls are thick, doors are locked, and the windows are boarded up. But I've taken the time to learn exactly where all the cracks are.

"Hey." My fingers tighten around his wrist, and he turns, dragging a hand down his jaw the way he does when he's fighting himself. "Never gonna happen. You're mine. You're ours. That doesn't change. Not now. Not ever."

His eyes fall to my mouth, dark with want, and fuck, I'd give anything to kiss him right here and let him take what he needs from me.

Roman's love isn't soft.

It's sex, skin, and the raw honesty of bodies moving together.

It's bruises on hips and fingers tangled in hair.

It's how he speaks the words he can't always say out loud.

"You said it yourself. It's all three of us or nothing. End of."

I press my thumb against the hollow of his throat, feeling his pulse race under my touch as I try to ground him and smooth out whatever darkness just chased the light from his face.

Some days, I think I could spend forever learning to read the silent language of Roman's fears. I want to understand every signal, every unspoken plea, and answer them all until he finally believes he's safe.

"Come on, let's get drunk," I say, and Roman's mouth curves into that devastating smile. "And when we get home, I'll show you exactly how much you've earned the attention I'm gonna give your cock."

"You're a motherfucker," he growls, palming himself through his jeans.

The way he gets worked up so easily—yeah, this man owns me.

We find Addie and Jasper in the kitchen, and of course, he's got her laughing. But that's Jasper—our joker, the glue that holds us all together. Right now, he's doing what he does best by keeping her entertained and, more importantly, far away from dickheads like Mikey King.

Empty red cups litter the counter, and music thumps through the walls, but in this little corner of the chaos, it's like they've carved out their own space.

"Hey, congratulations." Addie turns to face us with a smile that lights up her whole face.

"Thanks. Did you enjoy the game?"

"Watching you guys win the championship?" She tilts her head, and her eyes sparkle with mischief. "Meh. It was okay."

"I'm glad you got to see your dad achieve it," Roman says, stepping up beside me and taking a slow sip of his beer. "I mean, that's why you were there, right?"

Addie's smile fades. "Well, you would think that."

"Okay, you two play nice," Jasper cuts in, ever the peacekeeper. "Or at least remember that once we're drafted, you probably won't have to see each other again. Might as well make these last moments bearable."

He tries to keep it light, but the thought of never seeing her again hits harder than I was ready for, and the way Roman's fingers tighten around his bottle tells me I'm not the only one feeling it.

"We're young and hot and only have a few nights like this left, so could you guys kiss and make up for me?" Jasper's charm works its magic as Roman huffs out something close to a smile, and

Addie's lips twitch at the corners. He claps his hands together, grinning. "Good. Now who wants a shot?"

Once the party starts winding down, I find myself outside, taking in the view. Under the stars, the lake stretches out like black glass, while mountains rise behind Mikey and Mitch's house—*man, those names are a mouthful.*

The scent of vanilla and something uniquely Addie, which has been quietly driving me crazy for years, overwhelms me, and I don't need to turn around to know she's there.

"It's peaceful out here, isn't it?" She steps up beside me, arms folded across her chest. "It's why I came here tonight. I know they have this view, and when it gets quiet like this, you can actually hear yourself think."

I look over at her, and her eyes are focused on the water. Her cheeks are pink from the cold, and her breath clouds in front of her.

"I'll miss it, you know. All of this." The words feel heavy in my mouth because we both know the NHL draft means leaving this town behind us.

"It's going to be strange with everyone gone." She wraps her arms around herself tighter, and I fight the urge to pull her close.

"What about you? What's your plan?"

She blows out a breath, her blonde hair dancing in the breeze. "I have no idea, but I don't think my future is here."

"No?"

"I don't want to get stuck. You know what I mean? I don't want to settle for some dead-end job and a mediocre husband just because that's what's expected of me. But you know my dad... you know how he is about keeping family close." She shakes her head, looking torn. "It feels like I can either break his heart and leave or stay and lose myself completely."

"You can't live your life for him, Addie." Her eyes flick up to mine, and I take a step closer. "You have to make yourself happy first, even if it means hurting someone else, because staying somewhere you don't belong just to please other people? That's not living. That's a slow death."

The moonlight catches in her eyes, and suddenly, I can't think about anything except how much I want her.

"Are you happy, Zeke?"

My mind immediately drifts to Roman and Jasper and those lazy mornings when we're wrapped up in sheets and sweat and something that feels a hell of a lot like forever. I think about the way Roman kisses me like he's afraid I'll disappear if he stops, and how Jasper always laughs into the curve of my neck as if he knows the world is ours and nothing can ever touch us. I think about late-night talks that bleed into sunrise, warm bodies pressed close after long games, and the unspoken vow that no matter where the draft takes us, we go together or we don't go at all.

"So happy," I answer truthfully. "What about you? What would make you happy, Addison Hope?"

She tilts her head back, staring up at the blanket of stars above us, and I watch the moment something shifts in her eyes.

"Fuck it," she whispers, and before I can blink, her hands are fisting the front of my hoodie and her mouth crashes into mine.

Her lips are soft, but the kiss is anything but gentle.

It's heat, hunger, and four years of tension snapping in an instant.

I jerk back, fingers flying to my tingling lips, but when she tries to retreat, looking mortified, something inside me refuses to let her go. I catch her waist and pull her back to me. This time, she melts against me like it's the most natural thing in the world. My tongue slides past her lips, and the whimper she makes drags my cock to full attention.

We break apart at the sound of someone clearing their throat, both of us breathing hard, and when I turn my head, I see my guys.

Jasper's wearing that shit-eating grin of his, while Roman's expression is a dangerous mix of turned on and ready to rip my head off.

"We were gonna tell you we're heading out," Jasper drawls, "but it looks like you might have other plans?"

"You're leaving already?" Addie asks, her breath still ragged from our kiss.

"Yeah, princess, we're leaving," Roman says, leaving no room for argument. "Come on."

He turns away, but Jasper lingers, his eyes still on Addie. "You wanna come with us?"

Roman stops mid-step and goes completely still. His eyes cut to Jasper like he's already planning his punishment for the invitation, but our wild boy simply shrugs a shoulder as if to say, *Too late now.*

"Pretty sure she needs to get home before Daddy starts wondering where she is," Roman bites out.

"Screw you, Ashford."

"Been there, done that, got the marks."

Roman and Addie's history is messy as hell, and when everything fell apart between them, she was the one who left the deepest scar. She didn't hurt him on purpose. That's not who she is, but Roman doesn't open up easily. He keeps people at a distance, yet somehow she got through. For the first time in his life, she made him believe it was safe to let someone in.

Then she left.

They lock eyes in a silent battle until Roman surprisingly backs down first. "Fine, princess. Let's go."

CHAPTER TWO
ADDISON

I push past the solid wall of muscle that is Roman Ashford—god, even angry, he's devastating—while Jasper falls into step beside me.

Jesus, I just kissed Roman's best friend.

No wonder he looks at me like I'm poison.

That's a line you don't cross, and I knew better.

Roman already hates me. It rolls off him in waves, and I've earned every bit of that hatred from him. But losing him gutted me too, deep enough that I still feel it even now. And yeah, I know kissing Zeke was probably the worst possible move if I ever wanted to fix what was broken between Roman and me, but there's just something about Zeke that makes me forget every reason why I shouldn't want him.

"Why do girls walk so fucking fast when they're pissed?" Jasper's teasing pulls me out of my spiral.

"I'm not pissed," I mutter.

"You are," he says, breezy as hell. "But it's okay. I'm not offended that you're lying to me."

I can't stop myself from glancing back over my shoulder, my

eyes catching on Roman and Zeke trailing a few steps behind us. That kiss, as brief as it was, continues to play out in my head, and the truth is that I've wanted it for longer than I'd ever let myself say out loud.

My dad would have an actual heart attack if he ever found out.

His words from last season still echo in my ears: *"Date who you want, you're an adult, but stay the hell away from my boys. I don't want them distracted."*

But he doesn't see the way Zeke looks at me or how Roman burns beneath the surface, always protecting himself, his silence always saying more than his words ever could: *Don't come closer unless you mean to stay.*

And I didn't stay.

I walked away.

And Jasper... God, Jasper, he's the grinning golden chaos who makes everything feel possible, even the things that shouldn't be.

Thoughts of all three men linger somewhere deep inside me, hidden in the places good girls aren't supposed to go. The kind of thoughts that make heat crawl up my neck and my pulse quicken with equal parts lust and shame because wanting one of them should be enough, but it's not.

I fucked everything sideways when I started dating Roman a few years ago. When my dad found out, he came straight for me. He told me to end it, said Roman's future hung in the balance, and listed a million reasons why his star player couldn't be with me.

It was a conflict of interest.

Team dynamics.

He couldn't play favorites if things went south between us.

I was hopelessly in love with Roman when I ripped us apart, and we haven't managed a civil conversation since. He built this wall between us, brick by fucking brick, because of what I did, and the worst part is that even though I expected these feelings to fade or at least turn into something manageable, they haven't.

Some nights I still wake up remembering how his hands felt on my skin, how he'd whisper against my neck when he thought I was sleeping, confessing things he couldn't say to me in daylight. Now, he barely says my name. He calls me princess like it's a joke, but I know it's because it's easier than remembering the way *Addie* used to fall from his lips when he was losing himself inside me.

Then there's Jasper, who somehow makes everything feel lighter just by existing. He gets me. Hell, he gets everyone. But everything with him feels effortless. Those dark eyes of his don't miss a thing, and that smile could talk me into anything.

Zeke is different. He's like sunshine breaking through storm clouds—warm and steady and so kind it hurts. Black hair that always falls into his eyes, and those green orbs? Yeah, they could pull you under before you even realized you were drowning.

He's beautiful, inside and out.

Okay, so I might be a little bit of a mess over all three of them. Like, full-blown good-girl-gone-hopelessly-feral.

The guys' house isn't far from Mikey's place. I've only been here once before, when I dropped off some paperwork for my dad last semester.

Jasper pushes open the front door, and I step inside, my buzz from earlier fading fast, replaced by a nervous energy that makes my stomach flutter.

"We've got beer, wine, tequila, vodka...?" Jasper offers, already moving toward the kitchen.

"White wine?"

"Think we've only got red." Jasper rummages through their collection of mostly empty bottles.

"Just give me whatever you guys are having."

His wicked grin should've been my first warning. "Shots it is, angel."

We drift from the kitchen into the living room, and suddenly the space feels smaller than it looks. Maybe it's the way Zeke settles onto the couch beside me, his thigh brushing against mine, or how Roman lounges across from us like some brooding god of hockey.

Jasper returns with what looks like liquid death in shot glasses, handing one out to each of us.

"What are we toasting to?" Jasper asks.

"How about *'We just won the fucking championship'*?" Roman says with pride.

Jasper leans in toward him, fingers squeezing his knee. "To the future NHL stars in this room—may we always be this fucking spectacular."

We all drink, and I nearly gag because, holy crap, this is strong.

"Jesus." Zeke laughs, rescuing my glass before it slips out of my hands.

"That was... disgusting."

"You want another?" Jasper smirks.

"Absolutely not," I say, laughing, but he doesn't look away. He holds me with that steady, too-intense gaze, and then drops the question I know he's been dying to ask.

"Okay, so, can we talk about what happened between you and Zeke earlier?"

"Um, no." The words shoot out of my mouth as I accidentally catch Roman's eyes—a catastrophic mistake because he's fucking beautiful.

"What? Why not?"

"Because drunken kisses don't need a discussion... especially when—" I cut myself off, not wanting to acknowledge how Roman watching me kiss his best friend feels like some kind of betrayal, even now.

I'm the worst.

"Don't stop on my account, princess. I've been getting my dick sucked for the past year, so you're welcome to kiss whoever the hell you like."

Yeah... that hit exactly the way he meant it to.

Fury ignites in my chest, spreading like wildfire and burning everything in its path. I stare him down, my body vibrating with rage.

"Yet they haven't stuck around?" The words fall out before I can stop them, my voice colder than I feel, and cruel in a way that makes me want to bite my tongue until it bleeds. "Must be a you problem."

I know I have no right to feel this way, and I'm a major fucking hypocrite, but the thought of him with other girls makes me feel physically sick. He was the last man I slept with, and the truth is, I'm not ready to give my body to anyone who isn't sitting in this room right now.

"Wanna bet?" Roman fires back, and my stomach drops.

No way.

I'd know if he had a girlfriend.

"Jesus," Jasper mutters, dragging a hand through his hair like we're both exhausting him. "Can we exist in the same fucking space for five minutes without you two going for blood? Besides, I'm more interested in the fact that I'm now the only person in this house who doesn't know what it's like to kiss you."

Is he playing with me? It feels like his usual bullshit, but the way he's looking at me... There's heat there.

"So I guess you either kiss me"—he grins, cocky as hell—"or let me watch you two go at it again. Or..."

"Don't." Roman's voice cuts like steel, his eyes locked on Jasper.

"I'm fucking serious, don't. She won't understand, and it'll—" He catches himself, jaw clenching.

"Understand what?" I say, looking to Zeke, who's watching Roman like he's a bomb about to detonate.

"Nothing," Roman snaps, but my eyes narrow at the blatant lie.

Before I can call him on it, Zeke rises from his chair and crouches in front of Roman, taking the beer from his grip.

"Hey, remember what I said." Zeke's hand slides around Roman's neck, drawing their foreheads together.

They both close their eyes, and the tenderness of it catches me completely off guard. Jasper's watching me like a hawk, gauging every reaction, like he already knows this is about to break me wide open in ways I never saw coming.

Roman's face twists with something raw and agonized, like whatever he's been burying is finally clawing its way out of him. His jaw clenches so tight I can see the muscle jump beneath his skin, and his eyes burn with the kind of feral need that sends a sharp ache through my chest.

I recognize that look.

He used to look at me that way.

Roman's fighting himself, and I can feel the exact moment he loses. His hands shoot out, fingers wrapping around Zeke's throat, and he pulls him closer, unable to hold himself back for another second.

No way. No fucking way. How—

Their mouths crash together, and fuck—I should look away, but I can't. I can't tear my eyes from the way Roman's fingers dig into Zeke's skin or the way Zeke's thumb strokes along Roman's jaw as if he's the most precious thing in the world.

"You remember Roman's outlet is touch, right?" Jasper murmurs, just in time to stop me from spiraling. His voice is low and calm, like he's trying to talk me off a ledge without letting me know I'm even on one. "I bet he always had his hands on you." Memories flood back of Roman's desperate touches, his face buried in my neck, fingers seeking bare skin any time life got too much. "Right now, our boy isn't thinking about anything except what he needs to survive whatever the hell is going on in his head."

"Our boy?" The words catch in my throat as Jasper slides closer on the couch. "He's... You're..."

"He's the love of my life, along with the guy he's about to bend over right here if we don't distract them."

"You're gay?" I blurt, my eyes wide. "All of you?"

"You know we're not, angel, and I know you remember exactly how Roman fucks. Did that ever feel like a man who was anywhere but right where he wanted to be?"

I can't answer.

I can't even form words.

I'm barely able to string together a coherent thought as I watch these two men in front of me.

Zeke and Roman are still going at it like they're the only ones in the room—mouths colliding, hands roaming, bodies pressed so close there's no space between them.

When Jasper's fingers find my chin, he gently tilts my face toward his. My eyes drop to his mouth, and when his thumb traces slowly across my bottom lip, I swear my whole body trembles.

"Tell me they're not the hottest fucking thing you've ever seen," he murmurs, and I can't argue because he's right. They're devastating together, and I'm soaked just from watching them.

"Not only them." The second the words leave me, Jasper's smile turns savage, and that's all the invitation he needs.

He seizes my mouth, claiming me like he's waited long enough. His tongue pushes past my lips, and suddenly, the room is full of nothing but wet sounds and heavy breathing. I'm confused as hell, but I can't stop kissing him back. He dominates the kiss completely; it's rougher than Zeke's earlier tenderness but not as brutally possessive as Roman used to be.

God, those kisses with Roman still haunt my dreams, but this... this is something else entirely.

Jasper kisses like he knows exactly what he wants, how to take it, and he's unapologetic as fuck about it.

When I break away from Jasper, I find two pairs of eyes burning into us. My head's spinning, caught somewhere between every fantasy I've moaned into my pillow and the reality that's unfolding right in front of me. And now that I'm here, now that this is really happening, I feel way over my head.

"I... I need to go." Roman's eyes snap to Jasper, pinning him with a look that practically screams, *I fucking told you this would happen.* "I don't..." I start, my voice cracking. "I don't think I should be here. Do you do this often?"

"Make out with each other? Fuck yes." Jasper laughs, but it's Zeke who moves first. He must sense my spiral because he slides in beside me again, boxing me in with his warmth.

"No," I say quietly, my eyes flicking between them all. "I meant with other girls."

"Hey." Zeke turns my face toward his, using that same gentleness he did with Roman a few minutes ago. "You can ask us anything you want, but whatever we tell you has to stay in this room." He pauses, just long enough to make sure I'm really hearing him. "We've never shown anyone this side of us or let anyone see who we really are to each other. And this—whatever's happening right now—it's only ever been you."

"Because you guys are together in secret?"

"Has to be that way." Roman's voice is rough, like the words hurt coming out. "Look, I know we've got history, baggage, whatever the hell you want to call it. But I also know you care about them. I know their friendship means something to you. So for their sake, please..."

He has no idea that even after everything, I still love him. I probably always will, and now, watching him beg for their safety, for their secret—well, it just makes me love him more.

"I'd never betray any of you." Roman doesn't say anything, but he nods once, and that tiny sliver of trust still hanging between us feels like everything. "So you're all sleeping together?"

Zeke shakes his head. "It's not just sex. Not even close."

"How did I not see it?"

"We're good at hiding it, angel. We've had to be. No one would understand. Not the coaches, not the league... not the world we're trying to make a future in. There's no space for this."

I nod slowly, my heart pounding as I look between the three of them. "So why are you telling me now?"

"Because it's you. Because you kissed Zeke, and I know you want me," Jasper says, leaning in close enough that I'm already imagining kissing him again. "We're almost out of time, and I wasn't about to waste the chance to find out what this could feel like with you."

"What about you?" I force the question out as I meet Roman's whiskey eyes.

"We had our shot, and you left." There's no anger in his voice, but it's clear he's buried whatever we once were. "I won't stand in their way, not when it comes to you. Not when I know exactly how it feels to..."

He doesn't finish that thought. He doesn't have to. I broke something between us, and now those walls he's built are solid steel.

"The question is, what do you want?" Zeke asks in that gentle way he's perfected, making me feel like he's offering me a way in and out all at once.

Before I can answer, I'm on my feet, putting distance between us and this conversation I'm nowhere near ready to have.

Roman just sits back, legs spread wide, completely unsurprised because he's already watched me run from something that matters once before. The last time I tried to leave, he followed me. He chased me down, believing he could convince me to stay.

But this time, he doesn't move.

He doesn't reach for me because he expects me to go.

And he's ready to let me.

"I can't... Not because I don't want to. I just..." The words get caught in my throat. "You're leaving. All of you will leave, and I can't..." My hand presses against my chest, right where it feels like my heart might splinter. "I think I should go."

"No, Addie. Stay. You can take one of the bedrooms, and I'll take you home in the morning." Zeke stands, his broad shoulders and solid chest taking up all the space in front of me.

When he glances at the other two, it's Jasper who moves first. He crosses the room slowly, and there's nothing playful about him now. He lifts one hand, the backs of his fingers brushing lightly against my jaw before he leans in and presses a kiss to my cheek.

"Sorry, Addie. I didn't mean to push too far or make you uncomfortable." The joker gets serious, and I hate it.

"You didn't make me uncomfortable," I say quickly, my eyes drifting to Roman, who refuses to look at me now. "I just... I already miss you guys, and you're not even gone yet. I don't want to make it worse by doing something stupid that we can't take back." I take a shaky breath. "But I promise your secret's safe with me."

Zeke reaches out, taking my hand and guiding me down the hallway to what I assume is the guest room.

Do they share a bed, all of them together?

The mechanics of their relationship are a mystery to me,

though the image of them tangled up in sheets makes me groan quietly to myself.

Zeke opens the door to a small room at the end of the hall but doesn't step inside. He just stands there, looking at me like he can see every thought flashing behind my eyes.

"That was a lot to put on you tonight, but you have to understand that Jasper doesn't do well with masking his feelings. You're lucky he hasn't told you how he feels about you and what he wants sooner. And the way he's managed to keep his mouth shut about what Roman and I mean to him? Well, that should tell you just how deep it goes."

I turn, my back brushing the cold hallway wall, my pulse hammering in my throat. "And what about you?"

"Come on," he murmurs, his eyes sweeping over me. "You knew. You had to have known, or you wouldn't have made your move tonight."

"Will you kiss me?" I whisper. "Just once more?"

He doesn't hesitate. He cages me against the wall, his body pinning mine. One arm braces above my head while his other hand slides to my jaw, his thumb tracing my bottom lip. When he finally kisses me, it isn't hard or rushed, but fuck—it's hot, and when he pulls back sooner than I want, my lips are tingling, and my body is practically screaming for more.

"Goodnight, Addison."

"Goodnight, Zeke."

CHAPTER THREE
ADDISON

Now

Older me wants to shake the shit out of younger me for walking out on them that night.

What was I even thinking?

I brush off memories of the night they won the championship more often than I'd like to admit. I have to because walking away from Roman for a second time still gnaws at me.

"The ceremony's at Highland Lodge in a couple of weeks. We need to reserve some cabins if you want to stay—they said availability's limited."

I'm slumped in my parents' living room, which looks like Santa's workshop threw up everywhere, thanks to my niece and nephew. There's wrapping paper all over, screaming kids, fake snow, glitter that I'm pretty sure wasn't there five minutes ago, and a battery-powered reindeer blinking like it's on the verge of a nervous breakdown.

You and me both, buddy.

"Highland Lodge is less than twenty minutes away," I mutter into my hot chocolate. "Most people will just drive back to town."

"Well, I thought it might be nice, you know, in case you and Mikey…"

Ah, yes, Mikey. My soon-to-be ex-husband, who I wasted almost two years of my life faking orgasms for while he panted over me like a pug with asthma.

"What is wrong with you?" I stare at my mother like she's grown a second head. "Seriously? You know what he did."

I caught him four months ago, butt naked and flailing like a dying trout, inside Whitney, my closest friend turned backstabbing bitch. And I say "inside" in the loosest possible terms because, honestly, two pathetic pumps and a groan like he stubbed his toe hardly qualify as mind-blowing sex.

Hats off to the guy though. It takes a real overachiever to disappoint two women at the same time.

Now Whitney's in the trash pile where she belongs, and Mikey —thanks to his wandering dick—is back living with Mommy and Daddy while I get to keep the house we shared.

So no, Mom. I'm not staying in some cozy fucking cabin with my cheating ex just because he scored a pity invite to my father's ceremony. But thanks.

"I blame that floozy for flaunting herself at him when your back was turned." Mom sniffs like she's discussing a slightly overcooked pot roast instead of my blown-to-shit marriage. "And you know how he is. I don't think he was ever happy working for his father."

"Okay, first of all, he messed up his hockey career by being a lazy, entitled dipshit who thought talent excused effort, which is why his sorry ass came crawling back to town in the first place. And second, as a woman, you should know better than to blame the woman."

"She was your friend."

"And he was my husband."

"No relationship is perfect, sweetie."

"Mom, stop."

"Would you have stayed with Dad if he'd hooked up with Evie Quinn?"

"You know I can't stand that woman! Why would you even say that to me?" Mom snaps, turning to glare daggers at Willow.

"Exactly," my sister says, cutting straight through Mom's dramatics. "Stop sticking up for the man, especially when said man is a walking, talking sack of crap."

I catch Willow's eye and feel that rush of gratitude I always get around my big sister these days. There's something about the decade between us that works now—she's flirting with forty, and I'm closer to thirty than twenty, but we've finally found our rhythm. We're just women now—women, sisters, allies, and, right now, she's my favorite person on the planet.

"I'm sorry, but I just want to see you happy and settled, especially because... well, you know."

Because I can't have kids.

Mom's greatest fear is that I'll end up alone, as if my empty uterus is some kind of man repellent. But Mikey proved you can be plenty lonely, even with a ring on your finger.

"Listen, let's not worry about me and what I'm doing. I'm fine."

This conversation feels way too heavy when Mariah Carey is demanding her Christmas list in the background like a sugar-high toddler. At least she knows what she wants—all I want for Christmas is a time machine to go back and cockblock myself from ever touching my ex.

"So, is there an invite list, or are the awards people handling that?"

"They've asked your father about who he'd like there, and of course, he went through friends, family, and old players. Not that they'll necessarily come, considering he trained a few that made it to the NHL. I imagine they all have fancy lives now."

I nearly choke, marshmallows and hot chocolate threatening to shoot out of my nose. "Wait—what? Why is the guest list going that far? I thought this was just family and friends."

My stomach does that thing where it feels like it's trying to escape through my throat. Because *old players* could mean... No. No way. The universe isn't that much of a bitch. Except it is, and I know exactly which three "old players" are probably topping that sentimental little list.

"I'm not sure. Your dad handled most of it. He just asked me to look into accommodation for anyone who needs it. Oh, and to help him find something to wear."

"By help, you mean choose," Willow says, laughing.

"Yes, you know how he is."

But I barely hear them because now I'm picturing the past walking back into my present, and all I can think is how emotionally unprepared I am for that.

My father's being awarded for his lifetime achievement in coaching and player development. The fancy plaque will say something about his dedication to building one of the country's most successful collegiate hockey programs, but that doesn't even begin to cover it.

It won't mention the countless midnight phone calls from players spiraling after a bad game, a breakup, or a family crisis, or the way he'd open our home to every kid who needed a couch, a meal, or just someone who wouldn't give up on them. It won't talk about the dinners Mom would cook for entire teams or how Dad would sit at our kitchen table until ungodly hours, drawing up plays and reviewing game tapes.

He's a hard-ass, always has been. He's the kind of coach who'd make his players skate suicides until their legs felt like jelly, then turn around and drive them to the emergency room himself if they got hurt. His players either worshipped him or wanted to run him over with the team bus—sometimes both in the same day—but they all respected him. Because beneath that gruff exterior and the endless drills, they knew he'd go to war for any one of them. And now he's finally being recognized for twenty-five years of early morning practices, of molding cocky teenagers into solid men, and building not just a program but a legacy.

I stick around through lunch, working through Mom's never-ending to-do list. Eventually, Willow and I make our escape, slipping out into the crisp December air before Mom can find another reason to keep us hostage.

Don't get me wrong, I love my mom, but sometimes she lives in this Hallmark movie version of reality where every problem can be solved with a cup of cocoa and a heart-to-heart. Meanwhile, Willow and I are stuck in the real world, where ex-husbands cheat, and happy endings aren't guaranteed.

Willow buckles Aaron and Hannah in, shuts the back door with her hip, and leans against the driver's side.

"No matter what Mom says to you, do not go back to Mikey." I laugh, pulling my coat tighter around myself. "I'm serious. Even if you're pulling a full Bridget Jones on Christmas morning—wine, pajamas, and 'All by Myself' on repeat—do not call him."

"You don't have to worry. Not even in my worst state would I go back to a man like that."

Willow gives me that patented big-sister stare as I tuck my newly shoulder-length blonde hair behind my ears. The cut was my post-breakup rebellion. Nothing says *fresh start* like chopping off eight inches of hair, along with the last two years I wasted on a guy I'm pretty sure I never really belonged with.

"You're doing better than I expected."

"I guess that's what happens when you're stupid enough to stay in a relationship just because everyone else said it made sense."

"You should've told me you weren't happy."

"By the time I realized it, everything was already in motion. The wedding, the house, the life I thought I was supposed to want." I force a smile. "It felt easier to just go along with it."

"Nothing is ever too late…" She checks her watch. "Except me. I have to get these kids home."

She pulls me into a quick hug before sliding into the driver's seat, and I watch her car disappear down the snowy street until it's just a speck in the distance.

Later, after a hot shower and slipping into fresh pajamas, I crawl into bed. *Love Actually* plays in the background, the kind of comfort movie I usually fall asleep to this time of year. But tonight, my mind won't shut the hell up.

What if they come back?

I press my head deeper into the pillow like that might smother the unwelcome thought, but it's already too late.

What if they show up at the ceremony?

What if they're not together anymore?

Or worse—what if there's someone new?

Some other woman they all felt drawn to?

I roll onto my side and stare at the blinking Christmas lights I strung above my window last week.

What if I have to sit there, smile politely, and pretend it doesn't gut me?

Ugh. Don't go there, Addie. Jesus.

Still, I can't shake it.

Whether I'm ready or not, after five years of silence and space, I might have to face the three men who took pieces of me with them when they left to chase their dreams.

CHAPTER FOUR

ROMAN

"Fuuuck... that's it." My head hits the wall with a thud as my eyes roll back, fingers twisting hard in both their hair.

Jasper's got me buried so deep down his throat his eyes are glassy, spit slicking his chin as his lips stretch wide. Below him, Zeke's tongue moves slow and dirty over my balls, like he's trying to draw the orgasm out of me one flick at a time.

"You're sharing me so fucking good."

They pulled me from sleep and had their mouths on me before I could even open my eyes.

"Whose mouth am I filling?" I rasp, barely holding it together.

"Mine," Zeke growls, pulling off my balls with a pop.

"Motherfucker won rock-paper-scissors," Jasper mutters around my dick.

"I'm sure our boy will share. Now get your mouth around me, baby."

I tighten my grip in Zeke's hair, guiding him closer. He takes me in one greedy swallow—no hesitation, no easing into it, just lips stretched wide, throat open, like he's begging me to use him.

His eyes water when I fuck into his mouth, and when I finally fall apart, he swallows every last drop.

Falling back breathless, I watch Jasper slam onto Zeke with a messy, open-mouthed kiss, my cum shared between them. It's not sweet. It's not gentle. It's primal, frenzied, and completely fucking feral.

When they finally pull apart, they settle on either side of me, their bodies pressed close against mine.

"Hell of a way to wake up, birthday boy, huh?" Jasper nuzzles into my neck, and I can feel his smile against my skin before he sinks his teeth in.

My body's wrecked. My heart's pounding. And my cock's already twitching again.

"Makes me wish it was my birthday every day," I manage, still caught in that space between pleasure and consciousness.

"Christmas is coming." Zeke flashes that smile—the one I fall for all over again every single day. "What are you hoping for?"

"Don't care," I say honestly. "As long as I get to fuck both of you... mouth, ass, fist, any way you want me, I'm in."

We talked about our needs early on, and our sex life's never been anything short of phenomenal. But in the quiet moments, when we're just being... the love we have for each other is indescribable. And for a guy like me, who's still learning how to put emotion into anything other than action, that kind of love is fucking everything.

I don't always have the words.

But when I touch them, they know.

Every kiss says, *I'm yours*, every touch is a promise to stay, and every breath we share is a reminder that what we have is bigger than any words I could find to describe it.

But I'm working on myself. I have been for years. And I'm a hell of a lot more open now than I was after...

No. Can't go there.

I can't think about the little blonde who still lives somewhere inside all of us, no matter how hard we tried to bury her after she married Mikey fucking King.

What the hell was she thinking?

The thought slips in before I can stop it, and Jasper's hand tightens on my thigh. He always knows when I'm thinking about her. We all do because none of us ever really stopped.

Addison's haunting us all, and those three cream-colored invitations on the nightstand are a constant reminder that not only are we invited to watch her father accept an award for his contributions to college hockey, but they want me, the former captain who helped bring home the championship, to present it.

"Right, I'm going to shower. We need to be at the rink in an hour." Jasper rises from the bed, naked and hot as fuck, and I'm two seconds away from following him.

That guy buried himself inside my heart before I even realized it was happening, and the stubborn bastard made it clear that he had no intention of ever letting go.

I'm still staring after him when Zeke's fingers curl around my jaw, and gently pull my focus back to him.

"You okay?" he asks.

"I'm fucking awesome."

I lean in, my lips brushing against his.

Zeke's got this heart that's too big for his own good and the kind of empathy that makes him feel everyone else's pain like it's his own. But he also has these dark, filthy edges. He holds us like we're fragile, but the way he commands with just his body and his words... yeah, I'll never get enough of that.

Then there's Jasper. He's got that devil perched on his shoulder, but fuck, he loves harder than anyone I've ever known. He gets swallowed up by whatever's eating at him sometimes, but he saves those shadows for us, and for the place we've built between the three of us. A place where we keep each other safe when the rest of the world would never understand.

"You're officially older than us."

"True, but I get to say I'm fucking two younger guys, so I'd call that a win."

"Which you can do as soon as we get you home tonight." Zeke stands, tugging on a pair of black boxer briefs. "But first, we're taking you out, sound good?"

"Perfect."

"Great," Zeke says, grabbing a gray T-shirt off the chair and tossing it at my face. "Now haul your ass up and get ready, or Coach won't let you live long enough to see another birthday."

We pull up to the rink together, jackets zipped tight against the cold, and it doesn't take long before a handful of fans start gathering out front. Some are faces we know by name. Others are new, hanging around, hoping to catch a glimpse and maybe snag a photo or a signature to post online.

We sign a few posters, scrawl our names across some jerseys, and pose for the usual pictures—grins half forced while our hands are already half frozen—and then finally we head inside.

Chuck and Jonas stand guard near the entrance, the way they always do when the players roll in. They don't smile, but then they don't need to. Their presence says it all: *You're safe here. Now move your ass and get your shit done.*

They nod once, and we nod back.

There's no small talk or bullshit. Just the kind of respect that's built from years of standing in the same cold hallways, watching the same bruised-up guys chase the same impossible dreams.

"Yo, birthday boy!" Garrett's voice bellows across the room. "Retirement's right around the corner for you, huh?"

"By the time you're even considered for captain, Garrett, you'll be a corpse rotting under the bleachers."

"Fuck you, Ashford."

Screw you, Ashford.

Those words have been playing on a loop in my head ever since the night Addison found out what Zeke, Jasper, and I really mean to each other. It wasn't something I was necessarily ready for—hell, part of me was terrified—but deep down, I knew it needed to happen, not for me, but for them.

They'd been tied to Addison for years, bound by something that ran deeper than friendship but had never been touched or explored.

We'd had a relationship once, her and me. It was real and raw, and we had the kind of connection that buries itself under your skin and refuses to let go. We weren't gentle with each other. We were a fucking explosion. Every touch was a wildfire we couldn't outrun, and every fight was like two storms colliding.

I handed Addie every side of me—the good, the bad, the messy, even the parts I didn't always understand. But it all went to shit the day she looked me dead in the eye and said we were done, like I hadn't handed her my whole damn heart and trusted her not to crush it.

It wasn't that she stopped wanting me. Being with Zeke and Jasper all these years has taught me that a love like that doesn't just burn out. But eventually, someone else's rules got between us, and when it mattered most, she made her choice, and it sure as hell wasn't me.

Hockey was the dream I'd been chasing my entire life, but I would've thrown it all away for her. I would've chosen her above anything else because even now, if anyone tried to make me pick between the NHL and my guys, I'd let it all go without a second thought.

Our love isn't a choice.

It's a necessity.

Hockey might be the fire in my veins, but Jasper and Zeke are the air in my lungs, and I'd choose them in every lifetime.

I've been captain of the Vipers for three seasons now. Three years of bleeding on the ice and turning a group of individual players into a single, unstoppable machine.

Every time I pull on my jersey, I feel the weight of all the others hanging in that locker room pressing down on my shoulders. I carry their hopes, doubts, and dreams, and it's my job to make them believe in each other and themselves. Some nights, being captain means being the toughest bastard on the ice. You skate through pain, hit harder than you should, and bleed for the boys who'd bleed for you. Other nights, it means knowing when somebody's on the edge and pulling him aside. Not to tear him down, but to remind him exactly who the fuck he is and that he's not alone out there. That no matter how bad it gets, he's got a family fighting beside him.

The boys all give me shit. Constant chirping and endless jokes, the kind of brotherhood that could look like hate from the outside but is nothing but bone-deep love underneath. And when the game's on the line and everything comes down to those final few minutes, I know that these guys would go to war for me, just like I'd go to war for them.

"Happy birthday, Captain," Jacky, our goalie who matches my six-foot-two height, grips my shoulder and flashes me a grin. "Did you get anything nice?"

Birthday head from the two guys I'd walk through hellfire for? Yeah, I'd call that better than nice.

And they know exactly what I'm thinking the second our eyes meet across the locker room. It doesn't matter how many years pass—that fire, that pull between us—it never fades. It only grows stronger and hotter.

CHAPTER
FIVE
JASPER

Training was a nightmare today.

Roman convinced Coach to crank up the drills just to be a dick. And after the way Zeke and I had him coming apart this morning, you'd think he'd be a little nicer... But nope, Roman Ashford clearly gets off on watching us all suffer.

The truth is, I don't even care. I'll still offer him my ass later without a second thought. It is his birthday, after all, and God help me, I love how the man fucks.

My face pressed into the mattress, his hand fisting my hair, and his thick cock driving so deep it's like my body was made just to take him.

Yeah, he can be as much of a bastard on the ice as he wants, and I'll still be begging for him by the time tonight's over.

We rolled out of the rink a little after six, hit the showers and changed, and now, a couple of hours later, we're sitting at a corner table in Angelo's, celebrating Roman's birthday. To everyone around us, we probably just look like three friends grabbing a late dinner, laughing too loudly, and stealing each other's fries. But nobody sees the truth written into every part of me—that these men are mine. Zeke and Roman are carved into my soul, stitched into my skin, and burned into every choice I make.

There's no version of me that exists without them.

It feels just as good knowing it now as it did the day Roman finally stopped fighting what he felt for me and Zeke and let himself fall. The stubborn ass held out longer than I thought he would, but damn if the fall wasn't worth the wait.

We started off playing on the same team, built our bond in the grind of practices and the pressure of games, and forged a friendship I always thought would stay simple.

But it didn't.

The attraction didn't ease its way in—it crashed into us, violent and undeniable, hitting fast and hard until it was all Zeke and I could think about.

Every time I tried to get him to just fucking kiss me, because I knew he wanted to, he'd grit his teeth, mutter something about boundaries, and put another mile between us. He was determined to bury what was burning between the three of us, but desire like that doesn't just disappear. And the second he broke—fuck—it was one of the best days of my life. He stopped running and finally admitted with his mouth, his hands, and his whole body that he was just as desperate for us as we were for him.

From then on, there was never going to be anyone else for any of us.

That door closed the second we let each other in.

One day, I'm going to sit in this same restaurant, maybe even this exact seat, and I'm going to touch them the way I want to. I'll lace my fingers through Zeke's and lean over and kiss Roman without worrying who's looking or what they might say.

One day, the whole world will know that these two men belong to me, and anyone who doesn't like it can literally go fuck themselves into oblivion.

Face-first.

Bare-assed.

Whatever works.

But for now, I keep my mouth shut.

Not because I'm scared. I'd burn the world down for them without blinking, but they deserve peace. They deserve something that's just ours, without the cameras and the headlines and the bloodthirsty motherfuckers who don't know a goddamn thing about real love.

Tonight's supposed to be about celebrating Roman.

Not thinking about Colorado.

Not thinking about going back to where it all started.

And definitely not thinking about the blonde still living there.

Except sometimes I think I can still taste her lips.

Addison Hope is the only girl I've ever been crazy about.

From day one, I was obsessed—craving everything she tried to keep off-limits. She didn't reveal much back then, not with all the Roman shit weighing her down before we got close enough for her to trust me, but I knew. I wasn't blind to the way she looked at me when she thought I wasn't paying attention, and over time, I knew the pull wasn't one-sided. That's why, when the chance finally came, I didn't hesitate.

Addie never wanted to get stuck in that town, and yet, that's exactly what happened. She married some floppy fuckboy who could never deserve her, not in a million years. And the worst part is that there's a piece of me that hates her for it. I hate that she fell in love, and of all the people in the world, it had to be with Mikey King.

I'm not an idiot. I knew she'd move on. It's been five years. But if I had it my way, she would've been part of us. She would've fit into the life we built and the dream we crafted, just like she was always meant to.

"Have you heard from your parents?" Roman asks, spearing something green and boring as hell off his plate, and I nod as he chews on whatever rabbit food he ordered.

Roman's always been strict with his diet, but it fits him. It fits the part of him that needs to have his shit together at all times, no cracks, no slipups, just complete control.

Whereas I've got the biggest fucking steak on the menu sitting in front of me, bleeding just the way I like it.

"Are they okay?" Zeke asks.

"Yeah," I say, carving off a chunk of meat. "They're thinking of visiting for a week after the holidays and asked if they could stay at the house."

Roman raises an eyebrow. "And you said?"

"I told them if they want to torture themselves, be my guest."

Laughter ripples around the table because they both know damn well I'm not lasting a week without putting my hands on them. Zero chance. If that means Sandra and Hank have to hear their golden boy getting railed by these two men sitting next to me... well, that's on them. They've been warned.

My parents and Zeke's mom have always known about the three of us. It helps that my mom and dad are the kind of people who'd welcome a three-ring circus into their living room if it meant their kid was happy; open-minded doesn't even begin to cover it.

When they saw us together, when they realized what we had and how we just fit, they looked at us and basically said, "Cool. More people to love."

Zeke's mom is a whole different kind of incredible. Jules is the gentlest soul you'll ever meet, which is exactly why Zeke has a heart bigger than most people's entire personalities. She didn't even bat an eye when she saw the way we loved each other; she just opened her arms like it was the most natural thing in the world and pulled me and Roman in as if we were hers too.

And Jesus Christ, Roman needed that more than he'll ever admit. He needed someone to hold him without conditions or expectations—just arms around him to remind him that he was more than enough.

Roman's demons are carved deep by two piss-poor parents. One's probably strung out in a ditch somewhere, while the other is probably whoring herself through some dead-end town.

Thank God the selfish motherfuckers stay away.

Roman got chewed up and spit out by the system, and even if he swears he "had it better than most," we know he's spent most of his life feeling alone.

Until her.

Until us.

"Speaking of torture…" I mutter, resting my fork beside my plate.

"Don't," Roman snaps, his voice like a whip. "Not today."

"Come on, we need to talk about it. I'll call a vote if I have to."

"This can't just be a fucking vote, Jasper," Roman bites back, throwing down his fork. "It's got to be all of us agreeing, or none of us. We can't half-ass this." He leans back, dragging a hand down his face, like he's already exhausted by the conversation.

"This needs to be about Coach. Not Addison," Zeke adds.

"Chances are, we won't see her. Obviously, we'll see her at the ceremony, but it's one night. One fucking night. We're adults, and fuck me, it's been five years." I think I need to go. I think I need to see her, look her in the eye, and feel absolutely nothing. "Besides, she could be hideous now."

Zeke shakes his head, laughing under his breath. "You know Mikey wouldn't have been caught dead with someone who didn't look like a trophy wife."

"Unless he's let himself go too," I shoot back, grinning as I tear into another bite of steak. "Which, you know... I fucking hope so because we're hot as shit."

Zeke leans back in his chair, that beautiful smile curving his mouth as he tilts his head at me. "You think she's going to take one look at you and realize what a colossal mistake Mikey King was?"

"You know it, baby. I'm fucking irresistible."

The only reason we can talk about her like this and pretend we're unaffected by the situation is because she's the one exception—the only one there's ever been and the only one there ever could be. If any of us even so much as thought about touching another man or woman, it wouldn't just hurt. It would tear apart everything we've built. It would be over, done, crushed into dust before it even had a chance to bleed out and permanently stain what we have.

We belong to each other, and I've never—not even in my weakest, most loneliest moments—ever been tempted to fuck that up, and I never will.

"Fuck," Roman mutters, dragging a hand through his dark hair. "We're doing this, aren't we?"

I lean back, exhaling slowly. "I'll talk to Coach tomorrow. Explain that we're going to need a few days away."

"I'll find us somewhere to stay while we're there," Zeke says, already pulling out his phone.

"Make sure it has a large room, with one bed. Big enough for all three of us," Roman says, his tone leaving no room for argument. "I'm not sleeping away from you two."

I slide my hand onto his thigh under the table, pressing my palm against the hard muscle there, letting him feel me.

My big guy is strong as hell on the outside, but he carries a layer of insecurity he never should've been saddled with, all because too many people broke him before anyone ever thought to hold him together.

I'm pretty sure it started from the way he was treated at home, and when he landed in the system, things only got worse. He bounced between places that didn't give a damn about him, and he was battered mentally and physically until surviving became the only thing he knew how to do. If I could track down every asshole who hurt him, I'd rip their spines out without a second thought.

All Zeke and I can do now is give him whatever he needs. Let him take whatever he wants and ensure he never has to question if he's loved. And if he needs to keep us close, even while he sleeps, then that's exactly where we'll be.

"I'll take care of it, baby, okay?" Zeke whispers, and under the table, I feel Roman's leg slowly settle under my hand. "I do think we need to figure out how we're going to navigate going back there though."

"Pretty sure all we can do is face it head-on and get it the fuck over with," Roman mutters.

"Well, screw it," I say, shrugging, bumping Roman's shoulder. "We'll head up to the mountains and try to make the best of it."

CHAPTER SIX
ADDISON

Jasper Hastings, Roman Ashford, Zeke Adams.

My heart stops when I see those three names on the guest list. I blink, thinking maybe I'm seeing things, but the letters stay in place, laughing at me through the screen.

I'd asked my mom to email me the attendee list, but honestly, trying to teach a boomer how to open anything more complicated than a Facebook post is about as productive as trying to baptize a cat. After fifteen minutes of instructions and another five of her asking if "the internet was down," I gave up. I emailed Jenny, the event coordinator, who sent the file over in minutes, where it sat unopened in my inbox overnight.

Part of me wishes I'd stayed blissfully unaware, but here I am, late twenties, and having a full-blown meltdown over three men who probably haven't thought about me in years. And because my brain's an asshole, I find myself thinking about Zeke and Roman—specifically *that* night.

I've replayed that memory more times than I can count.

Jasper was right.

Nothing, and I mean nothing, has ever come close to touching how hot it was.

Groaning, I grab my phone, check the time, and shoot a text to Willow. I know she's awake. Her tiny humans seem allergic to sleep, and she's usually up at the ass crack of dawn.

> What are you wearing on Saturday?

It takes her about two seconds to reply, and when it comes through, I snort out a laugh.

> WILLOW: nn48mlm)))

> Seriously? Why are you still letting Hannah use your phone as a teething toy?

> WILLOW: Sorry. She grabbed it off the couch. Uhm… what am I wearing? Something someone my age can get away with that doesn't smell like spilled milk or a diaper explosion.

> Helpful.

> WILLOW: A long maroon dress that sucks in everything happening south of my boobs. And a coat. Because it's practically Christmas, and it's gonna be cold as hell.

> Thank you. Also, you're beautiful, spilled milk and diapers or no spilled milk and diapers.

The day I realized I'd be stuck in this town for good, I made a choice. If I couldn't leave, then I'd build something worth staying for, and that's how Eternal Chapter was born. I used to dream of seeing the world. I imagined myself on endless road trips, staying in tiny, crooked apartments in cities where nobody knew my name. About late-night conversations with strangers who'd feel like home, even if just for a brief moment in time.

I wanted to live it all. I thought I would, but I didn't, and there's no real reason why. I just... didn't move.

Eternal Chapter is my baby. My quiet little slice of heaven, tucked between a coffee shop that never quite gets my order right and a vintage clothing store that always smells like lavender.

Every morning, when I unlock the front door and the old brass bell chimes its familiar welcome, I feel that slight flutter in my chest because there they are—all my literary loves lined up on wooden shelves I stained myself.

In here, between these walls that hold more stories than I'll ever live, this life doesn't feel small at all. It feels like exactly where I'm supposed to be.

Imagine a bookstore bathed in every shade of pink and purple you can think of. Soft-blush walls, dusty-rose cushions slumped lovingly into the corner of a cream couch, and a faded lilac rug worn in by customers who caught their boots on the corners. Now imagine those shelves lined with books full of men who don't just blur the line between right and wrong—they set it on fire. Morally gray men who'd take their time ruining you, then make you crawl back and beg for more with your legs still shaking. And all of them, stacked neatly against pastel-pink shelving like filth disguised as fairy tales.

My phone sits on the desk, practically taunting me, daring me to do something I never have before and break the one promise I made to myself when Jasper, Roman, and Zeke left: no looking them up online.

Cold turkey worked until now, but with the ceremony looming, the temptation to learn everything about them claws at my throat. I need to be prepared. I need to know if they're married, engaged, or happy without me in their life.

My finger lingers over the purple social media icon when the doorbell chimes, making me jump like I've been caught watching porn in church.

Maybe it's divine intervention or the universe saving me from myself. Either way, I focus on Bing Crosby's voice drifting through the speakers instead of my racing heart.

I take a breath, flatten down my sweater, and when I finally lift my head, I find three sets of eyes focused on me.

The world grinds to a halt around me, and all I can think is how badly I wish I looked hotter, because this bookstore gremlin situation is definitely not how I imagined my hockey boys seeing me for the first time after all these years.

Zeke's eyes hit me first—deep emerald green that are still so soft it guts me. There's no resentment there, no distance, just that same devastating gentleness that always made me want to fall apart in his arms.

Jasper's gaze follows—dark brown and burning, sharp enough to slice through me, yet somehow he still feels like the safest place I've ever known. He stands with that same confidence he's always had, like he knows exactly what he does to me.

And then there's Roman.

Roman, whose amber eyes have darkened into something almost molten now, rich gold catching the wall lights like fire. His black T-shirt clings to his chest beneath the open coat, and I catch glimpses of tattoos I don't recognize crawling up his neck and disappearing beneath his collar. He stares at me as if five years away from each other didn't dent the hunger he once had for me, but that hurt... I still see it in his eyes.

They aren't boys anymore.

They're men now.

Men who didn't just survive without me, they thrived. It's there in the set of their shoulders and how they own every inch of space they occupy without even trying. Meanwhile, I'm standing behind the counter of a pink bookstore, clutching a half-cold cup of cocoa, wondering how the hell I'm supposed to survive this.

As Jasper steps forward, the smallest smile pulls at the corner of his mouth, and my heart stutters in my chest.

"Hey, angel," he says, his voice so heartbreakingly familiar it knocks the ground right out from under me. "It's been a while."

CHAPTER SEVEN
ZEKE

Once we were back in Colorado, it took us less than five minutes to figure out where to find Addison. Not that we needed to dig too deep—we've all kept tabs on her over the years.

Waiting until the award ceremony to see her was never going to happen. The three of us were wound too tight. We knew it'd be better to break the ice now, on our terms, than to play out our reunion in front of half the town on her father's night.

Of course, there was always the very real possibility that Addison wouldn't give a flying shit that we were here. She's married now and supposedly happy with the kind of simple, uncomplicated life her father always wanted for her.

The good daughter who fell in line.

But I know better the moment those navy eyes collide with mine.

Addison was always an open book to those who knew how to read her, and five years haven't changed that. Every emotion plays across her face like a movie I can't look away from.

Lost.

Confused.

Hopeful.

Anxious.

Happy.

Cornered.

Her energy pulses through the store, raw and real and so fucking intoxicating it makes my chest ache.

She's drowning in an oversized sweater, covering a body that was never meant to be hidden. The glasses she used to only wear when she was too tired to care what anyone thought are perched on her nose, and her hair's loose around her shoulders—soft, touchable... familiar.

And yeah, she might be married to Mikey King, but the way she's looking at us right now isn't the look of a woman who's living the dream she chose. This is the look of a woman seeing ghosts she never managed to bury and realizing the past isn't done with her yet.

Jasper's the first to greet her—no surprise there. He's never met a silence he didn't feel the need to fill, nor has he ever managed to find a filter between his brain and his mouth. He's got all the subtlety of a wrecking ball and the self-restraint of a kid in a candy store. But now, watching him break the ice while I'm still frozen in place, I'm grateful for his inability to shut the hell up.

Jesus, she's more beautiful than I remember.

Her hair's shorter now, brushing just past her shoulders instead of spilling down her back, and there's something different in the way she holds herself.

"How did you know where I was?" Her voice is steady, but her fingers twist in the hem of her sweater, a nervous tell she never outgrew.

"Small town," I answer, watching her reaction. "People know everything about everyone. You know that."

"Don't just stand there. Get your ass round here."

She circles the counter, and Jasper pulls her into a hug that looks so easy, like muscle memory, but I can see the way his hands tremble slightly against her back before he lets her go.

When she steps back, I take my turn, wrapping her petite frame in my arms. She melts into my embrace like no time has passed at all, and when I finally release her, she turns her attention to Roman.

"How are you?" she asks softly.

He just nods, rubbing his jaw as he takes her in.

"I can't believe you're all really here." She laughs, but it's got an edge of hysteria to it, like she's still trying to convince herself we're real.

"We wanted to come see you before the weekend," Jasper says.

"I've been thinking about it a lot, and… yeah. I'm glad you found me. Of course it's good to see you all."

"How's Coach?" I ask, resting my hip against the counter.

"He's living his best life, knowing all the fuss is going to be about him for once."

I let out a low laugh, shaking my head. "I guess it is his turn."

"Where's your husband?" Roman asks, blunt as always.

I reach for him instinctively, running my hand up and down his back. I have no idea if he can even feel my touch through his coat, but I don't stop.

"Mikey is…" Addison pauses, clasping her hands together before lowering them. "I actually have no idea where he is. You'll see him over the weekend though."

"Awesome," Roman mutters, his mouth twisting around the word. "Can't wait to catch up."

"Still can't believe you married a King," Jasper chimes in, grinning in that shit-eating way that only he can get away with. "What were you thinking, angel?"

"I was drunk when I agreed," she says, and we all laugh, too loud and too long. "So, where are you guys staying?"

"In a cabin up at the lodge," Jasper announces, sprawling across Addison's counter like he owns the place.

"They're really nice," she replies, offering a smile that's a little too tight. "Spacious."

"Perfect, because we take up a lot of room."

There's a hint of curiosity in her eyes, but she swallows whatever she was about to say.

"What?" Jasper calls her out instantly, cocking his head, daring her to say it. "Come on, angel. You're dying to ask. I can see it all over that pretty face."

Addison shifts, her fingers knotting together before she finally exhales. "I guess I was wondering…" She trails off. "I take it you guys are still—"

"Still fucking each other's brains out?" Jasper cuts in without a shred of shame. "Yeah, baby. Every goddamn day."

For a second, she just stands there completely frozen, pink flushing across her cheeks and spreading down her neck.

I reach out and grab Jasper by the back of his coat, yanking him off the counter hard enough to make him grunt.

"What the hell's wrong with you?" I growl at him, even though I'm half laughing because this is just who he is—wild, unapologetic, and way too much. But fuck, I love him for it.

"What?" Jasper just shrugs, grinning like the chaotic bastard he is. "Come on, you know she was desperate to ask. Weren't you, Addie?"

"Not quite the words I would've used," she mutters, her voice unsteady but her mouth twitching like she's fighting a smile.

"Doesn't make it any less true," Jasper fires back.

"You really haven't changed, have you?" She laughs, and that's when I hear my big guy speak up beside me.

"Have you?"

"I like to think so," she answers softly.

I snort, tightening my grip on Jasper's neck before finally letting him go. "Yeah, well, as you can see, this one's still fucking trouble."

"Don't pretend you two don't fucking love it." He flashes a smile that's all teeth, while Roman lets out a deep rumble of laughter beside me.

"How long are you guys staying?"

"We're heading back to Boston on Sunday. We've got some time to catch up if you're free. Maybe we could grab a drink tomorrow night?"

Before she can answer, Roman's phone starts ringing. When he mouths the word "coach," he's already moving toward the door, slipping outside to take the call.

"How is he?" she whispers, like she's not sure she's allowed to care this much anymore.

I glance at Jasper, and he's already looking at me, the same thought written across his face.

She still feels something for him.

"He's still Roman. He still carries everything like it's his alone. But this is a lot for him. It's a lot for all of us."

She nods, picking up what I'm saying without needing it spelled out. "I suppose we could do something tomorrow," she offers. "But I'm guessing you're still keeping your relationship under wraps?"

"For now," Jasper answers before I can.

"Then why don't you come to my house? You don't have to hide who you are there."

"Are you sure about that, angel? Last time we were all a little wasted in a house together, we ended up making out."

"I'm pretty sure we're all adult enough to know the past isn't an issue anymore."

Jasper laughs just as Roman steps back inside, pocketing his phone, his eyes immediately finding hers.

"Addie's invited us over tomorrow night," I tell him, watching his face carefully.

"Yeah, hard pass." He runs a hand through his hair, clearly uncomfortable. "No offense, Addie, but I'm not spending the night anywhere near Mikey. I know he's your guy, but I can't stand that dick."

Addison doesn't flinch. She just cocks her head and fires right back. "You could be one too, once."

Suddenly I'm not standing in her bookstore anymore. I'm standing five years in the past, watching Roman and Addison dance around each other like they weren't already on fire.

"Oh, I'm still a dick. I just don't hide it behind a fake smile and a snake's personality."

"Well, you'll be glad to know he won't be there, so the invitation stands."

Roman goes quiet, staring her down, and the silence stretches between them, charged with all the history they're pretending doesn't exist. There's still something there. We can all feel it, even if he's too damn stubborn and she's too married to admit it.

"How about you come to us instead?" Jasper cuts in, pulling out his phone and holding it out to her. "Give me your number, and we'll figure it out."

I watch as she punches in her number, her fingers steady even though I can see her pulse fluttering in her throat.

Addie, baby, you really have no idea what you just did.

Because she doesn't know what it means to give Jasper an inch when he's been starving for a mile.

The man is relentless on a good day—on the ice, in bed, in

every part of his life, and now that he has her number, he's not going to leave her alone.

"It was good to see you, Addison."

"You too, Zeke," she says, her smile touching something deep in my chest. "All of you."

With one last look at her, we turn and walk away, the bell over the door chiming behind us.

The bitter December wind whips around us, and I hear Roman take a shaky breath as we start walking.

"Are you okay?" I ask, fighting the urge to pull him close.

"Yeah, just seeing her again… It's a lot."

"Made you realize you still feel something for her?" Roman nods, and Jasper slides an arm around his shoulders, casual but grounding him with the contact I know he needs. "Well, you're not the only one, Captain, which is good. Means you're still just as stupidly gone for her as we are, right, Zeke?"

"Yeah," I breathe out. "She hasn't changed at all, has she? Five years, and she still looks at us like we never left."

"Let me grab some dinner," Jasper says, his thumb stroking Roman's shoulder. "You two head back. Take a minute to—"

"Don't go." Roman cuts him off, and I see that spark of need between them—that instinct to reach for each other when shit gets heavy. His fingers find Jasper's coat, holding on. "The restaurant up at the lodge is fine."

"Come on." I shove the keys at Roman because we all know he needs to move; he needs to do something before he combusts.

We had to book the largest cabin with enough rooms for all three of us to keep up the lie. I hate living like the best thing in my life is something I have to hide, but I don't see another way until we can all walk away from hockey for good.

Coming out would be like handing ourselves over to be ripped apart. The media would have a field day. The sports networks would dissect it, and fans would spit their opinions across every screen they could reach, as if loving each other somehow cancels out everything we've achieved on the ice.

I close the cabin door behind me, and Roman's on me like a starved animal. His big hands fist my hair, yanking my head back as his mouth crashes onto mine. His tongue forces my lips apart, taking what he needs, and within seconds, both our shirts are off. I bend to run kisses along his shoulder, tasting salt and skin and marking him with my teeth.

"On the bed," Roman growls as I strip off the rest of my clothes.

I watch him from the corner of my eye—watch how his muscles flex under tattooed skin as he yanks his pants down.

He doesn't bother waiting for me. He just drops onto the mattress and sprawls back against the headboard, fist tight around his cock, stroking himself. My eyes lock on the silver barbell glinting at the head, slick and swollen, his need for me already dripping from the tip.

"What do you need, baby?" I ask.

"I just need you close."

I crawl onto the bed, climbing straight into his lap, straddling him, wrapping one arm tight around his shoulder. When I spit into my palm and bring our foreheads together, I grip us both, working us slowly. Roman's hands bruise my back, pulling me impossibly closer as his hips snap up into my fist like he's lost all control.

"How long?" Roman pants against my mouth.

"He'll be quick. You know he'll be climbing out of his skin to get back to us."

CHAPTER EIGHT
JASPER

I've never chosen food faster in my fucking life, and when I tell you I practically ran back to the cabin, I mean it. I'd bet my left nut Roman and Zeke started without me.

I bust through the door, the freezing air following me before I kick it shut behind me. The takeout bags hit the kitchen counter with a careless thud, forgotten about completely. Without slowing down, I move to the bedroom, and my eyes land on the bed. Zeke's straddling Roman's lap, grinding down on him, while their mouths are fused in a kiss that's nothing short of desperate.

"Fuckers," I growl, already stripping my jacket off and dragging my T-shirt over my head. "I knew you'd start without me."

Not that I'm complaining—the view's fucking delicious.

Roman breaks away from Zeke's mouth just long enough to shoot me a look that could drop me to my knees. "Get over here and fill our boy's ass."

"Yes, sir," I mutter, shoving my jeans down my hips, cock already hard at the sight of them.

Zeke and Roman's grunts fill the air, and a shudder runs through me at how fucking beautiful they sound together.

Watching them like this is one of my favorite things in the world. These moments are the only time my brain shuts the hell up. Everything else disappears except for what's right in front of me.

Them.

Mine.

My guys.

My whole goddamn world, right here.

Desperate, filthy, and beautiful in ways nothing else could ever fucking touch.

I climb onto the bed and pull Zeke back, tilting his face and kissing him like the desperate bastard I am before leaning forward and giving Roman my tongue. Pulling back, I brush my nose against his and haul Zeke back by the hips, forcing him onto his knees between us.

"You lucky fucker," I growl, knowing Roman's about to get the show of his life.

"Getting to feel every thrust through his throat? Fucking heaven."

"Less talking, more eating my ass," Zeke demands, breathless and needy, grinding back against me like he's trying to get himself off by friction alone.

Bending down, I run my tongue up the length of Zeke's cock before dragging it over his balls and up to his ass, and fuck, my eyes automatically roll back because he always tastes like heaven. The noises he makes when my tongue's on him and the way his thighs start to tremble under my grip—nothing I've ever chased comes close to this.

When I push my tongue inside him, Zeke damn near loses it, rutting shamelessly against my mouth. I fumble open the nightstand drawer, not bothering to look, and grab the lube. My fingers are slick in seconds. One presses into him slowly, just enough to stretch and tease, while my other hand wraps tight around his cock.

"Fuck, Jasper," he pants out, pushing back onto my hand. "That feels so good."

Roman's hips snap forward as he thrusts into Zeke's mouth. "Open that throat. That's it... just like that."

I can barely fucking breathe watching Zeke choke himself on Roman's dick while he fucks back onto my fingers. When I finally drag them out of him, he shudders hard, already close to blowing.

"Easy, baby," I rasp, slicking up my cock, fist working fast because I'm right there with him—so damn close, I can barely see straight.

I line up at his entrance, pressing against that tight ring of muscle until he starts to give, and I watch every inch of me disappear.

It's never just sex with them.

It's worship.

It's fucking home.

I'll never get enough of filling Zeke up. One of these days, I'm going to break Roman down too. I'm gonna fuck the fight right out of him. He likes to play the big, bad dominant and swears he's strictly a top, but I see it. Every time we switch, his eyes track the movement like he's trying not to imagine himself there.

One day, baby.

"You want this?" Roman growls, fisting Zeke's hair as he offers himself again.

Lucky asshole—this time I mean Zeke because Roman's cock is exquisite, and that piercing hits spots that make you see stars.

Zeke groans, and fuck if it doesn't make me snap. I drive into him harder, faster, hitting deep with every thrust, using Zeke's tight, wrecked body to fuck with Roman from the inside out.

If this is the only way I can top our captain for now, then I'm damn well gonna take it.

"Fuck, Jasper. He's sucking me all the way down. Keep fucking him like that."

Zeke's got this gift—no-hands orgasm. Just a cock in his throat, another in his ass, and he's gone. Fucking prodigy our boy is, and knowing I can get him there every single time makes me feel like a god.

"Show us what our cock-drunk boy can do, Zeke," I growl, slamming into him so hard the bed rocks. "Let go for us."

Like it was written into his bones, Zeke pulls off Roman's cock with a filthy, wet pop, making these broken sounds as I pound into him harder.

"Fuck—yes—holy shit," Zeke cries out, his body locking up before shuddering violently.

Roman catches Zeke's release in his palm, that devil's smirk spreading across his face. He slicks his pierced cock with it, jerking himself off rough and fast, his head slamming back against the headboard as he chases his release, and Jesus, I can't tear my eyes away.

Zeke's gone boneless around me while our captain puts on a show, and between this vice-grip ass and Roman losing it, I'm about to fucking detonate.

"Keep going," I growl at Roman, fucking into Zeke like I'm trying to push him through the bed. "Fucking come for us," I demand, and Roman's whole body goes rigid.

The second his cum starts painting his abs, my orgasm tears through me, and I bury myself balls-deep inside Zeke, emptying into him.

"Fuuuck," I choke out, sagging against Zeke's back, still pulsing inside him.

Roman slumps against the headboard, chest heaving, his hand lazily dragging through the mess across his stomach.

I ease out of Zeke and collapse beside him, the three of us ending up in a sweaty heap of satisfaction.

"Jesus, I love you both so much. That was..." My voice trails off, words failing me as I try to catch my breath.

"Yeah, baby, it was," Roman murmurs.

"Permission to talk about she-who-must-not-be-named?" I mumble against his skin, still drunk off both of them.

"Go for it, but only because I'm still high enough from coming that I can't bring myself to knock your ass out." Roman laughs while his fingers trace lazy patterns on my skin.

"As much as being with you two is more than enough for me and always will be. Tell me you haven't thought about Addison sitting on your face while we're together like that."

Roman groans, throwing his arm over his eyes like that might block out the memories. Because he knows exactly how she tastes, and I can't pretend I'm not jealous as hell.

"She ruined me for any other pussy, but my dick wasn't enough, so let's not go down that road."

"Come on, man," Zeke says, reaching out to stroke Roman's skin. "You know that was all about Coach—"

"Still couldn't make her stay, could I?"

"You are enough. I know you know that now," I say, reaching for his hand and twisting our fingers together while my other hand strokes through Zeke's hair.

"I know Addie's with Mikey, but if she weren't, if you had the chance, would you take it?" Zeke asks.

"Without a shadow of a doubt, and I wouldn't stop until she was clawing me to pieces. You?"

Zeke nods. "The attraction never went away. But we know it's all of us or none of us."

I turn my head, locking eyes with Roman. "What about you, Captain?"

"Honestly? I don't know…" He lets the words sit there for a second before pushing through them. "But I get it. I always have, and she's never been off the table when it comes to you two. And yeah, I'd love to fuck you both while you're touching her, but my hands on her body? Pretty sure it would kill me a little, and I'm not willing to put myself through it."

CHAPTER NINE
ROMAN

It's just a drink.

It's just a catch-up with an old friend because that's what she was first.

Before I went and fell in love with her.

Why the fuck can't I let it go?

I don't mean the kind of letting go you do when something's finished and it makes sense. I mean the kind where every part of you knows it's over, but your body still tightens when you hear their name. The kind where your chest still fucking aches when you imagine them with someone else.

I know Addison's married now, and that should've been the end of it, but here I am, standing in front of the door, my heart punching against my ribs like it's trying to break free, while she knocks on the other side.

Maybe this is a step toward moving on.

Maybe tonight I can remember how to be her friend.

Maybe I should stop lying to myself.

I glance to my right at Jasper. He's so confident, so unapologetically himself. He's the kind of man you want to lean on forever, the one who doesn't wait for you to ask before he catches you. You just know he's already there, holding you up before you even realize you're falling.

Then to my left, there's Zeke, who's soft in a way that makes you literally fucking ache. He's all heart, all beauty, and there's something about how he exists in the world that makes you want to cover him in bubble wrap, but you know he's protecting you just as fiercely. One look from him and you understand that this man would burn the world down for the people he loves.

These guys make me a sappy bastard, but I'm more than good with it.

I'm grateful.

Jasper steps forward and pulls open the door, and there she is—Addison Hope, standing in the cold with her blonde hair tied back in a loose ponytail, soft wisps escaping to frame her face. She's wearing a black tank under a thick winter coat she hasn't bothered to button, the edges flaring open like she left in a hurry.

Maybe she wasn't planning to come and changed her mind at the last second.

"Get in here before you freeze your tiny ass off," Jasper says, and she steps inside, closing the door behind her.

Jasper reaches out and helps her slide off her coat, ever the gentleman when it suits him, and that's when I see those jeans. Low-slung and faded in all the right places, hugging her hips and ass like they were custom-made to destroy me.

"Hey." She smiles at me and Zeke, but it's clear she's nervous.

It's subtle, but the tells are still there—tight smile, fingers twitching at her sides, and blue eyes that won't hold mine for more than a second.

She might be trying to play it cool, but I've known Addison for a long time, and I can read her without even trying.

So can they.

"We bought you some wine," I force out, trying my hardest to act normal for all of us. "That okay?"

"I'll always be that wine-drunk girl you used to know," she says, and fuck if it doesn't feel like both a promise and a threat. "It's been decorated so pretty in here."

Zeke chuckles as he moves to the kitchen counter, already pulling out glasses. "Usually that's my job back home," he says, glancing at her over his shoulder. "But this place was already done up when we arrived."

Zeke's always the one who makes our home feel like Christmas. He's the one who decorates the tree, arranges the stockings, and lights the candles that smell like vanilla and pine. Jasper and I help, but mostly, we just drink whiskey and flirt until we become a distraction.

"What's your place like in Boston?"

"It's different from here," Zeke says, glancing at both of us before continuing. "Not homely in the traditional sense, but it is *home*. We've got an entire floor—big windows, city skyline, lights that never go out. It feels… alive."

"You're all happy there?"

Zeke nods slowly. "Happier than any of us ever imagined, I think."

"The only thing we'd change is hiding," Jasper cuts in. "We don't hide inside our home. We're just us there. But outside, when the masks come on, that's the part I hate."

"We all do, baby," I murmur, reaching out and resting my hand on Jasper's back, my fingers curling just enough to feel him there.

I don't pull away when Addison's eyes land on the way I touch him. If she recalls that I used to touch her in that same way, then so be it. Let her remember.

"So, is Addison Hope still the same wine-drunk girl who enjoys watching two guys make out while she's being kissed?"

She slowly turns her head and places a hand on her hip, and all I can do is stand there and watch because how she answers matters more than it should—especially considering she's wifed up now.

She doesn't wear a ring, but I know plenty of people who don't.

"Are you going to be like this all night?" she asks, raising a brow.

"Probably," Jasper replies, with zero apology in his voice.

"So, no offense when I ignore you?"

"You can try," he says with a smirk, "but we both know that never worked out for you before."

Zeke chuckles as he moves around the island, his hand lingering for half a second on her back before he pulls away, reaching for the wineglasses.

"Sorry about him," he says, pouring her a large glass. "He's never changing."

She accepts the wine, her fingers brushing his like she didn't once look at him like he hung the fucking moon.

But I see it.

A hint of pink rises beneath her winter-pale skin, while Zeke's jaw twitches like he's biting back the urge to step closer. I feel every inch of it as though it's stitched into my own damn bones.

"Also, for the record, you gave us shots that night. Wine-drunk me isn't nearly as reckless."

Jasper pushes off the counter, and I move with him, closing the space like it's instinct. My chest brushes his back as I settle in behind him, close enough to feel his warmth. His hand reaches behind him, gripping my thigh—not hard, not possessive, just there.

"My dad mentioned you made captain, Roman."

I'm curled around Jasper, my chin hooked over his shoulder as I breathe him in. The warm, woodsy scent he always wears fills my lungs like a drug—one hit and everything in me goes quiet.

"Like he was ever destined for anything less," Jasper says, and the pride in his voice makes something hot and possessive twist in my stomach.

I nip at his ear, letting my teeth graze the sensitive skin. When I lift my gaze, Addison's watching us—her lips are parted, breath caught in her throat like she wasn't expecting the intimacy. It's as if she forgot what it was, the way I used to touch her, and how I was always reaching for her too.

What we looked like before everything went to hell.

Because there was a time when it was all she knew.

My touch.

My need.

The way I looked at her like I'd tear the world apart just to keep her under my hands.

"Yeah, I've been doing it a while now." My fingers drift under Jasper's shirt, tracing slow circles into his hip. "It's probably about time someone else took over."

"They won't find anyone half as good," Jasper says, leaning his weight back into me.

"One bad hit is all it takes. I could go out next month and snap both legs, and that's my career over in seconds."

Zeke groans. "You just want to be taken care of."

"I mean... I wouldn't say no." I smirk. "A few weeks of rest. Someone feeding me, working out all those knots in my thighs... I could definitely use the break."

Jasper barks out a laugh, cracking open his beer. "What the hell do you think this is?"

"A few days off. Nothing more."

"So," Zeke says, turning toward Addison, "what's going on with you? Everything good?"

She nods as she takes a long pull from her glass.

Lying before she even opens her mouth.

"Yeah, everything's great."

Lying again.

"Did you tell your husband you were coming up here tonight?"

"Nope."

"Why not? Figure he'd want to know we're back in town and spending the night with his wife."

"Please stop calling me that, Roman, and since we're not living together anymore, I don't think it's any of his fucking business where I go or who I see." She quickly turns on her heel and walks into the living room, glass in hand, like she didn't just nuke the entire conversation.

"Like hell you're walking away from that, Addison!" Jasper calls after her, with a half-stunned laugh. He lets out a low whistle, rubbing his jaw with that wicked smirk he wears when he knows shit's about to get messy. "Well," he drawls, eyes flicking between us and the hallway she disappeared down, "guess this little reunion just got a hell of a lot more interesting."

Jasper follows her into the living room, and Zeke catches my eye. His look asks if I'm good, and I nod because, honestly, knowing she ditched that asshole makes everything better, even if it's about to blow our whole dynamic apart.

By the time we reach the living room, Jasper's already claimed the spot next to her on the couch. Addison sits with her legs folded beneath her. Zeke and I drop into the armchairs across from them, and for a moment, it's like we've slipped right back to that night.

"You better start talking, Addie," Jasper says, elbows on his knees, his focus pinned entirely on her.

"There's not much to tell. He tripped and fell inside my friend's pussy like the manwhore he is."

"He what?" The words come out like gravel, my grip tightening around the neck of my beer.

"Oh, save the righteous anger, Roman. You always hated him. Don't act shocked now."

"Yeah, well." I lean back, not bothering to hide my satisfaction. What I do hide is how much it guts me, knowing he might've hurt her. "When you're right, you're right."

What I don't say is how my hands are already itching, how the next time I see that piece of shit, I won't be playing nice. I won't be shaking his hand and swallowing my disgust. No, next time, I'm rearranging his fucking face.

"How are you holding up?"

"I'm good. Weirdly good." She meets Zeke's eyes, lets out a breath, and takes another sip of wine, like it might help the words come easier. "I don't think I was ever truly in it. There was always something missing, and maybe he felt it too. Maybe that's why his dick got lost inside someone else."

"At least you're not pulling that self-blame bullshit." Jasper's jaw tightens. "I hate when people do that."

"Another sign it was wrong from the start, right? I mean, shouldn't I be ugly crying into my wine or dissecting every fucking thing I did wrong?"

"We all could've told you the guy was an ass," Zeke says, leaning forward. "Pretty sure we did several times. And what happened to you getting out of here?"

"I don't know." She runs a hand through her hair, pulling out the elastic and letting blonde waves fall around her shoulders. "I can't answer that. But I don't regret spending the last few years around my family."

"You always wanted more. That's what Zeke's saying."

I'm not even sure what I mean by more.

Maybe freedom or love... Maybe us.

No—not us.

Them.

That door's sealed shut for a reason.

"Maybe the things I wanted changed somewhere along the way," she says, almost as if she's trying to convince herself.

She drags her hands down her face, and fuck me if I don't catch myself staring at the way it makes her chest rise and fall.

Focus, you dick.

"This is crazy," she mutters, fingers pressed against her temples. "I shouldn't be telling you all this. We haven't... There's been so much time, so much distance, and... Jesus, we don't even know each other anymore."

"That's bullshit, Addie, and you fucking know it." Jasper leans forward, his eyes burning into hers. "You're still you, and we still care. So let's get drunk, pretend time doesn't mean shit, and remind you what it feels like to be yourself with us again."

A few hours later and too many bottles of wine in, I'm watching Addison lose her filter one glass at a time. She's matching Jasper shot for shot, while I switched to water an hour ago. Someone needs to stay clearheaded, and right now, that someone's me.

"You know what else?" she says, leaning forward like she's about to tell us a secret, wine sloshing dangerously close to the edge of her glass. "He was bad. Like... tragically bad. And I've never... well, I have, but..." She waves her hand like it's gonna help the words make sense. "You know what I mean?"

Zeke nearly spits out his drink, and Jasper loses it completely.

Addison's grinning now, flushed in the prettiest fucking way. "I mean, I've had orgasms before—great ones—but not with him. And the worst part?" She slams back what's left of her drink and points at us like we're supposed to guess. "He thought he was the shit. Like he was doing me a favor by even showing up hard." The three of us crack up, and her laugh—that real, unfiltered sound I remember from years ago—hits me right in the chest.

"Have you ever had sex so bad it felt like you needed to exorcise it out of your body?" she asks, her eyes wide and dramatic as hell. "Like, full-on shower, bleach, holy water—scrub your fucking skin raw just to forget they ever put their disgusting hands on you?"

"Can't say I have, beautiful." Zeke grins, clearly enjoying this version of her.

"Never?" She gasps. "God, lucky you. I've had more 'what the hell am I doing with him' showers than orgasms. One time it was so bad I cried into my loofah."

Jasper's choking on a beer. Zeke's laughing so hard he nearly tips backward in his chair. And I'm ready to tell her to stop talking. Stop laughing. Stop being this version of Addison—messy, beautiful, and real as hell—because I'm sitting here, watching her come alive again, and my heart's remembering what it feels like to want her.

"I think it's time to call it a night, angel." Jasper drains his beer, laughing at the way she's sprawled across the couch like a queen.

"What? Why? I'm fine." She tries to sit up straighter, nearly dropping her empty glass.

"Fine, you are. Fuck me..." Jasper's eyes roam over her, and I recognize that look.

It's the same one he gives me when he's riding me hard with his hand wrapped around my throat.

God, I'd kill to watch him with her.

"But you're also wasted, and tomorrow's gonna hit you like a truck."

I lean close to Zeke, keeping my voice low. "She can't go home like this."

"I know," Zeke mutters back.

I catch Jasper's eye and jerk my chin toward the guest rooms. He reads me instantly, nodding in agreement.

"Looks like you're crashing here tonight," I say.

"What? No," Addison protests. "I should go home."

"And how exactly are you getting there, princess?"

The nickname slips out before I can catch it, and the room goes silent. Jasper's head snaps up, Zeke freezes mid-sip, and Addison... Jesus, the way she looks at me feels like a punch to the chest.

That name belongs to a different time, a different us, and we all know it.

Sure, I could drive her down the mountain. But leaving her alone, this drunk, with her mascara smudged and her words starting to slur, feels like a dick move.

"Uhmm..." She blinks like she's trying to remember how her brain works. "Where will I sleep? Where are you sleeping?"

"There's a guest room," Jasper says, leaning back with that cocky fucking grin that screams trouble. "And we sleep together. Always have, always will. We don't do separate beds, angel." His smirk widens, and I know he's about to set the room on fire. "And damn near every time we end up in one... someone's getting fucked."

Addison's mouth opens slightly, then shuts again.

I shoot Zeke a "what the actual fuck" look, both of us caught between laughing and shock. Honestly, I don't even know why we're surprised anymore. Jasper opens his mouth and filth falls out like it's a love language.

But then I catch the way Addie's whole body tenses. Not from disgust. No, this is something else entirely. She's turned on. I can see the heat in her eyes—that soft glaze of *fuck me* wrapped in confusion—and part of me wants Jasper to keep pushing, to see how far this goes. But nothing prepares me for what comes out of her mouth.

"Who... How does it work? Which one of you...?" I can't look away as Jasper grabs her chin and tilts her face to his.

"Tops?" When she nods, he slides his hand into her hair, tucking a strand behind her ear. "All of us."

"So you... all of you... together?" The words come out breathless, and it's not embarrassment holding her back from asking what she really wants to know—it's arousal, pure and simple.

"Zeke and I like to be fucked just as much as we like to do the fucking. Depends on the night and the mood." Then he glances at me, smirking. "But Roman's dominant to the bone and hasn't let either of us touch him like that." He looks back at her, his eyes dark. "But you know that already, don't you? You remember exactly how good he is when he's got your body under his. When he's fucking you so deep you forget how to speak, let alone scream his name."

I didn't need the reminder of being inside Addie, but here we are. Every second of it floods back, every sound she made, every whimper when I pushed her to the edge. The way her skin tasted like sweet summer peaches under my tongue, and those eyes that sparkled like she had galaxies trapped behind her lashes every time I whispered those three words against her throat.

"Why not?" Her wine-glazed eyes penetrate mine.

"Because being vulnerable is hard for me, and feeling out of control?" I shake my head, jaw tight. "Even harder."

"One of these days I'm going to fucking ruin you, Captain." Jasper grins, and Zeke just laughs.

God help me, I want it.

I want to give myself up completely.

I want to feel stretched and full and fucked out.

"That right?" I murmur, my eyes dragging back to Jasper like I'm already halfway to saying, *Yes, please, fucking do it.*

"Someone's not saying no anymore," he drawls.

"Maybe someone needs to shut the fuck up right now." My eyes go wide, begging him to drop it before this conversation goes somewhere we can't take back.

"Because of me?" Addison slurs, frowning like she just realized she's the topic of conversation. "I'm sorry… I wasn't trying to pry. Okay, maybe I was a little because…" She attempts to stand, immediately topples back down, and dissolves into a fit of drunk giggles.

"I'm getting her to bed," I say, already moving. "I don't trust her not to try and fuck one of you, and I definitely don't trust Jasper with his dick anywhere near her right now."

"Hey, I heard that!" she snipes back, still laughing. "But I promise I'd never try to take any of you…" Her eyes glaze over. "I'd be more than happy to just watch because you're all… Well, you know what you are. You have mirrors." Zeke snorts into his drink, and Jasper grins like he's won a fucking prize.

"Jesus Christ," I mutter, standing and swooping her up in one motion. She lands over my shoulder, laughing like this is all a game, when she doesn't even realize what she's doing to me.

I feel every curve of her body against mine, and it wrecks me. I want to put her down. I want to never let her go. I want to bury myself inside her and never come up for air, and I want to run as far away as possible so I forget how this ever felt.

I make it to the bedroom, lower her onto the bed, and she immediately melts into the pillows like they've been calling her name all night. The Christmas bedding—green and gold, and obnoxiously festive—feels out of place for the kind of thoughts I'm having right now.

"Are you sure you don't mind me staying?" she mumbles, wiggling her foot at me with a lazy little smile.

I kneel down, pulling off her sock, and immediately regret every decision that led to this moment. Her skin is soft and warm against my fingers, and I'm trying—really fucking trying—not to stare at the perfectly painted lilac polish on her toes. It's such a small detail, so insignificant, but it's Addie. She always painted her toes these soft, pastel colors.

"I don't want it to be weird, and I definitely don't want you to feel uncomfortable around me like you always used to."

"I'm fine, Addie," I mutter, tugging off her other sock, and she points at her jeans.

Fuck no. My dick's already semihard, and there's no way I'm letting myself see what's underneath.

"Sleep in them."

"Roman," she whines, her eyes still shut. "Sleeping in denim is a fucking crime, and I refuse to commit it."

"You say the weirdest shit sometimes."

"You used to love that about me."

Ignore it.

"Roman?"

"Yeah?"

"Please."

She's drunk, I'm weak and clearly a complete fucking idiot.

My hand moves before reason can catch up, finding the button of her jeans. I pop it open, drag the zipper down slow enough to feel every click of metal, then slide the denim down her legs.

Holy shit.

Pink panties.

Soft, barely there lace that's so thin I can see the outline of her pussy. My heart stutters. My cock throbs, and I want to bury my face between her thighs.

"I'm sorry."

Don't. Fucking. Ask.

"What for?"

"Hurting you," she mumbles as I pull her legs free from her jeans and stand, draping a blanket over her.

She sinks deeper into the bed, her eyes fixed on me like she's afraid the words won't count if she doesn't see me hear them.

"I know I did, and one day… I hope you'll like me again. Not for the girl who fucked it all up. But for the woman I am now, because I've changed, Roman. Not completely, but enough, and I swear I would've done everything differently if I could go back."

Fuck my heart and the way it shatters into a million pieces. "It's okay, Addie. Just get some sleep."

"No, it's not okay," she whispers. "I made shitty choices. But you have to know I did lo—"

"Get some sleep." I cut her off fast because I can't hear that right now.

She turns away without another word, burrowing into the blanket as if she's trying to disappear. I scrub a hand through my hair, feeling every complicated emotion crash over me at once. For a second, I just stand there, watching her breathe, before I shove the mess of feelings down and head back to my guys.

CHAPTER TEN
ADDISON

I have to be dead.

When I manage to crack open one blurry eye, it's pitch black in the room, and I have no clue where the hell I am or what time it is.

The sheets are caught around my legs, like I've spent the night fighting for my life, and my mouth is dry as hell.

I reach blindly toward where I hope there's a nightstand, praying my phone somehow made it here with me—though considering I can barely remember my own name right now, that feels a little optimistic.

But then my fingers brush against something cold and familiar. I flip my phone over, and the second the screen lights up, my eye snaps shut again like I've just been eye-fucked by the sun.

Squinting, I manage to catch the time.

Ugh, 2:49 a.m.

A groan punches out of me as I flop back onto the bed, dragging a hand down my face.

I flick my phone's flashlight on, blinking through what I'm pretty sure is one bloodshot eye, trying to get a read on where I am, and then it all comes rushing back to me. Drinking with Roman, Zeke, and Jasper, followed by Roman hauling my drunk ass to bed.

So, yeah. I guess I stayed the night. Or half the night. Whatever.

I swing my legs out of bed because my bladder is screaming at me. I push up to stand, wobbling slightly, but thankfully, I'm sober enough—or at least not dead enough—to think for myself. Shuffling toward the door like some sad zombie, I crack it open and step into the hall.

Of course these rich assholes have the biggest cabin on the mountain.

Stepping out of the room, I spot a light spilling down the hall —the bathroom, thank God. After taking care of business and rinsing my hands under water that I really wish was warmer, I start to tiptoe back to my room when I hear voices. I freeze, my heart thudding against my ribs as I strain to listen. That's definitely Roman, though the words are lost in the darkness.

I know exactly what I'm listening for, and yeah, maybe it's the alcohol still buzzing through my veins, or perhaps it's just pure curiosity, but my feet are already moving before my brain can catch up with why this is probably a terrible idea.

I follow the sounds, each step taking me closer until they're unmistakable. When I slowly push the door open, it feels like stumbling straight into a porno I didn't even know I needed— three almost-naked men, wearing nothing but boxer briefs, standing at the foot of the bed in what can only be described as a perfect triangle of lust.

Zeke drags slow, open-mouthed kisses down Roman's throat, his fingers sinking against Jasper's ass, pulling him closer in a way that makes my thighs clench. Roman groans into Jasper's mouth as they kiss, his hands roaming in a way that feels... familiar.

Jasper gasps when Roman fists a hand in his hair, yanking his head back to kiss him harder, rougher, while Zeke's fingers slip beneath the waistband of Jasper's briefs, teasing the crease of his ass. Roman's other hand grips Zeke's hair, yanking him closer, dragging him into the kiss until all three of them are a mess of greedy mouths and possessive hands.

I should look away, but I'm frozen.

I shouldn't be standing here, pressing my thighs together like some shameless voyeur, but holy hell, they're intoxicating.

Roman's body is a masterpiece. Tattoos cover every muscle, from his neck to his thighs, like someone took sex and sketched it across his skin. And yeah, I'm like many women who have a serious thing for ink, especially when it's wrapped around a body like his.

The other two are both unmarked, but no less lethal. Smooth, golden skin stretched over sculpted muscle that speaks to every hour spent in the gym and on the ice.

I need to drag my sorry, aching body back to the empty bed I crawled out of and pretend I never saw any of this. Pretend I'm not already imagining what it would feel like to be pinned between them.

But of course, the floorboard betrays me with a creak as I take a step back.

Stupid, ancient, noisy-as-hell cabin.

With Roman's mouth still claiming his throat, Jasper's eyes lift and find mine through the dark, looking at me like he knew I'd be here.

Heat floods my body, and I know I'm not just watching anymore—I'm prey, caught in a web I wove myself the second I followed their voices, and there's no chance in hell he's letting me walk away.

Jasper doesn't say a word. He keeps my secret, never looking away, even as his fingertips trace Zeke's spine. Zeke arches into his touch, turning his head until Roman's mouth finds his, and they start kissing like they've been dying to tear each other apart.

The last thirty seconds feel like thirty minutes. Jasper's eyes haven't left me once, and when I force myself to step back, his voice cuts through the air.

"I wouldn't do that if I were you, angel."

Jasper grips Zeke and Roman by the backs of their necks, forcing them to turn and look at me, standing there like an idiot in nothing but a tank and panties, caught red-handed.

"Don't even think about walking out that door."

"I-I didn't mean to... I'm sorry," I stammer, my voice so small I barely recognize it.

"For what?" Jasper asks, none of them making any attempt to send me away. "For watching the way we love each other, or for wanting to feel it?"

"Don't... not again," I plead.

"Not ever... because nothing happened before, did it?" Jasper fires back.

He steps forward, and I flick my gaze past him, catching the way Roman and Zeke watch, their eyes dark and their bodies coiled like they're just waiting for permission to pounce. When Jasper reaches me, he braces one hand against the doorframe, and his body heat wraps around me as his lips skim the shell of my ear.

"Five years, and I've never stopped wanting you. None of us have. But it's always your choice." My breath hitches, knowing this gorgeous man is mine to take. "But if it were up to me, angel, you'd be naked and crying my name before you could convince yourself you shouldn't want this."

I stumble back a step, caught between a desire so fierce it burns and the truth that, once again, these men will leave.

Sunday.

That gives me just a handful of nights to remember what it feels like to have them close before they get on that flight back to Boston, leaving me with fresh memories to torture myself with.

"Don't fucking move, princess." Roman's voice freezes me in place. "I mean it. Stop running and get your ass in the chair." He gestures to the corner while I stand there, struck dumb by the authority in his voice. "I'm not playing, Addie. Sit down and watch because I know you want them." *Them, not him*—and the way he separates himself from that equation makes my stomach knot. "But you need to see what we are when we're together and what it'll mean when you're a part of it."

"I'm not—" I whisper, my voice shaking.

"You. Are." Roman cuts me off, firm and final. "You always have been."

I take a deep breath, searching for either courage or sanity, anything to drown out the voice in my head telling me to run.

Jasper sees it—the second the fight leaves my body. He lifts his hand toward me, and I glance down at it before meeting his eyes, and what I see there guts me.

The cocky, confident man I've always known is gone, and in his place is something raw and exposed. This is Jasper stripped bare, needing me to choose him, to choose them. Not because he wants to take, but because he needs me to want this just as badly as he does.

I take his hand, and he pulls me against his chest, his lips hovering just above mine. I melt right there because this is really happening, and there's no going back from this cliff we're about to plunge over.

"Do as he says, angel."

My eyes drop to Jasper's mouth, to those full, perfect lips, but I already know he won't kiss me.

"If you want out at any point, no one will stop you." He pauses, his thumb grazing the inside of my wrist where my pulse thrashes wildly beneath my skin. "But if you stay, I'd love nothing more than to watch your fingers disappear into those little pink panties while you see our boy stretch me open and fuck me raw."

He could mean Zeke.

He could mean Roman.

But the way he says *our boy*, I know exactly who he means.

Our Roman.

Jasper threads his fingers through mine and leads me to the chair. My heart hammers, my body already on edge as he turns and walks back toward them. He reaches Zeke first, grabbing the front of his throat and pulling him into a kiss so fierce I swear I feel it tear through me. His eyes flick to mine for a brief moment before he groans, wraps a hand around the back of Zeke's head, and deepens the kiss.

Roman moves in behind Jasper, his hands sliding down Jasper's boxer briefs to tug them past his thighs. Jasper kicks them away, baring himself without shame, his body taut and trembling under their hands. Roman's mouth trails over Jasper's neck, lips and teeth dragging across heated, flushed skin, and the sound that rips from Jasper's throat is so erotic, so filthy, that I have to press my thighs together just to get the slightest bit of relief.

Roman reaches for something on the bed, the light catching the bottle in his hand—*lube*. He pours some into his palm, then slides his hand between Jasper's cheeks. With Zeke pressed tight against his front and Roman at his back, Jasper lets out a broken, needy groan.

"Feel good, baby?" Zeke murmurs, wrapping his hand around Jasper's beautifully thick cock.

"Jesus, don't stop." Jasper pants, grinding between them. "Keep touching me like that."

One minute, I'm alcohol-drunk, and the next, I'm soaked

between the thighs watching three men lose themselves in each other.

When I lift my gaze, I find all three pairs of eyes set on me. They're waiting for me to realize this is too much and bolt, but they don't know that I've never felt more alive.

Instead of running, I slide my hand beneath the hem of my shirt, fingers trembling slightly as they find my hardened nipple. When I drag my thumb across it, Zeke and Jasper's lips curve into smiles before they turn their attention to Roman, whose stare is so hungry it feels like it's already stripping me bare and marking me from across the room.

This is new territory for me.

I'm not shy, and I've never been afraid of my body or what I want. But I've never been this open or bold, not for anyone.

Only for them.

Because only with them do I feel like I can be anything, and I know they'll still look at me like I'm just Addie.

"Get on the bed, facing her," Roman commands, and Jasper moves to the bed, dropping his knees to the mattress. "Lie on your back in front of him, Zeke. I want him fucking you while I'm inside him."

Control isn't something Roman has. Control is who Roman is, so it's no surprise that he's the most dominant of the three.

I can see it in all of them, simmering just beneath the surface, but with Roman, it's unmistakable.

He was always the one in control of my pleasure. No one has ever touched me the way he did. No one has ever made me feel like I was burning alive just to be put back together by something as simple as a kiss.

"Come on, baby," Jasper growls, his voice dripping with hunger. "My cock's so fucking desperate it's about to start begging without me."

"Wait..." Zeke says, walking toward me.

When he reaches me, he curls his hand around my chin, forcing me to look him in the eyes. Without a second thought, I grab his free hand and lower it between my thighs, pressing his fingers into the soaked lace of my panties.

I'm wet enough that he can feel it, and there's no question of how badly I want this.

Zeke's eyes go wide, and for a second, he just stands there, breathing hard and staring at me like he's seeing me for the very first time. He bites down on his lip as I release his wrist, but he doesn't pull away. Instead, he presses harder, dragging his fingers across the thin lace, brushing my clit with just enough pressure to make my eyes roll.

"Touch yourself," Zeke rasps. "Let them see how much you want this."

He leans in and grazes the corner of my mouth with his lips. It's soft, almost sweet, if it weren't for the way his fingers are still teasing me over my soaked panties. When he steps back, his fingers hook into the waistband of his briefs, and he shoves them down, baring every perfect inch of his cock like he was made to be watched.

Jasper smirks as Zeke falls back against the bed in front of him.

"Let me guess, our girl's wet, isn't she?" Zeke doesn't answer out loud, but he must nod because the groan that rips from Jasper's chest is so deep, it vibrates through the room and straight into my bones.

Roman reaches around Jasper, his hand wrapping firmly around Zeke's cock, stroking him in slow, filthy pulls that make Zeke's hips jerk off the bed. At the same time, Roman's other hand slides lower, pushing between Jasper's cheeks.

"Jesus, get inside me already. You're killing me here."

Jasper turns his face toward Roman. "Hear that, Rome? Zeke's getting needy."

"What about you? Are you ready for my dick?"

"What do you think, Captain?"

"I think you've got a smart mouth."

"You fucking love it," Jasper teases against his lips before their mouths crash together.

Somewhere in the middle of the kiss, Roman must push inside him because Jasper's whole body tenses, and the groan that leaves both of them echoes around the room, making it impossible to tell where one of them ends and the other begins.

"Fuck, I'll never get over how good you feel," Jasper mutters as he dips his head and swirls his tongue around the tip of Zeke's cock.

The sound that spills from Zeke only makes the need between my thighs burn hotter until it borders on painful. I finally give in, letting my hand trail downward, fingers brushing over the soaked lace, and even that slight friction is enough to pull a shaky breath from my chest.

Roman catches it instantly. He fists Jasper's hair and yanks his head back, holding him there like he wants him to see every second of what comes next. Jasper's head falls back, lips swollen and glistening, and his dazed eyes find mine. When Zeke's head turns, too, all three of them watch me like I'm exactly where they always wanted me.

"Atta girl," Jasper praises, and it's enough to push me closer to the edge. "Play with that little clit. Get it nice and swollen for us."

"Get inside him. She's not gonna last," Roman growls.

Jasper coats himself in lube, lines up with Zeke, and drives in deep, burying himself to the hilt.

It doesn't take long before they find their rhythm, and sitting here watching them lose their minds, I realize I want to be part of it so badly it hurts.

"Fuck, this tight ass is perfect," Jasper growls, his hands crushing Zeke's waist like he's about to split him open, rocking back into Roman's cock every time he moves. "Keep touching yourself, Addie. It's not gonna take much longer with the scent of your pussy in the air."

Oh. Holy. Shit.

I slip my fingers beneath the waistband of my panties and start rubbing faster.

"Fuck!" Zeke roars, his body jerking as Jasper slams into him, his hand wrapped tight around his cock.

"Come for us, baby. I know you're right fucking there." Jasper jerks Zeke's cock once, twice, then lets go.

Zeke comes hard, shooting across his chest and stomach, and I have to physically stop myself from crawling across the bed and licking every drop off his skin.

"I felt that... felt you fucking squeeze down just from watching him blow," Roman growls, his hips snapping faster.

Jasper's whole body is trembling, sweat dripping down his chest, and when his gaze finds mine, I nearly lose it.

"I'm so close," he grits out. "You with us, Addie?"

I whimper, and my thighs tremble as I watch Jasper pull out of Zeke.

My fingers move frantically over my clit while he fucks his fist, Roman pounding into him from behind.

Roman's hands are planted on Jasper's shoulders, fingers digging into his sweat-slicked skin. Every inch of him is wracked with pleasure, but even when he's blinded by lust, Roman's eyes find mine.

It's no longer bodies colliding on the bed.

It's Roman and me, the way it always was, and that pull between us tightens until there's no space left to breathe.

Slowly, Roman gives me a single nod before his mouth shapes a single, soundless word across the space between us.

Come.

There's no fighting it.

My body answers for me, breaking wide open, like Roman reached across the room and touched me without laying a hand on me.

I twist in the chair as my orgasm hits, and a broken cry rips out of me as I grind against my fingers.

"Fuuuck," Jasper cries as he jerks his cock faster, chasing the same edge.

Roman lets out a savage roar and slams into him one last time, burying himself deep.

I watch Jasper fall apart, his release coating Zeke's stomach, just as Roman finishes inside him.

Seconds later, the four of us are panting and completely fucked out. Roman finally moves, pulling out with a low groan, and Jasper immediately slumps sideways onto the bed beside Zeke, who hasn't stopped staring at me.

"Come here," Jasper says, arms stretched out toward me like he can't stand the distance for one more second. "Come on, angel. Just forget whatever's about to make you overthink and get over here."

He always was an overly affectionate bastard, and god, if I haven't missed that about him.

I huff out a soft laugh and push myself to my feet, my body still trembling.

I make my way to the bed and crawl over Jasper's solid, muscular body, loving the way he instantly pulls me into him. His naked torso is hot against my skin, his cock still thick and pressing against my hip, but he doesn't move to do anything more than hold me.

Zeke shifts beside me, wiping himself off before settling on my other side, while Roman moves in next to Jasper.

Part of me feels out of place, as if I'm intruding on something that doesn't belong to me. But another part of me believes that this is exactly where I'm supposed to be.

"You okay, beautiful?" Zeke asks, looking down at me as his fingers thread through my hair.

I manage a nod and a smile before I look across the bed, and the second I find Roman, my heart kicks up.

I'm not sure what I hoped to see, but he won't look at me. He stares at the ceiling, his shoulders rigid with tension that screams *retreat*. My fingers twitch, aching to reach for him, to cross that impossible distance, but before I can touch him, his eyes drop, catching the movement—*catching the thought.*

One glance at my hand and his walls slam up so fast I can almost hear them. "I'm gonna clean up," he mutters, pushing off the bed hard enough to make the mattress dip. "I'll be back in a minute."

He walks away from me like it's a matter of survival.

Only when he's standing a few feet away does he turn back and look at me—at us—at the way Jasper's arms are wrapped around me and the way I'm clinging to someone else while he stands alone.

For a moment, I'm sure I see comfort flash across his face, maybe even a sliver of peace, but there's pain there too. Whatever it is, it's enough to make him look away and walk out without saying a word.

"I'll go with him," Jasper says, easing me into Zeke's waiting arms.

When I finally wrap my arms around Zeke's body, something inside me slots back into place. But even as I breathe him in and let myself be held, part of me is still twisted up in the man who couldn't let himself stay.

CHAPTER ELEVEN
ZEKE

Addison's curled up in my arms, warm and soft and exactly where I want her, while Roman's being comforted by the one other person in this world who gets him like I do. After everything that went down tonight, after the way Jasper took the lead and cracked something open between the four of us, I'm pretty sure I'll never be okay with letting Addie out of my sight again.

Her heart is racing, her energy a mix of confusion and contentment, but there's also concern. Jasper's got Roman. I trust that, so right now, my entire world narrows to the woman in my arms.

I run my fingers through her short blonde hair and press a kiss to the top of her head. "You okay, beautiful?"

She nods against my chest, pressing closer. "Thank you."

"For what?"

"For guiding me. I've never done anything like that before."

"Neither have we."

Her palm flattens against my chest as she lifts her head, those stunning stormy-blue eyes narrowing. "Never?"

I shake my head slowly. "The three of us, yeah, obviously. But never with someone else. Never like this."

"You never... There's never been another woman?"

I shake my head, holding her gaze, needing her to remember what we'd told her years ago—that it was only ever her.

"No, never."

"Wow." She bites her lip. "I guess I assumed you'd all need to find someone to fill that space."

"We don't need a woman to make us whole." When her eyes drop, I gently tilt her chin up, refusing to let her hide. "The right woman would add to our happiness, not complete it. She'd be loved, cherished, and become part of what we are. But we're solid even if that woman couldn't see herself with us."

She blinks, but I see the exact second it lands—when the meaning behind my words clicks into place.

If *she* could ever see a life with us.

"I think anyone would be dumb to give you three up."

My heart stumbles, caught somewhere between hope and fear. She means it. But I know Addison—she'll always hold a piece of herself back, especially with everything Roman's still fighting.

We lie there in the quiet for a few peaceful minutes, her head tucked beneath my chin, when she breaks the silence. "Tell me about your life, Zeke."

I smile, pressing a kiss to her temple. "What do you wanna know?"

"Everything. Hockey, your friends, Jasper, Roman... I wanna know it all."

"Well, you already know playing pro was the dream, and honestly, sometimes it still doesn't feel real that we actually made it." She hums softly, listening, so I keep going. "It's given us more than we ever imagined—careers we love, stability we didn't all grow up with, and yeah... stepping out onto the ice, hearing the crowd lose their minds? That never gets old. It's the kind of thing that gets in your veins and stays there. You crave it." I glance down at her. "Of course, it doesn't feel great if we're not winning—then we're just three overpaid assholes who didn't score enough goals."

"I was so proud of you guys when my dad told me. I wanted to reach out so many times, and then Mikey happened..." Her voice trails off, and I run my fingers through her hair, letting her know it's okay.

"We felt the same," I whisper. "Jasper almost got in contact once."

"Really?"

"Yeah, but you know how he is. He doesn't feel anything halfway, and Roman was worried about him opening a door he couldn't walk through."

"Is he okay?" she asks after a beat. "Because he always acts like he is, but I know he sometimes feels like he's got to be everything for everyone."

"Jasper's just... Jasper. I know not being able to be open about us chips away at him a little more each day. He loves with everything he's got, and holding all of that back? It's just not who he is."

"He shouldn't have to hold back. It shouldn't be like that."

"He and Roman had a close call not long ago, nearly outing themselves to the entire team."

"What happened?"

"Jasper went down after taking a bad hit and was out cold for a few seconds. I've never seen anyone move as fast as Roman did. The guy's a monster on the ice, but that was something else—he was across the rink and at Jasper's side before anyone else even realized what was happening." I pause, remembering the rush of panic we both felt. "I was right behind him, and for a second... all that love Roman tries so hard to hide, it was just right there, spilling out. I put a hand on his shoulder to ground him, and he caught himself. Jasper came to, laughing like a damn maniac, and the look he gave Roman? Swear to god, it was a challenge.

Like he was daring him to kiss him right there in front of everyone."

She bursts into laughter, her body shaking softly against mine. I wrap my arms around her, pulling her closer, and for a few perfect seconds, I let myself quietly hope we get more moments like this.

"So Roman's okay? He's doing good?"

"Yeah, beautiful. He's doing fine." I pause. "He hasn't changed though. So what just happened between us? He'll be overthinking it now."

She nods, biting her lip. "I don't want him to hate me anymore."

"He doesn't hate you."

"He still hates me being near him."

"Roman loved you, Addison. That's all it is. When he lets someone in, he gives everything he's got—he doesn't know any other way." She nods, her bottom lip trembling, and the urge to kiss her is instant.

I want to erase the hurt in her eyes, promise her we'll figure this out, but with everything still so raw—Roman's wounds still open—I can't. Not yet. So I press my lips to her forehead, lingering there, and gather her back against my chest, holding her for all of us.

"Stay here tonight, yeah?" I whisper.

She nods, and I ease us both beneath the covers. I know when morning comes, she'll be curled between me and Jasper, and that's when shit gets real. Because whatever this was tonight, it's not going away.

CHAPTER
TWELVE
ROMAN

EIGHT YEARS AGO

I hate sneaking around. But I'd do it a thousand times over for her. Somewhere between late-night texts and stolen glances across the rink, I fell for the one girl I should've stayed away from—my coach's daughter. The same coach who's made it crystal clear that if any of his players so much as look at her sideways, they're benched.

If it ever came down to a choice between keeping Addie or keeping my spot on the team... there's no question. It's her—every single time.

Right now, the guys and I are in the final quarter of the game, and we're head-to-head with one goal to score to win. There's no doubt in my mind that we're going to do it. No room for anything except the absolute certainty that we're about to bury this puck in the back of their net and walk away with the win. I've got the best guys around me, teammates I've bled with and fought beside. Most of them, I'd trust with my life. Others? I'd rather slam into the ice and pretend it was an accident.

The puck drops, and everything else disappears. Right now, it's just me, the ice, and the game I've loved since I was a kid. My blades carve *deep as I chase down the puck, adrenaline crackling through me like electricity.*

We move through plays we could run in our sleep. Zeke takes the hit, sending the puck along the boards. Jasper scoops it up, cool as ever, and just like that, it's back on my stick—right where I want it. We play as one; I don't even have to look to know where they are. I just know.

Twenty seconds left on the clock.

I spin past a defender, threading the puck to Chad, before he flips the puck right back to me. I don't hesitate. I shoot, and the puck sails to the back of the net. The red light flashes, the horn blares, and the game is ours.

The arena explodes around me, and the fans are on their feet, giving off the kind of energy only a win in the final seconds can deliver. Jasper barrels into my side, slamming me against the boards. Zeke and Grant are right there, piling on, all of us shouting, laughing, and letting the adrenaline take over.

When I finally break away, breathless, I scan the stands, and there she is—my girl, in her usual spot, on her feet and shining brighter than the arena lights. She's grinning, her eyes fixed on mine, and when she lifts her arm, I know exactly what's coming. She holds up one finger, and the rest of the world drops away.

One finger—our code. You're the one. I love you.

I can't help the grin that splits my face.

I lift my hand, two fingers in the air. I love you too.

Maybe it's dumb, but it's ours.

Jesus, what the hell is wrong with me?

I scrub a hand down my face, trying to erase the image, but the damage is done. The memory's already there.

I was more involved in Addie's pleasure than I ever meant to be—though if I'm being honest, if I really didn't want it, I wouldn't have let myself get lost in her and the way she touched herself.

It was… Fuck. I don't even have the words for what it was.

Beautiful.

Devastating.

Addictive.

Terrifying.

And now my head's a mess because deep down I know this is all going to blow up in our faces. The truth is, when I saw them all together in the bed—Addie, Zeke, and Jasper—I felt like maybe this crazy, impossible thing could actually work, and that scares the shit out of me.

I'm staring at my reflection, trying to make sense of the storm in my head, when I catch Jasper's dark eyes in the mirror as he steps up behind me.

I don't think I've ever needed to be closer to him more than I do right now.

He doesn't say anything at first. He just runs his hands over my shoulders, his thumbs dragging slow circles over the tense muscles before pressing a soft kiss to the back of my neck.

"Who are you running from?" he asks quietly. "Her or yourself?"

"Both," I admit.

He wraps his arms around me from behind, pulling me into his chest, and I let myself sink into him, resting the back of my head against his shoulder.

"You'd think I'd be over this by now."

"No, baby. You love too hard for that. You hold on tight to the things that matter, and when something hurts you, you shut it out."

"It isn't healthy."

"So?" he whispers, lips grazing the shell of my ear. "Nobody gets through life without being a little messed up."

I actually laugh, the sound surprising us both. Jasper grins, then starts peppering light, playful kisses along my neck, chasing the tension away one touch at a time.

His hands don't stop moving, one gliding over my chest, the other tracing the dip of my waist, not just touching but holding me.

"You think she's okay?" I ask.

"I think she's worried about you."

I hate that he might be right. If that's true, it means she still cares, and that's a whole other kind of mess I'm not ready to unpack.

"Maybe it's time you had a real conversation with her," he says.

"What's the point in dragging it back up now? We're leaving straight after the ceremony." I catch that brief spark of hope that lights up his eyes before he tries to hide it. "Don't go there. Get it out of your head because it's never going to happen, and I don't want you getting lost in something she'll probably run from by tomorrow."

"What if she doesn't?"

I turn to face him, pressing my hand to his chest, right over his heart. "Don't let this break, Jasper. I know what she means to you and Zeke."

He snorts, rolling his eyes. "Stop feeding yourself that crap and be real for once. Or don't, but don't lie to me."

"I just..." I pause, swallowing around the knot in my throat. "I just don't want you to get hurt, baby. That's all this is."

He brushes his thumb over my cheek and tilts his head. "I'll be fine. Zeke will be fine. You will be fine. And so will she." He says it like it's a truth he's decided on, and the universe has no choice but to fall in line. "It'll work out the way it's supposed to." Before I can say anything else, he steps in closer, his body moving into mine and caging me gently against the sink. "Now," he murmurs, pressing a slow kiss beneath my jaw, "weren't you supposed to be getting cleaned up?"

He doesn't say a word as he guides me into the shower, following close behind until we're both standing under the spray. He reaches for the shower gel and lathers it between his hands, then starts working it over my chest and arms in smooth, steady circles.

Our bodies move together in the steam and heat. We're skin to skin, both of us hard but completely untouched because this isn't about sex. This is intimacy and letting someone love you when you don't know how to ask for it.

When he's finished, I return the favor, washing him with the same care he showed me. My hands roam over the hard lines of his chest, back, and shoulders, taking my time with him.

Water drips from his hair, trailing down his cheeks and along the curve of his jaw.

He's beautiful.

I close the space between us, pressing my body flush against his, pinning him against the shower wall. His skin burns beneath mine, and the second our mouths meet, I forget how to breathe.

I kiss him slowly, my tongue gliding against his, his taste flooding my mouth and pulling me deeper until everything else just falls away.

Right now, there's only this—the feel of his body against mine, the quiet whimper he makes when I angle my head and deepen the kiss, and the way he kisses me back like I'm the only thing that exists in his world.

"I love you." He breathes those three words against my lips—words that still undo me, no matter how much time passes.

"I love you too. So fucking much."

We stay like that, foreheads pressed together, mouths barely apart, breathing each other in while the water beats down around us.

Eventually, I ease off him, and we stand quietly beneath the stream, both of us reluctant to break the moment, even though we know we have to. He steps out first, grabbing a towel from the rack and tossing one my way.

"You ready, Captain?"

"I think so."

But honestly? I'm not sure.

Jasper, who is without a doubt the most affectionate person I've ever met, doesn't hesitate to take my hand and lace our fingers together. He's always touching me or Zeke whenever he can, probably to make up for the moments he can't.

The second I step inside the bedroom, Addie's eyes go wide. She thinks I'm going to ask her to leave. It's written all over her face, that worry and uncertainty, but even if I can't bring myself to sleep right next to her tonight, I'd never send her away.

Not now. Not ever.

"Zeke said it was okay..." she whispers.

"Of course it is, angel," Jasper says, climbing into bed beside her.

I follow, slipping in on his other side as Zeke quietly gets out of bed, still naked. He grabs his underwear, pulls it on, and crouches down beside me. He runs a hand through my still-damp hair, searching my face for something I'm not sure I could name even if I tried. But I let him see it all—the worry, the longing, the fear. He exhales, leans in, and kisses my forehead, then presses a gentle kiss to my mouth. When he's done, he reaches for Jasper, kissing his cheek before switching off the lamp and climbing back into bed.

Time passes strangely after that. It could be minutes, but it feels like hours. Jasper's sprawled on his back, one arm tucked behind his head, the other resting on his stomach. Zeke's turned toward me, his chest to Addie's back, arms curled around her in that protective way he's held me so many times before

He's good at making people feel safe.

I let my gaze linger on them, watching Addie's chest rise and fall, and something inside me loosens just a little.

Maybe Jasper's right.

Maybe this doesn't have to fall apart.

Maybe we still have time to get it right.

CHAPTER THIRTEEN
ADDISON

"We're snowed in."

That's what Zeke told me an hour ago, and I'm still trying to figure out what the universe has against me.

Maybe this is karma.

Maybe this is what happens when you let go of the man you loved years ago, and your punishment is being trapped in one place with him, his two boyfriends, and the unbearable truth that you still have feelings for all three of them.

I glance out the window again, searching for any sign of hope, but the world's disappeared beneath a thick, relentless blanket of white. There's no chance any vehicles are getting up or down this mountain.

I'm completely stuck.

Last night we crossed a line. And not just any line. *The* line. The kind that doesn't come with a rewind button or a cute little apology. It's the kind that changes things permanently, and now we're trapped at this lodge for who the hell knows how long, with no distractions, no exits, and way too many unresolved feelings between us.

I'm standing at the front desk, phone pressed to my ear, trying and failing to get ahold of my mom. Now they're saying the ceremony might be canceled thanks to last night's surprise snowfall, and of course, she's not answering. She's probably sitting right next to the damn thing, squinting at the screen, still unsure which button actually picks up.

"Still nothing." I sigh, lowering the phone. "She's not answering."

"We can keep trying if you'd like," Joan offers.

She's the one running this place—calm, capable, with a reassuring voice that makes you feel like maybe everything will be okay even when it's clearly not.

I have to quickly remind myself that it's not just us stranded up here. The storm trapped all the staff and guests too.

"Would you? I want her to be prepared, just in case."

"I'm hoping we'll get it cleared by then—as long as we don't get hit with more."

"I'll keep my fingers crossed." I glance toward the window where snow piles against the glass. "Actually... you don't happen to have any other cabins available, do you?"

"You don't want to stay with your friends? They've got the biggest place—plenty of bedrooms."

"I'll talk to them, but if not..."

"If not, we'll find something for you. Although, fair warning, if the weekend goes ahead, we're booked solid."

"Thank you, Joan. Is everything still working in the restaurant?"

"Yeah, and Clive's not going anywhere, so there will always be food if anyone needs it."

I nod before stepping back into the cold, and the wind bites at my face as I approach the cabin.

Jasper throws the door open, standing there in nothing but a pair of gray sweats, looking so good I want to drop to my knees and thank whatever god made men like him.

"Get in here, you dumbass, before you freeze," he calls out, grinning like nothing's changed. His chest is bare, his abs are on full display, and his messy, light-brown hair looks like he's been dragging his hands through it for hours.

Roman's already at the kitchen island, sitting next to Zeke with a mug of coffee in front of him, his gaze following me the moment I step into the room.

"Did you find out what's happening with your dad's award this weekend?" Zeke asks.

"Yeah," I say, glancing between the three of them. "They're hoping the roads will clear—assuming we don't get hit again tonight." I drop onto the edge of the couch, fingers fidgeting in my lap. "They've got a cabin for me if I want it. At least until Saturday."

Jasper's head snaps up. "What?"

Jasper doesn't do subtle.

He doesn't do quiet either.

"What do you mean a cabin?"

"I mean…" I swallow hard. "You're all staying here, and I didn't want to assume anything. I figured I could just—"

"What? Leave?" Jasper asks, already crossing the room like he's about to argue this with his whole chest. "Seriously. Explain this to me, angel, because right now I'm wondering if I hallucinated last night. Wondering if you didn't actually fall asleep in our bed, and I just imagined you hooking your leg around me this morning when I tried to get up."

"I don't want to impose. I'm not supposed to be here."

Jasper slides in beside me, throws his arm around my shoulders, and pulls me into him until there's no space left between us.

"Don't ever say that. If there's anywhere you belong, it's right here with us. You know that, yeah?" He glances at Zeke for backup.

"No one's going to make you do anything you're not ready for," Zeke says, "but you're not staying in some empty cabin by yourself. Not when this place has plenty of room and not when we want you here."

My throat tightens as I glance over at Roman. He hasn't said a word, but his silence feels heavier than anything else in the room. I can't do this if he doesn't want me here. I need to hear it from him.

His golden eyes meet mine, burning with something real.

No walls.

No bullshit.

"Stay," he finally says, standing up and rinsing his mug before dropping it into the sink. "They're right. It'd be stupid for you to hole up somewhere by yourself for the next few days."

"Okay, well, I've got another problem, and this one's a little humiliating," I admit, my cheeks warming as I watch Jasper stand and saunter around the kitchen island, grabbing a bottle of water from the fridge.

Zeke raises a brow. "What is it?"

"I have no clothes. No underwear. No toothbrush. I'm pretty sure reception can hook me up with the basics, but…"

All three of them go still for a beat, and it's Jasper's reaction I clock first. His mouth curls into a slow, wicked smile, one arm crossing his chest while the other rubs a hand along his jaw, like he's trying and failing not to say exactly what's on his mind.

"I mean," he drawls, his eyes raking down my body and back up with zero shame, "I'm just not hearing a single problem in that sentence."

"I'm being serious," I say, rolling my eyes even though I can't keep the smile off my face.

"What? I can't help it if the idea of you wandering around here in my T-shirt and no panties sounds like a Christmas miracle."

"This," I mutter, waving a hand in his direction, "is exactly why I almost kept my mouth shut."

"Oh, come on. You drop a visual like that and expect us to behave? We're only human, angel."

Roman finally speaks from his spot at the island. "We've all got plenty. There's a washer and a dryer. We'll figure it out."

"It's only four more days," Zeke adds, stepping in close enough that I can feel his warmth. "Why don't you go take a shower, and we'll get you what you need."

"Okay, thank you." I give them a small smile and turn toward the hallway.

In the guest bathroom, I turn the water on and let it run, watching as steam immediately starts fogging the mirror and curling into the corners of the room. I strip off the clothes I arrived in last night and step under the spray, letting the water scald my skin, hoping it'll burn away the ache I'm carrying. But the truth is, no amount of heat could distract me from the simple, terrifying fact that I'm snowed in with three men I never stopped wanting. Two who look at me like we could somehow pick up where we left off and pretend that's a realistic option when we all know it's not.

Four days trapped in this cabin with them, with nowhere to run and no excuse to leave.

I press my palms flat against the tile and close my eyes.

How the hell am I going to survive this?

CHAPTER
FOURTEEN
JASPER

"Alright, we need to talk about this. All of us. We've gotta be on the same page." I spin around the second Addie's out of earshot, facing Zeke and Roman like it's go time.

Roman just laughs, shaking his head. "You look like you're about to explode with whatever you need to get off your chest."

"Just listen and don't judge, okay? I just need a yes or a no."

"Floor's yours, baby," Zeke says, leaning back with a smirk.

"Thank you." I blow out a breath, running a hand through my hair. "If she wants last night to happen again... are you in?"

They don't even blink. Two nods, two yeses. Not that I'm shocked, but I wanted to allow them the space to say no.

"If she wants to join us—actually insert herself into what we are, right in the middle, when we're fucking—are you both good with that?"

Zeke snorts, grinning away at me. "You really have a way with words, you know that?" I tilt my head, giving him a look, with one eyebrow raised.

"After the way you were begging me in the shower this morning, you can't say anything. What was it? *Please, baby, fuck my ass.*"

You're such a good boy, so fucking deep—don't stop, don't you dare fucking stop."

Zeke just grins, not an ounce of shame in him. "Yeah? Well, you were a good boy. Nearly had me seeing stars. I might've even blacked out for a second."

Roman groans and rolls his eyes, tugging on his sweatpants. "Are you two done?"

"Sorry, where was I?"

Zeke shifts forward, leaning his forearms on the island between us. "You wanna know how we feel about Addie joining us."

"Yeah. Zeke, I already know where you stand, so really, the decision comes down to you, Rome. Whatever you want, that's what we do."

Roman's jaw works, and his golden eyes dart away briefly before he finally speaks. "I'm fine with it. I just... can't."

"You don't have to do anything you're not comfortable with," Zeke says, leaning in a little closer to him.

"Watching you two with her? That'll get me hard as fuck, and I'm down for that. I just can't touch her again."

I get it. I understand. Even if part of me wants to believe the four of us could be more than temporary.

But how the hell could it ever work? We live completely different lives.

I'm trying not to let the doubt sink its claws in, but Roman's not wrong, and that might be what scares me the most.

"Okay, so what about one-on-one with her?" I ask, watching them both closely as they nod.

"Are you sure, Captain?" I press, needing to hear it from Roman, needing to know this won't in any way break us.

"It doesn't change what we have. I'm not worried, and I'm not jealous—only because it's her. I know we all miss pussy sometimes, but don't get any ideas."

"Never," Zeke murmurs. "It's always us."

Then, as if it's instinct—like we're three parts of one whole—the space between us disappears. Zeke's thigh brushes mine, and Roman's hand settles at the nape of my neck. I reach out, curling my fingers around Zeke's wrist. We don't say a word, but we don't need to. Shoulders bump, hips press, and hands slide into familiar places like they were made to be there.

Our foreheads meet—three points of contact, three pulses syncing in the space between us.

Fuck, I'm so in love with them.

It's that perfect fire-to-the-veins kind of love. The kind you fight for, bleed for, burn the fucking world down for. And they're mine. Every beautiful and brilliant inch of them—*mine*.

"One of us needs to get her some clothes," I say, breaking the quiet.

Zeke steps back a little, running a hand through his onyx hair. "You go. She's most comfortable with you."

"Not true," I say, already turning toward the door. "I just know how to nudge her without overwhelming her."

Roman looks at me, that rare soft smile tugging at his mouth. The one he only gives to us that says, *I'm so gone for you, and you know it.*

I turn and head down the hall with a pair of clean underwear and a white T-shirt. There's no way they'll fit her—she's so damn tiny—but it's better than nothing.

The sound of the shower drifts through the doorway of the guest room. I set the clothes on the bed and sit down on the edge, elbows to my knees, trying to get my shit together. But the longer I sit here, the more my mind drifts to her. Wet. Bare. Just a few feet across the hall, behind that closed door.

My fingers flex against my thighs, jaw clenched so tight it aches, and I shut my eyes and count to five before I force myself up and knock gently on the bathroom door. The last thing I need is for her to walk out naked and catch me lurking like some kind of creep. Not that I wouldn't fall to my knees for even a glimpse of her, but I want her to want that.

"Addie? I grabbed you some clothes. I've put them on the bed."

She doesn't answer. Instead, the bathroom door opens, and she steps out. Her skin is flushed, and her blonde hair is soaked and dripping down her collarbones.

The white towel clings to her damp skin, hanging on by a thread as it skims dangerously high on her thighs. She has my brain short-circuiting, and for a second, I can't string together a single fucking sentence.

She's breathtaking.

"Thank you," she says, and I just nod, unable to take my eyes off her as she walks into her room. She tilts her head, a slow smile playing on her lips. "You're staring, Jasper."

"Course I am," I mutter, stepping in close. "Look at you. I'd have to be stupid not to be thinking about what I need to say to get you out of that towel." She laughs, but I'm dead serious. I close the distance, my heart pounding. I reach out, sliding a strand of wet hair from her cheek. "Addie..."

"What happened to angel?"

"This feels like an Addie moment."

"Why?"

"Because in about ten seconds, that towel's hitting the floor, I'm dropping to my knees, and I'm gonna eat your pussy until your legs shake." I reach forward, brushing the spot where her towel is tucked in. "Tell me to stop," I murmur, giving her the out. "Say the word, and I'll walk out that door."

"I can't..." she breathes out.

I loosen the towel, holding it up with one hand. "Last chance, Addie."

She shakes her head, and that's all I need. I let the towel drop to the floor, but I don't look yet. Not when all I want is her mouth. I reach out and tilt her chin up, my thumb brushing her jaw, and then I kiss her. The second our lips meet, she gasps against me. Her arms wrap around my neck, fingers digging into my hair as she devours me. There's no hesitation, no second-guessing. Just her, melting into me like she's been waiting to kiss me like this again.

She opens for me, and when our tongues meet, it's all I can do not to lose my mind. My cock's already hard as hell, throbbing against the inside of my sweats, and every second her mouth is on mine, it winds me up tighter.

I love it, but it's fucking unbearable.

She pulls back first, her breath ragged, lips swollen. Then she steps away and presses her bare back to the edge of the wooden dresser behind her.

"You can look at me now," she whispers.

I let my gaze wander down her face, over the elegant line of her throat, to the perfect swell of her breasts, nipples tight and begging for my mouth. My eyes drift lower, over the dip of her stomach, lingering on the small patch of hair nestled between her thighs. I follow the length of her legs, over those sculpted calves, all the way to her lilac toes.

"Holy shit... I wasn't prepared for how perfect you are."

"I'm not perfect."

"To me, you're everything, and I don't want to hear otherwise."

I step into her space and kiss her again, letting my mouth trail down her neck, across her collarbone, until my tongue licks across one of her tight, peaked nipples. She gasps, her body jerking like even that's too much. Sliding down to my knees, I feel her thread her fingers through my hair, keeping me close as I place a gentle kiss on her stomach before inhaling the heady scent of her arousal.

It's been a long time since I've gone down on a girl, but I figure it's like riding a bike—once you've made a woman come on your tongue, it's not something you forget.

And god, she wants this. I can smell it. I can feel it in the way she's trembling. I start with soft kisses along the inside of her thighs, letting my breath tease her. Finally, I drag my tongue through her center, groaning against her as I watch that pretty clit twitch for more.

"Let's take care of that, baby." I dip my tongue inside her, then slide it up, circling her clit before sucking it gently. Her hands tighten in my hair like she doesn't know whether to push me away or pull me deeper.

So I stay, and I feast.

I flick and suck, my tongue working in rhythm with the way her hips start to roll. She's clenching, chasing it, and I want to give her everything.

In the middle of it all, I can't stop the thought that punches through me: Zeke, inside me. Roman and Addie, devouring each other. My mouth on her, my fingers gripping his ass, all of us frantic and ravenous.

Yeah, one day that's happening, and I already know it'll ruin me in the best way.

My hands slide up her thighs, her skin now prickled with goose bumps, and I grip her waist tight, burying my face deeper between her legs. She starts to buck against me, and her pussy pulses beneath my tongue. Her fingers clench in my hair, holding me there like she never wants me to stop. And fuck, I wouldn't, not for anything. She cries out quietly, lost in it, and I keep going until I feel her melt, until I know she's wrung out. I finally pull back, wiping my mouth with the back of my hand, giving myself a quiet nod like, *Yeah, you did that.*

I stand, reach for her towel, and wrap it around her, allowing my hands to brush over her warm, still-quivering skin.

"Beautiful," I murmur, watching as she blinks up at me. "Perfect."

Her navy eyes are wide, and she's glowing in the way only someone fully satisfied can.

"Clothes are on the bed, angel," I tell her, pressing a soft kiss to her temple. "Take whatever time you need. We'll grab some lunch in a little while, yeah?" She nods slowly, her eyes fixed on mine like I just handed her the stars.

She's so damn cute, and right now, utterly breathtaking.

"You're welcome, by the way, baby," I toss over my shoulder with a wink, shutting the door behind me as I head back down the hall with the taste of her still lingering on my tongue.

Roman is where I left him at the island, nursing another coffee. I like that he's treating this trip like a real break, not dragging his strict diet or brutal morning workouts along with him. He needs the pause, whether he admits it or not.

"Where's Zeke?"

Roman looks up at me, his brow raised. "He's on the phone with his mom."

Something in my face must scream, *I just went down on Addie,* because his eyes narrow instantly.

"What have you done?"

"Me?" I step closer and turn his barstool, positioning myself between his legs. He sets his coffee down, and his hands slide around to grip my ass before settling on the small of my back. "Why don't you find out what I've done, Captain?"

I watch as he inhales, and I see the exact second it hits him.

His eyes darken, and I know he's figured it out. He knows I've had my mouth on her.

"You smell like her."

I drag my tongue slowly across my bottom lip, not even trying to hide it. His eyes follow the movement like he's hypnotized, pupils blowing wider with every second that passes. He shoves to his feet, grabs my face in both hands, and presses his lips to mine. His tongue drives into my mouth, seeking mine like he needs to taste what's left of her on me.

"You taste like her too."

"Fucking delicious, isn't she?" I murmur against his lips. "I knew you'd remember, and I get it. Her pussy's exquisite."

His mouth crashes back onto mine, and I drop my hand to grip his cock through his shorts. He growls deep in my throat before I pull back just enough, lips brushing against his.

"Are you kissing me or eating her?"

"Both," he breathes out, thrusting forward, tongue sliding back into my mouth before he pulls away again. "Tasting you two together though... Fuck, it's everything."

We're both gasping, rutting, and kissing like we're trying to claw our way inside each other when I hear Zeke's voice cut through the haze.

"I will never tire of this view."

Roman jerks his head up, breath ragged, and he turns slightly. I look over his shoulder just in time to see Zeke standing there with his arms crossed over his chest, and fuck me, the heat in his eyes says *he's next*.

"Get your ass over here," Roman growls, reaching out and yanking Zeke straight into us.

"Roman's had one taste of Addie off my lips, and now he's gone feral."

Zeke's jaw tightens. "Share."

Roman's hands thread into both our hair as we lean in—three mouths, one kiss, and fuck, it's the best kind of chaos. Zeke groans when our tongues meet, licking into my mouth as if he's chasing her down, too, like he needs to taste what's left of her in the mess we've made. Now we're just three hard-as-hell men, wrecked by one woman's scent and the taste of each other.

"I've had her," I pant out between kisses. "Now I want you. Both of you."

"Get on your knees," Roman commands, giving zero fucks if Addie were to walk in and find us like this.

Zeke's already unzipping his jeans. "You're gonna choke on both of us. You'll swallow every drop, and you're gonna stroke your cock while you do it, understand?"

"Got it, baby. Now shut up and put my throat to use."

Roman fists his cock. "You've got the sluttiest fucking mouth, Jasper."

I swirl my tongue over the tip of Roman's cock, tasting the first salty drop, then turn my head toward Zeke, giving him the same attention.

"I know... now fucking fill it."

Roman's cock is in his hand one second, the glint of his piercing catching the light, and the next it's sliding into my mouth before I can even blink. My hand slips into my sweatpants, fingers wrapping around my dick as he grips my head and starts to thrust.

"God, you're so good," he says, groaning.

"Fuck his throat, Rome," Zeke growls, his fist pumping slowly next to him. "He can take it."

"Can you, baby? Can you take every inch of this cock?" I moan around him, eyes watering, spit slicking my chin. I don't pull back. *I take it.* I'm on the edge, ready to fucking lose it when he pulls out and tilts my chin up to meet his eyes. "Think about that while Zeke fucks your mouth."

My attention shifts to Zeke. He's not as long as Roman, but he's a fucking monster in his own right, and he knows exactly what to do with it. I glance up, my lips parted, and he slaps the head against my tongue, owning me. I open up and let him in, my tongue working over him as he sinks deeper, until my nose is pressed tight against his groin. One hand grips his ass, fingers digging in hard enough to bruise. My other hand is still buried in my sweatpants, pumping myself fast, already so far gone I could come just from the sound of their breathing.

"That's it," Zeke growls. "Such a good fucking boy."

The words hit me right in the chest. Praise like that only winds me tighter.

I look up just as Zeke leans into Roman. They kiss like they're starving, and the only thing keeping them standing is each other. Both cocks push past my lips, switching back and forth until my jaw aches, and I'm dizzy with it.

"Tongue out for us," Zeke murmurs, both of their hands stroking through my hair.

Roman stands over me, eyes wild, cock in hand, and his muscles are pulled tight. "You ready?"

I glance up between them, smirking through my parted lips. "Give it to me."

"You don't swallow," he growls, fist working faster. "You keep it on your tongue until I say."

"Yes, sir."

Roman groans as his cum shoots across my tongue, thick and hot.

I hold it there.

My eyes focus on Zeke, watching as his fist tightens, and his cock swells as he nears the edge.

What I don't expect is Roman suddenly dropping to his knees in front of me and taking my cock down his throat. I buck hard, barely managing to keep my mouth open for Zeke as he steps in, moaning as his cum coats my tongue.

Pleasure crashes through me, and I shoot into his mouth, and when he finally pulls off, my whole body sags. Roman stands, grips my jaw tight, and spits my cum right back onto my tongue—him, Zeke, and the ghost of Addie all mixed together. A taste of all four of us and everything we could be.

"Now be a good boy and swallow," Zeke commands.

And I do, with a huge fucking smile on my face.

Both of my men lean in, hungry for what they left behind. They lick my lips and suck my tongue, chasing the taste of themselves, her, and me.

When Zeke finally helps me up, I just laugh and shake my head. "You're an animal, Roman, you know that?"

"You love it." He grins like the asshole he is, presses a kiss to my neck, then slaps my ass hard enough to make me flinch. "I'm going for another shower, then we'll get lunch, yeah?"

"I just swallowed a whole fucking buffet," I fire back, and I hear his laugh follow him down the hall.

I turn to Zeke, who's perched on a barstool, his legs spread, watching me like I'm the center of his universe.

"Come here," he says, pulling me between his legs and pressing a soft kiss to my bare chest. "You good?"

"You kidding?" But I know him—Zeke always checks in. It's who he is, and I love him for it. "That's easily in the top five mornings of my life."

I slide my fingers into his hair and gently tilt his head back so I can really look at him.

"Are you okay?"

"Always," he answers with a smile.

"I'm serious…"

"I know. And I promise I'm good. I'm just thinking about those two."

"Roman and Addie?" He nods. "Whether he wants to admit it or not, things will move forward between them. And yeah, it's gonna mess him up, but it's the only way he heals. The only way they both do."

"He's going to get so lost in his head," Zeke murmurs.

"I know." I pause, pressing my forehead to his. "But I also know this is going somewhere. I know she's not walking away from us."

"You do, huh?"

"Yeah," I say, brushing my thumb across his cheek. "I really do."

CHAPTER FIFTEEN
ROMAN

By the time we finally got food today, we were all a little wrecked. I lost my damn mind over what went down between Addie and Jasper, and I didn't even try to hide it. Tasting her again took me straight back to those winter nights when she'd grind against my face, soaking my mouth and my chin, always so desperate to come she'd barely let me breathe.

I wonder if Jasper got her to tremble the same way.

Of course he did.

The guy could probably make her come with nothing but a look.

There's been a weird energy hanging over us tonight—a kind of restless tension none of us seem able to shake, no matter how many casual conversations we attempt or how hard we try to pretend everything's normal. Maybe we just need a little time to ourselves, to rest and breathe and get used to sharing the same space over the next few days.

Or maybe we're all quietly dreading what comes after the weekend, when we pack up and return to our lives and Addie stays behind.

I know I'm not making things any easier for anyone when it comes to Addison, but the truth is, I don't know how to do this any differently.

When you grow up being passed around from house to house, feeling like you mean nothing to nobody, you learn not to get too comfortable, and you stop expecting to matter. Nobody asks what you need. Nobody cares what you want. They just count down the days until you're someone else's responsibility.

Then one day, when you finally find your home in someone—the kind of home that feels safe, that feels like yours—only to have her burn it to the fucking ground, it doesn't just change you. It rewires you and forces you to keep people at arm's length, even when part of you is still desperate to be let in.

I've been lying beside Zeke for over an hour now, staring at the ceiling like it might finally give me the answers my brain won't stop chasing. Both of my guys can fall asleep as soon as their heads touch the pillow. Me? I've got insomnia that fucks me sideways and a brain that won't shut up, no matter how tired I am.

Addison went to bed early tonight. We had a quiet dinner, and afterward she said she wanted to read on her phone for a while. Disappearing into a book and finding peace between the pages has always been her thing, so it didn't surprise me one bit that she opened a bookstore.

I'm never getting any sleep if I just lie here thinking about her.

I haul myself out of bed and drag my restless ass to the kitchen. What I want is coffee, strong, black coffee, but that's a hell of a stupid idea when I'm already wired, so I reach for the whiskey instead.

Screw it, it's almost Christmas, and at this point, I think half the country is running on booze anyway.

Leaning against the counter, the cold marble bites into my spine, but I barely notice anymore. Years on the ice have conditioned me to the cold and made it something I seek rather than avoid.

I'm standing here in nothing but black boxer briefs, glass half full in my hand, sipping slowly and letting the whiskey spread fire through my chest when footsteps echo down the hall.

I figure it's Zeke or Jasper—those two always track me down if I'm not where I'm supposed to be.

Needy bastards, but I wouldn't have them any other way.

Except it's not either of them standing in the doorway.

It's Addie.

She's barefoot and drowning in one of my T-shirts because she asked for the biggest thing we had, and Jesus, it's giving full post-fucking energy.

She used to walk around in nothing but my shirts.

Her eyes widen, lips parting like she's caught somewhere between running and staying right where she is.

We just stare at each other for a few long seconds, the silence stretching between us as the whiskey slowly burns my throat. But it's nothing compared to the heat crawling under my skin just from being alone with her.

It hasn't been just the two of us like this in years. Not since the day I begged her not to walk away from me. I can still feel the agony of that moment. I can still hear the way my voice cracked when I told her I'd spend the rest of my life loving her. I didn't care how pathetic I looked or that I was falling apart in front of her. I just wanted her to stay.

Not my finest moment—not by a long shot. But I was so gone for her, so fucking in love, I would've walked through hell if she'd promised she'd be mine.

Do I still love her? Pretty sure I do, but I wish I didn't. I wish the feeling would just disappear, shrivel up, and die.

But it doesn't. It never has.

What's worse is how my body and brain—both traitors—agree on one thing: I still want her.

I want to close the distance between us, pull her into my chest, and kiss her like the last few years never happened. Because in my mind, she never really left—not my head, not my heart, not the place where my soul still fucking aches for her.

She was mine once, but there's a voice buried deep inside me that's loud as hell tonight, screaming that maybe she was never meant to be just mine. Maybe she was always meant to be ours.

"I'm sorry... I just wanted to grab some water," she whispers as she edges into the kitchen.

I can tell she's cautious about being alone with me, and I don't blame her. I haven't exactly been the warmest.

"Can't you sleep?" I ask, watching her as she crosses the room. She moves past me to reach the cabinet, close enough that her scent surrounds me.

She smells like strawberries, always strawberries.

She shakes her head. "No... you?"

"No... that hasn't really changed." Her eyes catch mine, and something glimmers there, before she forces it down. "What?"

"I just assumed you'd have found another way to deal with it."

She was how I survived the sleepless nights. She knows that. She remembers it.

"It's not always bad," I say.

"Is it worse because I'm here?"

Yes.

But I shake my head and reach for the bottle, pouring just enough to take the edge off.

"It's probably just being stuck here, and I have no idea when the hell we're getting out. We might as well bend over and hand Coach the goddamn paddle ourselves because if we roll in even a day later than we told him, that man's gonna murder us, drag our asses back from the grave, and kill us all over again just to prove a fucking point."

"Hopefully it won't come to that," she says, filling her cup with water.

"I hope not." I push off the counter, forcing a smile that doesn't reach anything inside me. "I'll take this to bed and give you some space."

I manage two steps before her voice breaks through the tension hanging between us.

"Wait... Roman, please. Can we just—"

I stop and exhale before I finally turn to face her. "What?"

Addie's midnight blues are glassy with unshed tears, and in that moment, every wall I've built between us feels paper-thin. I feel myself slipping, ready to drop everything just to hold her together.

"I can't..." She looks away, but I watch as a single tear escapes and tracks down her cheek before she can swipe it away. "I can't keep living with you hating me the way you do. It hurts me, Roman."

All the resentment I've been clinging to—the thing I thought was keeping me safe—suddenly feels like it's choking me instead. The despair in her voice, the heartbreak etched on her face... it guts me in a way nothing else ever has.

"I don't hate you, princess."

She lets out a bitter little laugh. "Liar."

"I don't," I repeat, shaking my head as if that'll somehow make her believe it. "I wish I could."

"Really? Because nothing you could ever do would make me want to hate you."

"I didn't break you, Addison. That's the difference. I would've given it all up for you." She looks at me, her eyes narrowing like she wants to argue, but I don't let up. "Don't look at me like I wouldn't have. You know I would. I would've walked away from the team, from the season, from all of it if it meant keeping you, and you ripped my fucking heart out instead."

Her arms wrap around herself as her shoulders curl in. "If we'd stayed together after my dad found out, you would've ended up off the team. I couldn't live with that, and if I hadn't done it, you wouldn't have what you do now. You wouldn't have Zeke and Jasper; you wouldn't have the NHL. I'm not trying to justify hurting you. I'm not saying it didn't kill me, too, but I believed you were meant for so much more. If I had to lose you to make sure you got it all... then I did what I had to do."

Tears spill over now, one after the other. "I loved you. Jesus, I loved you so much, and I'm sorry, Roman. I'm so fucking sorry I ever hurt you. For me, it was a mistake, one I've been living with every day since, but it was the best thing I could've done for you. I see how you love them, and it kills me as much as I love it because I'm jealous. You used to look at me like that. You used to touch me like you touch them, and I destroyed it. And before you leave, before I never see you again—because I know this is it, that this is all we've got—I just need you to know I've hated myself every single day for what I did to us."

A sob catches in her throat, tears spilling faster, and that's it. I'm done. I can't stand here and watch her break for another second. My pride, my anger, all my bullshit—none of it matters. I'm not that guy.

I step forward and wrap my arms around her, pulling her in like I've been waiting years to do it one more time. She's so small in my hold, fragile in a way that makes every old instinct to protect her flare up.

"Please don't cry," I whisper, burying my face in her hair. "You know it kills me."

She clings to me, hesitant at first, like she's afraid I'll push her away, but I don't let go. I can't, not when she's hurting. Right now, it isn't about our history or heartbreak. It's about being human and holding someone when the world feels too heavy.

"I only want one thing from you, Addie."

She tilts her face into my chest, her voice muffled. "What?"

"Be careful with Zeke and Jasper. They're not ready to lose you. They're not ready for whatever goodbye you think is coming."

She looks up at me then, her eyes swollen and red. "But you are?"

"It's just the way it is. What are you going to do, pack up your life and come to Boston?" I cup her face in my hands, her palms pressed to my ribs, holding on like we're both afraid to let go. "If that's a life you could see, then you need to tell me right now."

"Of course I could, but it's not that simple." Her lip quivers, and a tear slips down, catching on my thumb as I hold her still. "I just want to be happy, Roman. I'm so tired of feeling alone."

"How long have you felt alone?"

"Since the day I lost you," she whispers. "It got worse when you all left after college. I thought I could move on. I told myself I had to, but something's been missing ever since, and nothing's ever really filled the space where you all were."

My gaze drops to her mouth, back up to her eyes, then down again—caught in this pull I've been trying to resist since the second we walked into her bookshop. I lean in, closer, close enough to feel her breath stutter, and suddenly her lips part, and my name falls from her.

"Roman..."

God, she says it like I'm still hers.

My eyes close, and I force myself to pull back.

"I can't, princess," I say, my hands still cradling her face. "I can't kiss you unless it's forever."

My lips brush her forehead, and I feel her tense before I let her go. I walk away, every step heavier than the last, leaving her standing there holding all the pieces of my heart that never stopped belonging to her.

I slip back into bed and reach for Zeke. My fingers brush over the bare skin of his back, searching for something solid to keep me from spiraling, and for a moment, I just let myself breathe.

Seconds later, I hear the bedroom door creak open.

I reach out blindly, hand extended, a silent invitation I'm not sure she'll take. But she does, and I'm so damn relieved when I feel her small hand in mine. She climbs in quietly, careful not to disturb them. Her body brushes against mine briefly as she moves across the mattress, then she slips into the space between Zeke and Jasper. I feel the mattress shift as she settles, and for tonight, at least, I know that none of us have to be alone.

As soon as I know she's there, tucked safely between the people I love, my body lets go. The ache in my chest eases, the noise in my head fades, and sleep finally claims me.

CHAPTER SIXTEEN
ADDISON

When the sun comes up and I remember where I am, there's this weird kind of calm that settles over me, something I haven't felt in a long, long time. Last night, something in me broke, but in that exact moment, I felt a piece of myself start to stitch back together.

Jasper's arms hold me tight, his body pressed so close it feels like we're sharing the same heartbeat. His chest rises and falls against my back, and for a moment, I know I'm exactly where I'm meant to be.

When I blink one eye open, adjusting to the light filtering through the curtains, I find Zeke watching me.

"You know that's kind of creepy," I whisper, my lips curving into a sleepy smile as my eyes flutter shut again.

"Just taking it all in, beautiful," he murmurs.

His fingers slide into my hair, brushing it back from my face with a tenderness that sends a shiver down my spine. When I open my eyes, the look on his face has changed—still gentle and full of care, but there's heat simmering beneath it.

I hold his gaze for a long, breathless second before he shifts closer, moving carefully so he doesn't wake Roman or Jasper.

"I really want to kiss you." He leans in, brushing his lips against mine. "It's been so long, Addison."

Our noses bump, and his mouth hovers close enough to tease but not enough to satisfy.

God, it's torture.

Finally, I close the space between us. Our lips meet, and his hand cradles my face.

It's heated, but more than that, it's relief. It's as if we've been aching for this moment without even realizing how deep the need ran. It's exactly like the first time, and somehow more.

"I've missed you," I whisper, and he runs his fingers through my hair.

Jasper stirs behind me, his arm slipping away, and then Zeke's hands are on my waist, pulling me on top of him. I can't help but laugh, the sound breaking free as our chests press together. He kisses me again, deeper this time, and I end up straddling him, my breath catching when I feel just how hard he is beneath me.

His grip tightens as I gently rock, grinding down just enough to ease the pressure coiling low in my belly.

But I want more.

I need more.

I want to feel him, all of him. And even though I'm almost certain he wants it too, a part of me wonders if this is the line he won't cross.

Roman has his limits. He'll hold me and soothe me but never push past the boundaries he's set for himself. I understand that. Jasper, I'd bet anything, would have me seeing stars and not think twice, but Zeke is harder for me to read.

I freeze, holding perfectly still on top of him, searching his face for something—permission, maybe, or a sign that he wants this as badly as I do. His eyes lock on mine, and it's like he's trying to unravel everything I'm thinking. Suddenly, he's sitting up beneath me, one strong arm curling around my back, pulling me flush against his chest. His lips brush mine, and everything else fades away except the heat thrumming between us.

"There's nothing you want that I haven't thought about every single day, but I have to be sure you won't regret it."

"I couldn't," I whisper. "Not with you... not with them."

"Fuck, Addison." His breath shudders out, his mouth brushing the shell of my ear. "You have no idea how much I want to keep you."

If I give myself over to this, it won't be a secret. Everyone will know I belong to three men. And yes—three, because the truth is, I've never stopped loving Roman. What I feel for Jasper and Zeke burns just as bright, and I know it's our history, the mess and the magic of it, that's pulled all of this back into the light so quickly. It scares me how right it feels, but when I look at Zeke, I see the truth shining in his eyes. I know it with the kind of certainty that lives in your bones.

I want all of them. I always have.

How would this even work? Would I be tucked away the same way they keep themselves hidden from the world? God knows they've done it for years, loving quietly, sacrificing more than anyone should ever have to. But I see the way it eats at them and the way it hurts.

They've barely been back in my life for a week, and I'm ready to flip my whole world upside down just for a chance at this.

"Get out of your head, beautiful," Zeke murmurs. "There's no pressure, but I'm not gonna pretend I don't want you, and I don't just mean your body." His lips find that spot on my neck, and I can't help the shiver that rips through me. "If you're this responsive to my mouth, how are you gonna feel when I'm inside you?"

"How about we find out?"

Roman.

My body goes still, and my heart skips.

Zeke pulls back slightly, his eyes flicking over his shoulder just as I do the same. Roman's propped up against the headboard now, sheets low on his waist, his tattooed chest glistening in the soft light. He runs a hand through his messy hair, and those amber eyes pierce mine like he's already inside my head.

"Yeah, I'm done. I've been lying here hard as fuck since Zeke said he wanted to kiss you. I figured I'd give you a minute, considering I've already had my mouth on both sets of lips."

"So, what do you say, beautiful? You want me to fuck you while they watch?"

I bite down on my lip and nod, my gaze bouncing between Jasper and Roman as the idea of watching them together again lights me up from the inside out.

"Ah, you wanna watch Roman stuff Jasper full of his cock while you're dripping down mine?"

Roman's palm moves over the bulge in his briefs, eyes gone dark with want, as Jasper trails a line of wet, open-mouthed kisses down my neck before catching Zeke by the jaw and kissing him hard.

"You hear that, Captain? Addie wants a show," Jasper teases, sliding out of the bed and finding a bottle of lube in one of the drawers. He tosses it in the air and catches it with a smirk as he strolls back toward the bed, his eyes on Roman the whole time.

"Both of you on your backs," Roman commands.

It's not a question or a suggestion.

It's an order, and it includes me.

Roman slips out of bed, making space for Jasper to stretch out, and Zeke wastes no time spinning me around and easing me back beside Jasper.

At the foot of the bed, Roman and Zeke turn to face each other, and when their mouths meet, it's like watching fire devour oxygen. Zeke fists a hand in Roman's hair, and Roman growls low in his throat.

They're devastating together.

"Still the hottest fucking thing you've ever seen, huh?" Jasper smirks, watching Roman's mouth move over Zeke's like he owns every inch of him. "Can't even pretend I'm not obsessed."

I reach for Jasper, my thumb stroking his cheek, and when my eyes drop to his mouth, it's like tumbling straight back to five years ago, to the first time I ever wanted this.

"Not just them," I whisper.

Jasper doesn't kiss me.

He devours me.

One second, I'm breathing, and the next, I'm drowning in him. I hook my leg around his waist, hauling him closer like I'll die if there's any space between us.

His hands are everywhere—raking up my sides, gripping my ass, and sliding under my T-shirt like it's not even there. When he shoves his thigh between my legs, I grind down on him, chasing the friction without a hint of shame.

"Touch her, Jasper. I want her ready for me when I slide inside," Zeke growls from the foot of the bed, but his words barely register as Jasper's hand slips into the front of my borrowed underwear.

"No problem there, she's fucking soaked," he mutters as he pushes a finger inside me, fucking me before adding a second, stretching me until I'm arching off the mattress. "When was the last time someone made you feel good, Addie? When was the last time you were fucked so right you couldn't do anything but beg for more?"

Before I can stop myself, my eyes lift. Roman stands still, his jaw clenched, and those gold-flecked eyes hold mine like he's living inside the memory I just slipped into.

Yeah, baby. Yeah, it was you.

I don't need to say it out loud. We can all feel it.

"The way he fucks... it's everything, right?" Jasper whispers in my ear, and I nod, my body strung so tight I feel like I might snap. "Zeke will make you see stars, too, angel. His cock... fuck, it feels so damn good."

Heat climbs up my spine, and my hand lowers, closing around Jasper's cock through his underwear. I tighten my grip around him, dragging my palm down the length of him.

"Take these off."

Jasper strips off his underwear, and holy shit, his dick is beautiful.

Of course it is.

It's Jasper.

He wraps a hand around the base, giving it a slow stroke. I reach out and cover his hand with mine, sliding my thumb over the precum already smeared across the head. I bring it to my lips, tasting him, loving the way his breath stutters and his eyes go dark when I swallow.

"Fuck..." A groan cuts through the air, but it doesn't come from Jasper.

Roman stands there, fully naked. Zeke is flush against his side —just as bare and just as unfairly beautiful—his lean frame pressed tight to Roman's bulk. He's got his mouth on Roman's neck, dragging slow, wet kisses down his throat. His hand wraps around his cock, and that's when I see his piercing for the first time. Silver gleams at the tip like it's begging to be played with. Now all I want is to drop to my knees and wrap my lips around him, feel that metal drag across my tongue as he fucks my mouth with those tattooed hands buried in my hair.

"You two look so good together," Roman rasps.

"Both of you need to get over here," Jasper orders as he begins to strip me of my clothes, leaving me naked for the first time in front of all of them. "Pretty sure we're both more than ready to get fucked."

"Get inside her, Zeke," Roman bites out, his voice ragged as he steps closer. "She doesn't want it sweet. She wants to be fucked like she's the only thing that's ever mattered." His gaze drags down my body like it physically hurts him to look and not touch. "That's what gets her off. When it's so fucking raw, she'll still feel you the next day, every inch of her marked by how badly you needed her." He exhales hard, his jaw tight. "She wants to be reminded that she's it, that she's the one."

The way Roman gets lost in his memories of us—it does something to me. I feel like I'm one second from falling apart, from tears or release, and I can't even tell which.

Roman and Zeke move in, slotting themselves above me and Jasper like they've done it a hundred times before. Their focus is absolute, all that hungry attention zeroed in on the only thing they want—us.

Roman pops the cap off the lube with a snap, and before I can even catch my breath, Zeke's mouth is on me. He licks a line straight up my chest, taking his time as he circles my nipple, sucking and biting until pleasure sparks along my spine.

He drops between my thighs, flattens his tongue, and drags it right across my clit.

"Holy shit—"

"She tastes phenomenal, doesn't she?" Jasper pants out.

"Fucking beautiful."

When I glance down at Roman, he's a perfect mirror of Zeke—his mouth wrapped around Jasper's cock, fingers buried deep, working him open.

Watching the way Roman touches Jasper makes my pussy throb, and I know Zeke can feel it. He wraps his lips around my clit, and I break. There's no slow build, no teasing edge, just a brutal, blinding orgasm that leaves me gasping and my legs trembling as I squeeze his head between my thighs.

"Zeke... Jesus—"

He doesn't stop licking me through it, moaning into my pussy like he can't get enough. Then his hand shoots out, grabbing Roman by the back of the neck, and he slams their mouths together. Roman groans into it, tongue-fucking Zeke like he's desperate to suck every trace of me off his lips.

"See how much Roman misses your pussy, baby," Jasper murmurs as his hand slides between my shaking thighs. "Fuck... you made a beautiful mess."

Zeke pulls back from Roman and presses their foreheads together, both of them breathless, sweat slick, and wild-eyed.

"Share, big guy," Jasper teases, and Roman's smirk is pure filth as he lowers his mouth to his.

"Addie?" Zeke's voice pulls me back in, and I turn my gaze to where he's settled between my thighs, the thick head of his cock brushing against my clit. "Listen, we can stop right now if you want. We don't use protection because it's always just been the three of us, but we should've had this conversation first. Honestly, I don't think any of us expected this to actually happen."

"I did... Fuck," Jasper groans. "They're in the nightstand beside you... Shit, Rome, keep fucking my ass like that."

Zeke laughs, reaching over to grab the box of condoms, but I cover his hand with mine.

"Can I just feel you? If you don't want to, I get it, but I'm on birth control, and I got tested after Mikey... and I haven't been with anyone since."

"You think I want anything between us after all this time?" he says, pressing a kiss to the swell of my breast before he starts to push in slow, thick, and bare. My back arches as he stretches me open, every part of me straining to take him. "Breathe, beautiful girl. This pussy was made for us."

Roman suddenly ignores his own no-touching rule and grabs my chin, forcing me to look at him.

"I'm only going to say this once, princess." I'm strung tight, the stretch of Zeke's cock still pulsing through me, but all I can focus on is him. "If you ever say your ex-husband's name while one of us is touching you again, I'll get Jasper to fuck your throat so deep that the only name you'll remember is the one making you gag."

He tenderly strokes my cheek, and I realize that this possessive bastard is still *my* possessive bastard, and I can't help what that does to me.

"It's not an empty threat, angel. I'll fucking do it," Jasper growls, but Roman shuts him up with his mouth, kissing him hard as he starts to pound into him while Zeke does the same to me.

The whole room dissolves into a mess of grunts, moans, and slapping skin, and I swear I've never been this turned on in my entire life.

Whatever this is—this wild, filthy, perfect fuckfest—it's exactly what I've always dreamed of with them.

"Holy shit, don't stop... I'm so close."

"You gonna come for us, Addison?"

"Yes, god, yes—"

"Come on my cock. Let me feel that pussy grip me." I clutch Zeke's shoulders, clinging as my body locks up, and I tighten around him. "Good girl." He groans, fucking me rougher right through my orgasm, drawing it out, and making every nerve in my body spark and burn. "Such a good fucking girl. Keep squeezing me, just like that."

Zeke drops his mouth to mine, kissing me hard as he slams

into me one last time. He finishes inside me, and when he pulls back, those green eyes hold me still, the world narrowing to nothing but this.

"Get on my dick, angel. Can't let Zeke have all the fun." Roman shifts onto his knees, eyes darkening as the seconds pass, and he gives me a small nod. I move to climb over Jasper, facing him, but his hands catch my waist before I can settle. "Uh-uh, face our guy... Make him remember what it's like to be inside you."

"You really think I could ever forget?"

I turn slowly, straddling Jasper in reverse, my back arching as I settle onto him.

Roman's right there.

He's so close.

If I leaned forward just an inch, I could press my cheek to his skin and lose myself in the comfort of him again. If I reached out, I could weave my fingers through his hair and pull him to me like I used to.

Like I still want to.

I don't look away.

Neither does he.

"Holy fuck, you feel... Jesus fucking Christ, Addie, you feel so good." Jasper groans, his hands gripping my hips tight as he helps me ride him.

Roman picks up the pace, his thrusts turning rougher and deeper. His eyes never leave mine—golden fire pinning me in place as he watches every flicker of pleasure that rolls through me.

"You got one more in you, baby? You came so fucking perfect for Zeke... Think you can come just as pretty for me and Rome?"

With Roman, it always happened easily. He knew my body better than I did. Zeke only has to look at me, and I'm halfway gone. And now, with Jasper buried inside me, it's like they've all found the switch and can flick it whenever they want.

Zeke slides in close, fingers finding my clit, circling it while his mouth locks onto my nipple. I cry out, my whole body tightening as another orgasm tears through me so hard I'm pretty sure I see the entire universe.

"Fuck, fuck, fuck—" Jasper chokes out, pulling me down hard as he spills inside me.

Roman pulls out of Jasper and moves in, his eyes wild. "Look at me," he growls. "Eyes on me, princess."

I hold his gaze, not daring to look away as he fists his cock and strokes fast. A broken roar rips from his throat as he unloads all over my pussy, painting me like I still belong to him.

I slide my fingers through the mess and bring them to my lips, tasting him, probably tasting Zeke and Jasper too, but this is for Roman. I want him to know I still ache for him, even if he can't bring himself to touch me right now.

He inhales sharply, freezing as he watches, his gaze dropping to my mouth. I see him teeter on the edge for a moment, torn between restraint and hunger. He jolts forward like he's going to kiss me, ready to take what he wants, but catches himself at the last second, stopping just shy of me.

"I am fucking ruined in the best way." Jasper moans from beneath me, shattering the moment.

Eventually, all four of us end up sprawled across the bed. I know I'll need a shower soon, we all will, but I'm not ready to break this afterglow just yet.

"I hope Coach's ceremony still happens Saturday," Zeke says, his fingers threading lazily through my hair. My head rests on his chest, his body pressed against Roman's, while Jasper is spread across my legs like he plans to stay there forever. "If the date changes, I don't think we'll get the chance to come back."

"I hope so too, otherwise, my mom's going to be unbearable."

"Give the woman a break," Roman says, chuckling. "She's had to put up with your dad for decades."

Jasper lifts his head just enough to chime in. "Don't talk about Brenda like that, Addie. She used to send the team cookies."

"She still does."

"Your dad's lucky to have a good woman," Zeke adds.

"Yeah, maybe."

There's a beat of silence, then Zeke gently nudges me. "Okay, explain that."

"I just think she could've been firmer with my dad sometimes. You know how he could be, but I don't know... She'd have me back with Mikey tomorrow if she had her way."

"Why the fuck would she be okay with that?" Roman blurts, saying exactly what everyone else is thinking.

"She's never believed in divorce. To her, marriage is something you endure, no matter what. Not that my dad would ever actually hurt her, but I think she'd stay with him even if he did."

"Did you ever consider staying with Mikey?" Zeke asks.

"Not once. I think I was already looking for a way out, and thankfully, he handed it to me."

"So what's next for you, princess?" I turn my face toward Roman, meeting his stare. "Do you think you'll get divorced?"

The question catches me off guard—not because I haven't thought about it, but because no one's actually said it out loud. Everything's just been sitting in limbo, suspended in this awful in-between where we're separated but not moving forward.

"I don't want to stay a King any longer than I have to," I say honestly. "So yeah, the sooner I can start the process, the better."

"Does he know there's no chance you're getting back together?" Jasper cuts in, sitting up slightly. "Because Mikey was always a persistent fuck. You know I always hated you around him."

"I was lost for a long time, and he was there when I needed someone, but marrying him was never truly what I wanted."

"So what does Addison Hope want now?" Zeke asks, deliberately using my maiden name.

"Happiness. That's all. What about you three?"

Roman glances at Jasper. Jasper looks to Zeke. Zeke's gaze finds Roman, and I suddenly feel like I've been left out of something I didn't even know was happening. Silence stretches between us until I sit up slowly, shifting Jasper off my legs so I can see all three of them properly.

"What aren't you saying?"

"Don't act like you don't know what they want."

Jasper sits up, pushing his hand through his hair. "Dude, I love you, but I swear, if you keep acting like the way you feel about Addie is somehow separate from the way Zeke and I feel, I'm gonna knock you the fuck out. There's no just 'me and Zeke,'" Jasper says, looking between us. "Whether you admit it or not, we all feel the same. You can guard that big, messed-up heart of yours, but it doesn't change the fact that you're still in love with her." Roman's silence says more than any denial could. "What we want is you, angel. All of us, including Roman, and I'm sick of pretending like that's not what this is. We're already all in, every single one of us, and I'm done dancing around it."

"Jasper..." Zeke says softly as Jasper stands, grabbing his underwear and yanking it on like he can't stand to be exposed for another second.

"No. Fuck that—no. I already have to hide the most important people in my life. I'm not doing it here too. Not with Addie. Not with Roman. Not with whatever the hell is still going on between them—whatever's always been going on between them." He rakes a hand through his hair, pacing like he's trying to outrun the chaos in his mind. "I can't do it. I can't keep up. I'm drowning, and I can only hold it together for so long."

"Jasper, I'm sorry," Roman says, his voice gentler than I've ever heard. "I know this is hard. It's hard for all of us, but I love you, okay? No amount of hiding changes that."

Jasper turns, and the look on his face shatters something inside me. "I don't want to do this anymore."

Roman's face crumbles. "What?"

Zeke's already moving, grabbing his underwear and crossing the room in seconds.

"Why can't I kiss you out there? Why can't I kiss Zeke? I don't even need you to answer. I already know why, but it shouldn't matter."

"Baby, look at me," Zeke says, forcing Jasper's frantic pacing to still. "If you want to go public, we'll do it the second we're back. If that's what you need, we'll figure it out. You know we only agreed to live like this for as long as it worked for all of us."

Roman's already pulled on a pair of shorts and moves in beside them, and I watch Jasper visibly ease the moment both his men are close.

"I'm sorry," Roman says, pressing his forehead to Jasper's. "I'd give anything to kiss you out there. And the day I do, I'll do it so fucking proudly. You know that."

The moment is wrapped in the kind of love most people never get to see, and suddenly, I'm painfully aware that I don't belong here—at least, not right now. I slip off the bed as quietly as possible, my feet barely skimming the floor, as I try to slip out of the room without anyone noticing.

"Stop, Addison," Zeke says, reaching out his hand toward me. "He needs you too. Or do you still not get that?" The softness in his green eyes practically breaks me. "We all do."

My chest tightens as I step back into them. Jasper pulls me into his arms immediately, pressing me to his chest. Roman and Zeke close in around us, their arms sliding around our bodies until there's no space between us.

"I'm sorry, baby," Jasper murmurs into my hair, pressing his cheek to the top of my head as he cradles me.

"Rome." Zeke's voice breaks the quiet, acknowledging something unspoken but deeply understood by all of us.

"I know," Roman answers, his tone heavy with the same realization.

It's there in the silence and in the way we're all holding onto each other—the confirmation that together we're whole.

CHAPTER SEVENTEEN
ADDISON

The awards ceremony is going ahead as planned tonight. We got the confirmation late last night, and now I'm standing here in the same outfit I arrived in days ago, somehow both ready and completely unprepared to say goodbye to these men, even if it's only for a few hours.

The past few days have been almost perfect. I say almost because Roman still won't touch me. Not intimately. Not the way Zeke and Jasper do. He's right there with us, but there's a line he won't cross.

But I know I love him. Whether he touches me or not, I love Roman. I love Zeke and Jasper too. I think I always have, even if I didn't have the words for it back then. Only now, it's more than that. It's so much bigger and deeper than anything I've ever felt. Even when I stood at that altar, dressed in white and promised forever to another man, my heart was already spoken for.

"So, we'll see you tonight?" Jasper steps closer, fingers threading through my hair before his lips land on mine.

"Yeah, I'll be arriving with my parents and Willow."

"Ah, man, I remember your sister. She was hot..." he teases, and I laugh as I smack him in the arm. He stumbles back dramatically, clutching himself like I just hit him with a brick.

"Jesus, woman! You see that? She assaulted me."

"You deserved it." Roman chuckles, and I grab Jasper's shirt, yanking him back to my mouth for a quick kiss.

"No flirting with my sister. She's a mom now. Show some respect."

"So when you're a mom, does that mean we can't disrespect you anymore? Because last night, you were pretty okay with being disrespected."

It's been years since a couple of doctors sat me down and rattled off a bunch of medical crap that barely made sense, trying to explain why my body won't do what it's supposed to. But standing here now, it suddenly feels huge. Because these three men might actually want a future with me, and they deserve to know exactly what that future can and can't look like before they start making promises they can't keep.

I need to tell them.

"You were right by my side getting your throat fucked by Roman," I answer.

"And my hand between your thighs, don't forget," Jasper adds, biting down on that full lower lip. "You were shaking, angel."

"Okay, you two." Zeke groans, dragging a hand over his face. "It's difficult enough letting you go, Addie, without the three of us being left here with our dicks hard."

"What a shame that would be," I purr, leaning in just enough to be a menace. "Because if I imagine the three of you together while I'm gone—fucking, touching, all sweaty and desperate—" Jasper slaps his hand over my mouth before I can finish, but I'm already laughing against his palm.

"No more out of you," he growls, grinning. "Now get your ass out of here, and we'll see you in a few hours."

I nod and turn to leave, but I can't stop my eyes from drifting back to Roman. He hasn't moved. His chin is dipped slightly, arms crossed tight over his chest, doing that whole silent, protective thing he does when he's trying too hard not to feel.

But then his eyes finally lift to meet mine.

I don't want you to leave again.

Please stay.

I still want you.

I wish I knew how to be what you need.

A thousand unsaid things, packed into a single look.

He doesn't speak or reach for me, and even though I pretend it doesn't, it hurts.

The snow crunches beneath my boots as I make my way to the car, my breath fogging in the icy air. I slide into the driver's seat, my fingers stiff and numb from the cold, fumbling with the keys before finally getting the engine started. I crank the heater up as high as it'll go, and Bing Crosby's voice drifts through the speakers. Christmas lights blink from distant cabins tucked between the pines, turning the whole drive down the mountain into something that belongs on the front of a holiday card.

I reach my house and step through the front door, and the cold hits me hard. I haven't been home in days, so yes, it's physically freezing. But it's more than that. The warmth I'd felt wrapped up in them—the comfort and the closeness I'd just started to get used to—are gone now.

This house, the place that once felt like my safe haven, suddenly feels lonelier than ever. As I stand in the kitchen, taking it all in, I realize I've never felt more detached from this space or the life I thought I wanted. The only things that truly keep me here are my bookstore and my family, and even then, if I ever had to leave, I know I could. There's always a plane ticket, and I can always visit.

But my store... that's different.

My bookstore is my baby.

I took it from a dusty, forgotten space and turned it into a place where stories breathe, ache, and burn. It's a home for every kind of romance, especially the ones with men who make you want to crawl inside the pages and never come back out.

But is it more important than *them*?

No. Not even close.

I think they want me to commit to them, but none of us have actually talked about what that would look like. We've been living in this perfect little bubble, and now that I'm out of it and back in my own space, my mind won't stop racing.

I have a thousand thoughts and even more what-ifs.

Tomorrow, they'll be gone.

All I've got left is tonight to figure out what the hell I'm going to do.

"I am one proud father," my dad says as he takes in my sister and me for the first time tonight. "You're both so beautiful."

"Aren't they just?" my mom adds, beaming as she slips her arm through his.

"Are you ready for tonight?"

"Of course," he says with a grin. "You know I love a bit of fuss, Addie."

Trailing behind them toward the waiting car, I feel my purse buzz with a message. Assuming it's Zeke finally texting me back, I pull out my phone, a smile already forming on my lips, but the second I glance at the screen, the smile vanishes.

> MIKEY: I figured I'd try one last time since you keep ignoring my calls and texts. We're going to run into each other tonight, so maybe grow up and talk to me like an adult. I just want five minutes, Adds.

God, I hate when he calls me that.

"Everything okay?" Willow asks, eyeing me as I stare at my phone.

I hand it over without saying a word, and she takes one glance before pulling a face.

"You know he won't stop until you talk to him, right?"

"Yeah, I know." I sigh, shoving the phone back in my bag.

"Forget that dickbag for a minute—I know you've been with Roman this week, and don't even try to lie to me. Something had to have happened."

I shrug, biting back a smile. "Nothing happened… with him, anyway."

She stops dead and spins around, pointing a finger at me. "Okay, I'm driving."

"What?"

"I mean it," she says, already fishing her keys out of her bag. "I have zero desire to parent tomorrow with a hangover, and I need the full story, start to finish." I can't help but laugh as she herds me toward her car, calling out, "Mom, Dad, I'm driving Addie!"

Dad frowns, already halfway to the car. "Why? I'd really like us to arrive together."

"We'll be right behind you, Dad," Willow says sweetly. "But I need to talk to Addison about my cycle, unless you want all the details?" Dad immediately backs off, muttering something under his breath. For a guy who's been a girl dad for years, periods still send him running every time.

"See you in a bit, girls," Mom calls, and the second I'm buckled into the passenger seat next to Willow, she turns to me with that look.

"Start talking. I want every single detail."

CHAPTER EIGHTEEN
ZEKE

What was supposed to be a quick shower before the awards tonight turned into Jasper pressing my chest against the tile and fucking me like he was trying to etch himself into my spine. Roman just leaned back against the wall, stroking his cock, eyes glued on every thrust, every sound, and every shudder that tore through us.

The things that came out of Rome's mouth while he watched… *Fuuuck.* They were the kind of words that make your knees buckle and your back arch because Roman doesn't just talk. He speaks to ruin you, and I don't know what got me off harder—Jasper's cock driving into me like he couldn't get close enough, his breath ragged against my ear as he whispered how much he loved me, or Roman telling me I was taking it like a good boy while he just watched as if we existed purely for his pleasure.

Both, always both.

Now I'm standing in the living room in my charcoal suit pants and crisp black button-down when Roman strolls in, wearing the same, except his pants are navy and his shirt's white, top buttons undone, giving me a flash of tattooed skin at his collarbone. It's enough to make my mouth go dry, and he just grins. He knows exactly where my mind's gone and lets me look as long as I want.

"You're in so much trouble," I say, my lip twitching as I give Roman a slow, obvious once-over. "You know what seeing you in that suit does to him."

"Why do you think I wore it?" He just smirks, spritzing cologne on his neck.

Not even a minute later, Jasper strides in and stops dead in his tracks, eyes going wide as they sweep over the two of us.

"Fuck me," he growls. "You two in suits give me an instant hard-on."

I laugh, but Jesus Christ... he's in all black, and it's doing things to me. The shirt, the slacks, the way every inch clings to him like it was stitched with the sole purpose of being ripped off. He looks so good it's criminal.

"You don't have to pretend," I tease, moving closer and brushing my lips over his. "We all know this is your favorite version of Roman."

Jasper grins, shaking his head. "Not true... I haven't seen my favorite version of Roman yet."

He crosses the room, slides his hand up to Roman's jaw, and buries his face in the curve of his neck. He inhales, breathing him in like he's chasing a high.

"Pretty sure the day you finally let me sink my cock in you, that'll be my favorite look." Roman's whole body tightens, pupils blown, and his gaze is pure heat as it lands on Jasper. "You like that idea? Me getting you out of this suit and fucking you full for the first time?" His hand catches Jasper's and presses it to the thick line of his cock.

"What do you think?" he rasps, ghosting his lips over Jasper's like he's about to lose control.

Jasper smirks, his hand still flexing possessively over him. "One of these days, I'm gonna watch you dripping my cum, baby."

I barely manage to catch my breath before I clear my throat and try to sound like I've got my shit together.

"Okay, guests have started arriving. I saw them coming up the drive, so you two need to shut your boys down. Tell them they'll get to play later, but right now, we have to go."

"Like you're not desperate to fuck him too," Jasper fires back, and the rumble of laughter from all three of us fills the room.

We head out, making the short walk from the cabin to the main house, where the celebration's already in full swing.

"What's the plan with Addie tonight? We're leaving tomorrow, and we have to figure shit out," Jasper says as we walk through the snow.

"Neither of you is to try and talk her into anything," Roman warns, glancing between us. "Tell her how you feel, fine, but she's got to want you enough on her own." Jasper pauses, slowing his pace, and exhales hard. "You know what I mean. Whatever happens between me and her... it's gonna take time."

"We've all felt it, Rome," I say, jamming my hands into my pockets. "This isn't just screwing around. I know she scares you, but she loves you. She might not have said it, but she loves all of us."

Jasper's grin breaks out wide. "She does, doesn't she?" he says, almost in awe, and just like that, the heaviness lifts. The tension eases, and we keep walking toward the party with just a little more hope.

The place looks incredible—silver and black everywhere, winter-themed, and sparkling like fresh snow. It's elegant, festive, and exactly what you'd expect a week before Christmas. But none of it really registers when Addison is the only thing I'm looking for.

"Do you see her?" Roman asks, his eyes scanning the room, and I can tell he's restless.

"No, but if she's coming with her parents, I bet they'll wait until most people arrive. Tonight's all about her dad, after all."

"I can't wait to tell him I'm going to steal his daughter," Jasper mutters, "which I'll do in front of everyone if that prick even breathes near her."

I follow his gaze and spot Mikey King pushing through the crowd, still wearing that smug grin and that same overinflated ego, like time hasn't touched him at all.

"Play nice," Roman says under his breath. "I don't want to ruin the night for Coach and his family."

"I'm always nice, Captain."

"You're also a sarcastic ass," I shoot back, grazing my fingertips along the back of Jasper's hand. "Come on, let's get a drink."

We've spent the past twenty minutes mingling—close, but never too close. There's a careful rhythm to the way we move around each other. We're always within reach but never quite touching.

We've been catching up with people we haven't seen in years, nodding along to old stories and smiling through polite conversations, when my body lights up without warning. I turn, mid-sentence, no longer hearing a word coming out of Grant Baxter's mouth as he drones on about his brother's messy divorce. I leave him mid-ramble, already forgotten, because standing at the entrance is Addison Hope.

I'm met with deep-blue eyes, a vision I wasn't even remotely prepared for. My gaze flits left and finds Roman and Jasper across the room. They've gone still, staring at Addie the exact same way I am, like they've just seen something holy.

She's wearing a dark-blue gown that clings to her body like it was sewn onto her skin, hugging every curve, the color a perfect match for her eyes. The fabric slides down her body and pools at her feet, elegant and tempting all at once. The ruched neckline hides those perfect breasts I've spent the last few days worshipping, and her hair's pulled back, with a few loose blonde strands framing her face, making her look even more devastatingly beautiful.

She's on her dad's arm, who looks exactly like he did five years ago. Her mom and sister walk beside them, but all I see is Addie. My focus zeroes in on her, and everything else becomes background noise.

She belongs to us.

I want to cross the room, pull her into my arms, and show her how much she means to me in front of everyone. But until we've all figured out what this is and what we're doing, it wouldn't be fair to her or any of us. So I stay rooted to the spot, my hands clenched at my sides.

Mikey King is on her like a fly on shit, and despite the way she clings harder onto her dad's arm, Coach doesn't tell him to back off, which blows my fucking mind. If I ever have a daughter, and some asshole who cheated on her had the balls to show up smiling like nothing happened, I'd be the first one dragging him out by the throat.

I turn to the left and catch Roman's eyes across the room. He tilts his chin subtly toward Jasper, who's standing rigid, looking the way he does right before he forgets to hold back. I shake my head once. It's not a warning, just a reminder that you don't leash Jasper. You don't cage that kind of fire. You just make sure he knows he's not alone, and he'll find his ground. He's got more restraint than anyone gives him credit for, but we know the signs. We know when that control starts to splinter.

So I go. I move through the crowd, my eyes focused on the family, who are now surrounded by well-wishers and old friends.

My body slots in behind Addison, close enough to touch but not enough to draw attention.

Until I do touch her and let my fingers drift across the bare skin at the small of her back, right where the dress ends above the swell of her ass. Her skin prickles, and I swear I hear her gasp. The corner of my mouth lifts before I slip seamlessly into the moment, throwing an arm around her dad like I've done a hundred times before.

"Hey, Coach."

The man who's the reason I ever made it to the NHL turns around, his face splitting into that huge, beaming smile I grew up chasing approval from.

"Zeke... look at you," he says, giving me a once-over.

I catch Addie doing the same, but the only thing in her eyes is pure, unfiltered want. I get it—hell, I can't look at her for too long either. I'm already half hard, and that's not going away anytime soon.

"How's it going, Coach?" I ask, and he opens his arms wide, looking around the room.

"I'm going to soak all this in before it's back to the ice next week."

"You deserve it."

He claps my shoulder, pride shining in his eyes. "Thanks, son. How's Boston treating you? I've been keeping up with you, Jasper, and Roman—watching every game. You boys make this old guy proud."

"Couldn't have done it without you, you hard-ass," I say, and he lets out a big booming laugh, shaking his head.

"Some of you boys needed someone to give you a serious kick up the ass to get moving, and I guess that had to be me." I nod, grinning, when someone calls his name from across the room. He claps my shoulder once more and excuses himself before stepping away.

Mikey suddenly appears again, sliding his arm around Addie's waist, but she instantly shrugs him off, not even being subtle about it.

"Don't touch me."

"Adds, come on, don't be like that."

"Problem?" I ask, stepping beside her.

Mikey turns toward me, his smile as fake as it is forced. "Zeke... didn't expect you to grace us with your presence. Surely you're too good for us all, now that you've made it pro."

"Well, as you can see, I'm here."

"What about Jasper and Roman?"

"They're over there," I say, tipping my glass toward my boys. He follows my gaze, glancing over his shoulder before looking back at Addie.

"Did you know Roman was coming?"

"Yeah," she says with a shrug.

"No one told me."

"Why would they? You shouldn't even be here, Mikey."

His jaw tics, and his eyes bounce between me and Addie. "I don't think we should be having this conversation right now."

"I agree," I say, finishing the last of my whiskey in a single swallow. The burn trails down my throat as I set the glass on the side table with a quiet clink. "Which is why I'm leaving." Relief washes over Mikey's face, and he doesn't even bother to hide it. "Addison, are you coming? We can catch up."

I hold my arm out like the gentleman I can be, and she laces her arm through mine. We fall into step as we make our way across the room straight toward the only two men here who matter because I know they'll need her close, even if Jasper's the only one who'll ever admit it.

"Thank you," she murmurs, and the scent of her perfume wraps around me like silk.

"You're lucky it was me who came to get you. If it had been Jasper, you'd already be tossed over his shoulder with his hand halfway up your dress."

"I believe you."

I lean in closer, letting my mouth brush the shell of her ear. "You look breathtaking, baby."

She turns her head toward me, her gaze dropping to my mouth, and the whole room falls away. The music, the crowd, the low hum of conversation—it all fades. There's only her and the heat building in the space between our lips.

"Easy, you two..." Roman's voice cuts in, and suddenly he and Jasper are right there beside us.

Jasper leans in, brushing a kiss over her cheek. "You look so damn beautiful, angel, but I really want that dress on the floor before the night's over."

She tilts her head and smiles, while her sapphire eyes dance with mischief. "I've got nothing on underneath it."

Jasper groans low in his throat, and Roman tries to play it cool, but I see the way he subtly adjusts himself. The three of us just stand there, caught somewhere between restraint and desperation, and Addie looks like she's loving every second of it.

"Fuck, baby. You can't say shit like that to me... Jesus." Jasper's voice cracks on the next line. "One of you better suck me off right now, or I'm gonna lose it."

Addie bursts out laughing, loud and unfiltered, and that sound is the kind of happiness I want to bottle and keep giving her for the rest of our lives.

"Roman, back at the lodge, looking like a fucking wet dream and practically begging for my dick. Zeke's just walking around like sex, just existing like he doesn't know how close I am to snapping, and now you, strolling through the room with nothing underneath that fucking dress." He drags a hand through his hair, his chest heaving. "You're all gonna fucking kill me. You know that, right? And I know I'll probably thank you for it, but seriously, if you're trying to drive me over the edge... Congratulations. I'm already there."

Roman leans across and lowers his voice beside his ear. "I swear to god, the second we get back to the cabin, I'm gonna fuck you so hard you won't remember your own name. You'll be dripping, shaking, and so dick-drunk you'll forget how to speak. But if you keep making me this hard out here, I'll drag you to the nearest closet and edge the fuck out of you until your cock's so swollen you're begging me to let you come."

His hand slides slowly and possessively over Jasper's lower back, fingers trailing down the dip of his spine.

"You're so fucking gone, I could unzip you right now, and you'd be moaning for me in front of every single person here, wouldn't you?"

The thirst between the three of us only deepens the longer we have each other.

Our love is filthy.

It's feral and fierce, a craving we've never learned to tame.

We show it with tongues in mouths, hands under clothes, and bodies colliding like we're trying to crawl inside each other.

We don't touch—*we claim.*

We don't kiss—*we devour.*

We don't fuck—*we obliterate.*

Now we've crossed into something untouchable with Addie, and there's no coming back from it.

"How do any of you ever get anything done?" Addie asks, clearly just as affected by Roman and Jasper as I am.

"With great difficulty," I snap back, dragging my gaze off the two living temptations at my side and focusing on her instead. "Can we get out of here for a minute? I need to talk to you." She nods, slipping between Jasper and Roman. I catch the way her hands brush their thighs as she passes, and I stay close, trailing after her.

"You good, big guy?"

Roman lets out a low chuckle and nods, and something in my chest pulls tight. I wish I could show him how proud I am of him, but for now, the look we share is enough.

There's nowhere in this place you can really hide from prying eyes, but what I want to say to Addison is meant only for us. I don't want an audience. I need to do this where I can have her to myself and kiss her the second I get the words out.

I spot a curtained-off nook behind the stage, and, after a quick glance to make sure no one's watching, I pull her in with me. The second we collide, the breath I've been holding all night finally leaves me—relief, hunger, and that deep-down satisfaction that comes from knowing she's been just as desperate for this as I have.

"Are you okay?"

"I am now," she whispers, biting down on her bottom lip. "I missed you guys. It felt weird being home without you."

"Yeah?"

"Yeah," she says quietly. "Those few hours... they felt longer than all the years you were gone, and that was bad enough."

"So I take it you're gonna miss us when we leave tomorrow." My hands cradle her face, thumbs sweeping over her cheeks as I search her eyes. "Because we have to go back, Addison."

"I know."

"I'm not going to ask you to come with us," I say, even though every part of me wants to drop to my knees and beg for it.

Her chest rises and falls, and I lower my hand, pressing it flat against her heart, needing to know if it beats for me.

"I'm not asking because you already know what we want. You know we want you with us. Not for a weekend, not for this stolen time. We want forever with you, Addison." I brush my thumb along her jaw, watching her blink back the tears building behind her lashes. "Could you walk away from the life you've built here for one with us? Because that's what you need to figure out—not for me, not for them... but for you."

Her heart thunders beneath my palm, and her eyes glaze over. But I don't give her room to look away, not when I've laid it all out.

"I'm in love with you, Addison," I whisper, finally letting the words tear free from where they've lived in my chest for far too long. "And if you told me right now this is what you want, we'd build a whole life around you. We'd give you everything." She trembles, and when a single tear slides down her cheek, I lean in and kiss it away.

"I'm not here to pressure you. I'm not asking you to decide tonight, but you need to know—we've already chosen you. All of us. And we'll keep choosing you, even if we have to wait." I pause, swallowing the lump that rises in my throat. "And when you're ready... When your heart finally catches up to the way you look at us, we'll be right there."

"You love me?" she whispers.

I pause, let her question settle in my chest, then brush my lips across hers.

"Yeah, beautiful. I love you. I always have."

"I love you too."

CHAPTER NINETEEN
JASPER

Fuck, he's hot.

Roman's on stage, and I can't take my eyes off him. That dark hair I love to tug on, the tattoos I've traced with my mouth, that body built for pleasure. He's mine in ways I still can't believe.

Then there's Zeke, just to my left, leaning against the wall like he's not the most dangerously beautiful man I've ever seen. All golden Mediterranean skin, and black hair that always falls into his unreal green eyes.

Honestly, I've somehow landed the two hottest men to ever exist, and I have no idea what I did to deserve them.

Then there's Addie—the light. The one girl we've always wanted. She's softness and fire, everything we didn't know we were missing until she walked back into our lives and made it impossible to imagine a world without her in it. She's the most beautiful woman I've ever known… not just to look at, but to belong to.

I'm obsessed, and not the cute kind.

No—I'm sick with it.

It lives in my bones and burrows under my skin like it's always belonged there. I love them so deeply it hurts in a way that feels physical, as if my body was never meant to hold this much want, but I wouldn't change it for anything. I need them desperately, wildly, and in ways that would scare anyone who hasn't felt the kind of love that borders on madness.

It's not healthy. It's raw and overwhelming at times, but fuck if I care because I know with absolute, soul-deep certainty that I could never live without them.

"Without Coach Hope, I wouldn't be living in Boston. I wouldn't be captain of the Boston Vipers or winning championships. I might not even be standing here at all. And it's not just me. So many of us in this room owe him more than we could ever put into words. The hours he poured into us, the way he pushed us harder than we thought possible, and the care and determination he showed to make us not just better players, but better men. He believed in us, even when we couldn't see it ourselves."

Watching Roman up there, talking about the game he loves and how he got here with the help of Addie's dad, I can't help but think back to when I used to watch him from the bench, or across the locker room, or flying down the ice.

That's how our friendship started. Not with words, but with sweat, bruises, and a kind of respect you can only earn on frozen ground.

I was in awe of him.

Still am, if I'm honest.

No one moves like Roman.

No one reads the ice like him.

But when it came to attraction, it started with Zeke—just him and me, hiding in the shadows, brushing fingers when no one was looking, but the day Roman caught us together, everything changed. The second I saw that unmistakable flush creep up our captain's neck while Zeke and I had our hands wrapped around each other's cocks, I knew he was going to be part of this.

Two weeks later, I'd found out exactly how Roman tasted. The three of us just fell together, fast and reckless, like it was always supposed to be this way.

"So, to the man we're all here to celebrate tonight, I ask you to raise a glass. To Coach Hope. To the early mornings, late nights, and the long bus rides where you never let us forget what we were fighting for. To the losses that taught us grit and the victories that made every second of your hard-ass riding us worth it." A few laughs ripple through the crowd, and I catch Coach's eye. He's shaking his head, but he's smiling. "To your beautiful family, who deserve medals of their own for sharing you with us all these years. For standing by you through the wins and the heartbreaks, the rink schedules and the chaos, and every single one of us lost kids who walked through your doors and left better for knowing you. You didn't just teach us hockey, Coach. You taught us what it means to show up, to push through when everything hurts, and to be part of something bigger than ourselves. Congratulations. This night is for you, and you've earned every second of it."

I raise my glass right along with everyone else as the room echoes with cheers and applause, but my head's somewhere else entirely.

Zeke.

Roman.

Addie.

We've been living a damn good life. Hell, a great one, actually. But I'm getting older, and I want more. I want everything. The hockey, sure, but the hiding? The loving in silence? I'm over it. Yeah, I'm living my dream, but lately it feels like only half a life.

The way Roman and Zeke have both said they're ready to step out together—god, it's everything. I swear I fell even harder in love with them for it.

And with Addie... there's no way in hell that's starting as a secret, let alone staying one. If I'm loving her, I'm doing it out loud from the very beginning. I'm not asking anyone for permission to be happy. I'm taking it.

I watch Coach make his way up to the stage, suited up and grinning like a man who's finally letting himself enjoy a little of the spotlight. He takes the award from Roman, shakes his hand, and I'm sure I see something pass between them in that moment —pride, maybe.

When Roman steps aside, his eyes sweep across the crowd until they find mine. I give him a wink, letting everything I'm feeling show on my face because fuck it, he needs to know how damn proud I am. He held it together, made the speech, and didn't disappear into his head the way he sometimes does. I'm fiercely proud of him.

Coach launches into his speech, thanking every player he's ever coached, the friends he's made, and, of course, his beautiful wife and daughters. It's warm, it's humble, and it's full of that no-bullshit charm that's made him such a legend.

An hour slips by in a blur of handshakes and catching up with old teammates. Eventually, I find myself scanning the crowd when I spot Addie's mom standing alone.

"Brenda!"

"Oh, Jasper!"

I throw my arms around my future mother-in-law, clinging to the hope that she'll remember just how much she used to adore me, especially when she finds out I'm happily sharing her daughter with my boyfriends, usually in the same bed, at the same time.

"You're looking beautiful," I tell her, and she blushes.

I've always liked Brenda, but that shitty advice she gave her daughter? Yeah, that I haven't forgotten.

I've been keeping an eye on Mikey all night, and his gaze hasn't strayed from Addie, not once. I can't say I blame him—she's fucking radiant, but he lost her, and that's on him. Even so, it eats at me watching him watch her like he's reliving every second he ever touched her. He's looking at her like he thinks he still has some kind of claim on her. Maybe legally, sure. Her name might still drag his behind it, stuck there for a while because she made the stupid decision of saying yes, but she's not his.

What if I wanted to marry her one day? What would it look like if we all did? It's not exactly something the world makes space for—three men and one woman bound together in every way that matters.

It might not be traditional, but I don't give a shit about tradition. Whatever we create and build together, it'll be ours, and that's all that matters.

I'd take her name without a second thought. I'd take Roman's or Zeke's, too, if it meant being tied to them. Because the truth is, it doesn't matter how we do it or what it looks like on paper. It's not about what the world sees—what matters is the truth of what we are.

Her mind? *Ours*—fucked so full of us she can't think straight without one of our names in her head.

Her soul? *Ours*—claimed and bound so completely, she can't imagine a life that doesn't include us.

Her perfect pussy? *That's definitely fucking ours*—to worship, to ruin, and to crawl to on our knees just for the chance to taste it.

That prick in the corner can keep staring for the rest of his life, but it won't change a thing because she's never going back to him.

"Me? Look at you. You're looking so dapper, Jasper," Brenda says, her blue eyes sparkling as she takes me in.

Before I can respond, I catch a glimpse of Addie weaving her way through the room, heading straight toward us.

"Addison... don't these boys scrub up well?" Brenda says as her daughter reaches our side. "I don't remember seeing them in anything other than their kits."

"They do," Addie says with a small smile. "They all look like gentlemen."

I've been the opposite of a gentleman to Addison, and she's loved every second of it.

"Oh, speaking of..." Brenda continues, "Mikey's been asking after you."

"And?"

"Well, he wants to talk to you. Like it or not, you're still married."

"Not."

"What?" Brenda blinks in surprise.

"You said, 'like it or not,' and the answer is not. The sooner I can get that fixed, the better."

"Divorce?" Brenda's face shifts from shock to realization as she looks at me. "I'm sorry, this probably isn't a conversation we should be having in front of others. Sorry, Jasper."

"Don't worry about it," I say with a shrug, shooting Addie a teasing look. "From what I hear, Mikey's been quite the naughty boy."

Brenda looks between the two of us, clearly trying to piece together more than she's being told.

"Mom, not everyone has to stay in a bad marriage just because they took vows."

Brenda frowns. "But divorce? You're not even thirty... and what about—" Addie's eyes widen slightly. It's quick, barely a flicker, but I catch it. That look right there? It's hiding something. "You're not getting any younger, is all I'm saying, and nobody wants to be alone."

I want to pull Addie into my arms. I want to tell her mother that she'll never be alone again.

"Do you have a girlfriend, Jasper?"

"I've got a girl," I say, keeping my gaze steady on the blonde goddess standing in front of me. "No label yet."

"Yet?" Addie repeats, her eyebrows lifting slightly.

"Yeah, yet... But I'm really hoping that changes." I hold her gaze, letting every ounce of what I feel pour into it. I want her to see everything I'm not saying out loud. No games. No pressure. Just my truth laid bare between us because whatever this is, whatever it's becoming, it matters, and I want her to know I'm all in.

"That's sweet," Brenda says with a fond smile. "See? Jasper understands. Love is meant to be forever."

"I agree," Addie says softly. "Love is forever... but only if it's the right kind."

I watch her carefully, something tightening in my chest. "And what does the right kind of love look like to you, Addison?"

Her eyes shift away from mine, and her teeth catch her bottom lip like she's holding back everything she wants to say. But before any of it slips out, she clears her throat. "Excuse me, I need to use the bathroom."

I'll give her two minutes, then I'm going after her.

"I'm sorry about that, Jasper. She's been through a lot."

"I know. But don't try to push her back toward someone who doesn't value her. She's beautiful, and there are men out there who would kill for the chance to love your daughter. Now, if you'll excuse me, I'm going to get myself a drink."

I make my way through the crowd, eyes scanning until I spot the bathrooms. The second I see the sign, I don't hesitate. I slip inside, and I'm immediately hit with the scent—it's so much nicer in here than the men's room. It smells like perfume and something floral, maybe jasmine or lavender.

Addie's standing at the counter, both hands gripping the edge, staring hard at her reflection in the mirror. Her eyes lift and catch mine just as I reach behind me and turn the lock.

Three strides and I'm right behind her, close enough to breathe her in and bury my face in the curve of her neck. My lips find her bare shoulder, lingering there while my fingers trace the delicate strap of her dress and ease it down her arm.

"Jasper…"

"Tell me," I murmur, sliding my hands over the silk of her dress until my thumbs brush her nipples, feeling them tighten under my touch. "Tell me I'm not the only one who's fallen in love."

"You're not," she whispers. "You know you're not."

My hand glides down her side, over the dip of her waist, and I don't dare look away from her reflection.

I find the slit in her dress and drag my hand up her thigh, slow enough to drive us both mad, until my fingers slip between her legs, and I cup her bare pussy. I just hold her there, fingers spread, feeling how she flutters against my palm.

"You feel that?" I whisper, my eyes holding hers in the mirror, as I push my fingers to the edge of her entrance. "That's not just need. That's your body begging for me, not just to fuck you, but to love you."

"I love you, Jasper," she whispers, turning her face toward mine. "I don't know what will happen tomorrow. I don't know what this becomes when you leave, and there's still so much I need to figure out here… But I do know that I want to love you out there. I need to love you out there in the real world, where it's loud and messy and hard. Because, god, Jasper… you're everything."

That's it. That's all it takes. I kiss her like I might never get another chance, tongue sliding past her lips, needing her everywhere, needing her always. We don't stop, not even as my fingers find her clit, brushing slow circles over her, my heart thundering so hard it feels like it could break right through my chest and fall into her hands.

She loves me.

The thought drives my fingers lower, and I push one inside her, slow at first, then deeper, rougher, as need takes hold. Our kiss turns savage, and her moans melt into my mouth as I start fucking her with my fingers.

When I finally tear my lips away, her eyes find mine in the mirror. My left hand covers her mouth, catching the sounds she can't hold back, and her body tightens around me as I curl my fingers just right.

She's shaking, her breath hot against my palm. "Keep your eyes on me. Don't you dare close them."

My fingers keep moving inside her, and the way she looks at me is like she's high on everything we are.

On everything I give her.

On me.

"I'm so in love with you, angel," I whisper against her skin. "Can I keep you forever?" She moans loud enough against my hand that I'm taking it as a *hell yes*.

My fingers stay buried inside her, knuckles deep, still moving, when the door handle rattles behind us, and everything stills.

"Adds?" I roll my eyes and drag my teeth along her shoulder, biting down just hard enough to leave proof. *My girl.* My name on her body. "I know you're in there. Your mom told me."

I slip my fingers from inside her, but I don't stop touching her. I bring the wetness up and over her clit, while my other hand leaves her mouth. She looks at me, her eyes wide with panic.

I raise my brows—*answer him.*

Her eyes narrow back—*are you fucking crazy?*

For her? Always.

"We need to talk. Let me in."

"Leave me alone, Mikey."

"Atta girl," I murmur darkly. "Now keep talking while I make you come with him right outside the door." She shudders, and I feel it all—every twitch, every shake, the way her body begs to break for me.

"We're not done, Adds," Mikey barks from the hallway. "Open the door."

"Maybe we should let him in," I whisper. "Let him see it just once. The first and last time he ever gets to watch you come. Watch you fall apart for someone who actually knows how to touch you."

She lets out a broken whimper, and her pussy clamps down on my fingers. I slap my hand back over her mouth, dragging her closer to my chest.

"I can feel it," I growl into her ear. "You're gonna come for me, aren't you, angel? You're going to soak my fingers while he stands there begging for a piece of something that was never really his."

Her whole body jerks, her moan muffled against my palm, and I don't let up. I can't. I'm too far gone, and she's too perfect like this.

The door handle rattles violently, and I slide my hand away from her mouth again, just enough for her to speak.

"Will you fuck off, Mikey? Only crazy people barge into women's bathrooms." My brow arches slowly, my head tilting as I catch the grin curling across her lips.

I'm the crazy bastard who came in here uninvited, backed her into a corner, and didn't ask for permission—and she let me because she loves me.

"You think that's crazy?" I whisper, dragging my tongue across her skin. "You don't even know what crazy looks like yet." I pinch her clit between my thumb and forefinger, rolling it slowly. "Tell me, angel... Are you really ready to tell the world you're mine? Because once you do, there's no going back."

She stills, breath hitching in her throat, and then she nods.

"Yo, Mikey," I call out, loud enough to carry through the door.

There's a pause—longer than I expected—and I can't help the wave of satisfaction that rolls through me.

"Who's that?" he finally asks, and I can hear the crack in his voice.

"I'm trying to make my girl feel good, so maybe do what she asked and fuck off."

"Hastings?" he yells. "Is that you?"

At the sound of my name, her whole body pulls tight. She's about to snap in my hands, and fuck, she's right there, fluttering, soaked, and desperate to break.

"Call out to me, angel," I whisper, my forehead pressed into her hair. "Let me belong to you."

I slip my hand from her mouth just as she comes undone, her body shuddering against mine, her cry—"Jasper"—tearing from her throat, and it's fucking stunning.

I keep stroking her through every aftershock, holding her up as she melts back into me, both of us ignoring the pounding at the door. Thank God this bathroom is tucked away from the party, or Mikey would have the whole place witnessing this.

For the next few minutes, all I want is to kiss her. Then I'll make damn sure Mikey King knows he's never getting anywhere near her again.

CHAPTER TWENTY

ROMAN

"Thank you, son." A hand lands heavy on my shoulder, and when I turn, it's Coach Hope standing beside me—the man I used to respect more than anyone, even when I hated him for taking Addie from me. "The things you said up there… they meant a lot to me. More than I probably deserve."

"What do you mean?" I ask, though part of me already knows.

He gives me a long look, one that makes my chest tighten before he even says a word. "It's been a long time, you know. I've had a lot of time to think."

I look away from him, forcing myself to let go and swallow the bitterness that wants to rise. "It's in the past. No point digging up something that can't be changed."

"I didn't always get things right, Roman, and looking back, I probably could've handled things differently, especially with how much pain I caused Addison. But when I told her to stop seeing you, it wasn't out of spite. I was thinking about your future and what I knew you could become."

"And what about her? Did her happiness not factor in?" He

doesn't answer right away. Maybe because we both know the truth—he made a call that cost both of us something.

"I love my daughter, but I didn't want her to be the reason you missed your shot, and I couldn't stand the idea of her heart breaking when you went off and did something huge with your life while she was left behind."

"You shouldn't have taken that choice from us. Do you know I almost quit the team after I lost her? I couldn't think straight, couldn't focus. And yeah... some part of me understood what you were trying to do. I get that you thought you were doing the right thing. But losing her?" I pause, the ache crawling up my throat. "That was the worst pain I've ever felt. Worse than any time I've been slammed into the boards or had a bone snap clean."

"Yet you always pick yourself back up after the knockdowns."

"Because I have to."

"No, it's because you're stubborn as hell," he says, trying to soften the air between us with a small smile as he lifts his glass for a sip of champagne.

"So I've been told."

"And you're a fighter. You never stop chasing what you want, which is why you made it to Boston."

"Took a hell of a lot of work," I admit. "And some damn good guidance along the way."

"Maybe, but please don't forget—no matter how hard you fight on the ice, you've got to fight for a life too. You deserve more than just the game. You've got to be happy, Roman."

"I am mostly."

"That's all we can hope for."

"I could be happier."

He lifts an eyebrow. "Yeah?"

"Yeah, you see, I'm just missing one thing..." My heart's pounding so hard I'm sure he can hear it. "I'm still in love with your daughter, Bill." I look him dead in the eyes as I use his name for the first time ever. "I never stopped, and I don't think I can walk away again. Losing Addie once nearly destroyed me. I don't think I'll survive losing her twice."

There's a flicker of surprise in his face, but it fades quickly.

"Then don't," he says. "Because if anyone deserves her, it's you. I knew it then... and I know it now."

The weight that lifts off me just from saying how I feel about her out loud—it's heavier than I ever realized, and bigger than I expected.

"I'm proud of you," he adds. "You, Jasper, and Zeke... I always knew the three of you would make it."

Always together. Always us.

"Does Addison share your feelings?" I nod because I'm certain she does. "Then, please, for the love of God, don't let Mikey King worm his way back in. That kid shouldn't have been allowed to marry her in the first place. Just don't tell my wife I said that. She's got this whole belief about vows and *for better or worse* that doesn't exactly line up with mine—especially when it comes to some egotistical prick who wouldn't know loyalty if it bit him on the damn dick." He pauses, his jaw tightening like he's forcing himself to stay calm. "You know what his excuse was? Why he did it?"

I hesitate, not sure if I want to hear this, but I lean in anyway, needing to understand how anyone could cheat on Addison.

"He blamed her," he says, his eyes narrowing with disgust. "Not to her face—he didn't have the balls for that. But to me, her father. He said he couldn't come to terms with never being a dad and blamed her for not being able to carry a child. He said that's why he started chasing tail."

It hits me like a fist to the chest.

Addie can't have kids.

And that son of a bitch made it her fault?

"Why are you telling me this?"

"Because if you love her, you need to be okay with it. *Really* okay. Not just in the way people say it when they're still figuring out how much they can carry. You can't use this against her, not ever."

"I would never," I snap, and suddenly all that's fueling me is pure anger and the visceral need to break Mikey's fucking legs.

He nods, as if that was the answer he expected, but he just needed to hear it out loud. "I know she's been up here the past few days. Addie's sister already chewed me out tonight about her happiness, about you, and what you mean to her—about what *they* mean to her." He means Zeke and Jasper, and that throws me for a second, but he just keeps talking. "Judging by the look on your face, I'm guessing Addie didn't tell you about her fertility issues herself, so please don't tell her you heard it from me. She needs to feel safe, not exposed, and I don't want her to think she's being talked about behind her back."

"I trust you with her, Roman. I know I'm just an old man who probably doesn't fully understand how what the three of you have works. But I see it. I see the way you all look at her and the way she looks back, and if she finally gets out of here… I want to believe you'll take care of her the way she deserves."

"I appreciate you saying that, and if that's what Addie wants—if this works—then none of us would ever hurt her. I swear to you."

Bill looks like he wants to say more, but I catch Zeke in my periphery, practically jumping out of his skin, trying to get my attention.

"Sorry, Coach, give me a minute," I say, already moving.

Zeke doesn't say a word, just flashes his phone as I follow him into the hall. A message from Jasper lights the screen, and I hear the chaos before we even turn the corner.

"Open the fucking door!" Mikey's voice cracks through the hallway, completely unhinged. Zeke's there in seconds, grabbing him by the arm and yanking him back hard.

"What the hell is wrong with you?" Zeke snaps, shoving him hard enough that he stumbles.

It's just us out here, for now, but the shouting is going to pull everyone's eyes in this direction if we don't get a handle on it, and I'll be damned if I let this dickhead ruin the night for anyone.

"Your fucking friend is in there with Addison," Mikey spits, practically foaming at the mouth.

I should probably be trying to diffuse this. But instead, I feel this sick, satisfied pull in my chest. I love that Jasper's in there with her right now while Mikey's out here, red-faced and rabid, and losing his mind.

"And?" I say flatly.

He whips around to face me, his eyes wild with fury. "What the fuck do you mean *and*?"

"You're not together anymore, so what the hell does it matter?"

"She's still my wife."

Yeah, see, I don't fucking love that.

"For now," Zeke cuts in, calm as hell and twice as confident.

That's when I hear the bathroom door creak open, and Jasper strolls out, his arm slung casually over Addison's shoulders. Jasper's hair is tousled, but he's wound tight. I can see it all over his face. I've edged him enough times to know the signs—jaw clenched, brown eyes darker than usual, hands twitching like he's seconds from snapping. Addison's lipstick is smeared just enough to give her away, and there's a fresh bite mark blooming on her shoulder where one strap of her dress has slipped down her arm. She looks thoroughly kissed and almost fucked.

Out of nowhere, I get butterflies—actual, honest-to-God butterflies. Do guys even get those? What's the guy's version—

adrenaline? Nerves? *Love?* Hell if I know, but whatever it is, it's happening.

"Hey, man," Jasper says, cocky as hell, flashing Mikey a smile that could get him punched. "Bathrooms all yours."

God, I love this idiot.

"I'm gonna kick your ass, Hastings."

I ignore Mikey's threat because if I let it land, I'll knock him flat on his ass, and this whole thing will explode. But Jasper doesn't even blink. He keeps smiling like the smug bastard he is, grinning like the cat that got the cream. Or, in this case, the lucky fuck who just got his fill of Addison's pussy and isn't even trying to pretend otherwise.

"You're not gonna do anything, Mikey," Addie says, stepping forward. "This has to stop. I can do whoever and whatever I want. You don't get a say, not anymore."

"Bullshit," he spits. "We're still married."

She lets out a quiet, bitter laugh. "Don't pretend those vows ever meant anything to you. They didn't when you were inside my friend, and they sure as shit don't now."

"Addison, please, can we talk about this away from them? I just—I want to talk."

"All I want from you is a divorce and for you to never come around my family again."

There's my strong girl.

"You shouldn't even be here tonight. My father might have respected you once, but not anymore. Now go. We're done."

"You think I'm just going to accept that you're with Hastings now?"

She stares him down, unblinking. "Not just him."

Zeke steps forward, moving in behind her, and presses a kiss to the side of her head like it's the most natural thing in the world.

I know this is a pivotal moment—one of those times that won't wait around for you to figure your shit out. I have two choices here: I can step forward and claim her with them, showing her that I'm in this, that I want what we could be, or I can stay exactly where I am and let Jasper and Zeke have this moment without me.

So I move, but I don't reach for her. I don't kiss her or wrap my arm around her like Zeke and Jasper do. But I step forward, standing beside her and them. I place myself in the space she's held open for me and let her know without a single word that I'm still here.

"N-No..." Mikey stammers, eyes darting between the four of us like he's just starting to piece it together.

"Whatever you're thinking?" Jasper says, his voice calm but lethal. "Yeah. Go ahead and believe it."

"Did you fuck them all before they left?" he spits, the words dripping with disgust.

"Not that it's any of your business, but no. The only one I've ever had a relationship with is Roman, but you already know that."

Mikey sneers, his eyes narrowing. "You wait 'til your mom hears about this."

"You're not gonna fucking do that, Mikey." He opens his mouth like he wants to argue, but I step in closer, just enough to make my point hit home.

"You need to leave, Mikey," Zeke says, like he's just making a suggestion, but everyone in this hallway knows better.

Zeke is the calm in the center of the storm, always reading the room and feeding off everyone's energy, and right now, he's soaking up all of ours, making that calm crack.

Mikey backs up a step, scrubbing a hand through his blond hair like he's trying to steady himself. But I watch it happen in real time—the shift from desperation to something darker. It takes a single breath, and his eyes go cold, his mouth twists, and then he points.

"Now that I know this is actually happening," he sneers, motioning toward the four of us, "I wouldn't want to be anywhere near you again."

He's disgusted—like we're something toxic, as if we're the ones who should be ashamed. Screw him. He won't be the last to have an opinion, and I've stopped caring what people like Mikey think.

"Make sure you get enough use out of her. She's good for a fuck. Shame her pussy can't do the one thing it's supposed to."

Motherfucker.

Everything inside me goes still, and my vision goes white. My fists clench so tight I feel my nails digging into my palms, and it takes everything in me not to lunge and break his face. This isn't just cruel, it's calculated. It's meant to humiliate her in the lowest, most unforgivable way. I glance at Zeke and Jasper and see the shock flicker in their eyes, but they hold steady. They don't rise to his bait or give him the satisfaction of reacting.

"How could you say that to me?" Addison's voice cracks, disbelief and heartbreak crashing together. "After everything you've done—how could you throw that in my face?"

"You're fucking three men, Adds. That shit stings, and I won't feel guilty about what I did anymore. At least now that I know I was married to a whore, I can walk away with my head held high."

I don't know which one of us moves first—me, Zeke, or Jasper—but it doesn't matter. We all surge forward. I just get there fastest. I fist my hands in his shirt, dragging him through the hallway and out of the building. He pushes back and swings wildly, but Jasper is there in an instant, delivering a solid punch to Mikey's stomach. He doubles over, choking on the pain, which is pathetic because Jasper held back. That was just a warning, not what he's fully capable of.

I spin, making sure Addie's okay, and see she's in Zeke's arms, face buried in his chest as he takes her back inside. Out of all of us, he's the one who knows how to hold her together when she's falling apart, and right now, she needs that more than anything.

I throw Mikey out into the snow, and he hits the ground hard, landing flat on his ass with a grunt. Jasper steps forward, towering over him like the final blow hasn't even landed yet.

"You don't step foot near her again, do you understand? I'm getting her out of this town and this life you tried to cage her in. She's gonna have everything she ever wanted, while you—one of the worst hockey players I've ever seen—can sit here and wallow in your self-pity bullshit. You couldn't satisfy your wife, couldn't step up as a man, and couldn't even fucking keep her. And now she's gonna spend the rest of her life wrapped around me, Roman, and Zeke, and she's gonna love every second of it."

Mikey tries to push up from the snow, but Jasper just steps closer, pushing him back down.

"I know it fucks with your ego that we made it while you were too lazy to get your shit together, and now we've taken Addie, so maybe there's a sliver of pity buried in me somewhere. But only because you've never actually known what it means to be loved by her. You got the version of her that was still trying to believe in you. The one who only ever wanted us but stayed with you anyway." Jasper laughs, and it's cold and smug. "That's gotta fucking burn, huh?"

"Go ahead, take her," Mikey sneers. "She's ruined now anyway. I only got with her because I thought her dad could set me up with a team." Jasper glances at me, and I give him the nod. His fist flies before Mikey can say another word, connecting with his jaw in a clean, brutal hit that snaps his head back and sends him stumbling.

"You fucking asshole!" Mikey screams, his hand pressed against his busted lip.

"You're lucky it wasn't Roman, because if he hit you, you'd be out cold and waking up drinking your meals through a straw." Despite all his sarcasm, Jasper's the one you want beside you when the shit hits the fan. "You don't get to talk about Addie like she wasn't a fucking gift. So here's what you're gonna do—you're gonna get the hell out of here, and you're not gonna look back. You're done here."

"You realize she hated you, right?" Mikey barks, jabbing a finger in my direction. "She told me once that you were her biggest regret." I hold my ground, jaw locked, refusing to give him the reaction he's so clearly starving for.

"Did he not just hear me?" Jasper snaps, whipping his head toward me, his dark eyes wide with disbelief. "Is he seriously that fucking dumb? I just told him, and he's still running his mouth?"

Mikey scrambles to get his footing as he tries to stand, and I step in, closing the space between us until I'm so close I can see the flicker of fear in his eyes.

"She never hated me. She hated that she lost me, and yeah, maybe I was her biggest regret, just like she was mine, but guess what? I'm the one who gets to spend the rest of forever between her thighs, reminding her exactly how much she *doesn't* hate me. That privilege is mine now. So I suggest you move, Mikey, because my hands are itching, and the only reason I haven't put you in the ground already is because you're not worth my career or my girl."

This time, Mikey doesn't say another word. He pulls out his phone and disappears into the snow, slipping away like the coward he's always been. When he's out of sight, Jasper steps in front of me and rests his forehead against my chest. I wrap my arms around him, my hands moving slowly up and down his back, doing my best to soothe him.

"We don't ever tell Addie what he said," I murmur against his hair. "He's in her past, and that's where he stays."

He finally lifts his face to mine, and I kiss him. Nobody's around, but even if they were, I wouldn't care. My lips would still be on his, and I wouldn't pull away.

"Let me see your hand," I say, and he lifts it for me. I check his knuckles, turning them over, and press a kiss to each one. "What he said about Addie. Does it change anything for you?"

"Fuck no, not even a little," he says, his eyes holding mine as if I should already know that—like it was never even a question. "Did you know?"

"Coach told me right before we came to find you. He knows Addie's been up here, and he wanted to make sure I wouldn't hold it against her the way Mikey did." My hands slide up his arms, fingertips brushing his skin, trying to share the warmth I don't really have myself.

"I hate that she didn't get to tell us on her own terms. It doesn't change anything, but it was her story to tell." I can feel the tension rising in him as his muscles coil under my hands. "You need to talk to her," he says quietly, his voice breaking a little at the edges. "Baby, please. I *need* you to talk to her. I need you to just say what you feel because you don't have to be scared. She's so in love with you, Rome."

He's overwhelmed, and I know words won't help right now. So I pull him in, wrap my arms around him, and hold him tight. I stay quiet, keeping the world at bay for him until I feel his breathing start to slow and his body settle in my embrace.

CHAPTER TWENTY-ONE
ROMAN

My feelings for Addie are complicated. At least, that's what I've been telling myself.

But tonight, she didn't hide from what we are when we're all together, and something shifted in me. The part of me that's been keeping her at a distance has cracked wide open, and with morning closing in and us leaving tomorrow, it suddenly hits me just how little time we have left with her.

Jasper finally shakes himself free from whatever dark place he'd slipped into, and once I'm sure he's steady, we head back to where we left Zeke and Addison.

Zeke is towering over her, gentle in a way that only he can be—his hands cupping her face like she's something precious. He's speaking softly, close enough that I can't make out the words, but I know he's reassuring her.

He leans in and softly brushes his lips against hers before turning his head toward us. His eyes find mine first, then shift to Jasper, and I watch the way his gaze sharpens, assessing us both, needing to be sure we're okay.

I give a slight tilt of my head toward Jasper, just enough to guide Zeke's attention to where it needs to be. His eyes drop immediately to Jasper's hand, the one he's still rubbing without realizing it—the hand that landed the punch.

"Show me," Zeke says, his focus narrowing completely on Jasper now.

Jasper lifts his hand and flexes his fingers, already trying to wave it off before Zeke can say more.

"It's fine. It's just gonna bruise. Busted that fucker's lip good though, didn't I, Rome?"

The corner of my mouth twitches, and even Zeke lets out a breath that's almost a laugh. But Addie doesn't smile. She hasn't since we returned. Her eyes are red, her cheeks blotchy, and she looks like she's holding herself together by a thread.

I should've done more. I should've broken Mikey in half and left him face down in the snow with a hockey stick for a headstone.

"Where is he?" she asks, her voice so small it barely carries.

"Gone," I say. "Hopefully, he freezes out there, and you won't have to waste another fucking minute waiting on that divorce."

Addie exhales, her shoulders trembling as she shakes her head. "I feel like such an idiot."

"Why?" Zeke asks.

"Because he's a piece of shit, and I actually married him. Jesus, what the hell was I thinking?"

"It's okay, angel," Jasper whispers beside her, trying to offer her comfort.

"No, it's not," she snaps, her bottom lip trembling. "I'm not okay. Nothing feels okay."

"Then help me understand that, baby, because right up until that asshole came in here trying to piss all over you, you were glowing. You were fucking radiant, and you were more than okay," Zeke says as he lifts a hand to gently tuck her hair behind her ear.

"How am I supposed to be okay after what he told you?" she says, and the laugh that slips out is so broken it makes my chest ache. "I should've told you myself. I know that, and I'm sorry for blindsiding you, but it's not something I can talk about easily. If it's a dealbreaker, then I'll understand. But please… please don't stand there and pretend."

"It's not even close to a dealbreaker. It's something we'll talk about when you're ready. But it doesn't change a damn thing for us."

"Zeke's right. Nothing's changed, beautiful girl," Jasper adds, stepping up behind him. He slides an arm around his waist and presses his lips to the side of his neck. "Do you wanna come to the women's bathroom with me? It's way nicer in there, and I'll get you off like I just did Addie."

I know Jasper too well not to see that he's trying to give Addison and me space and the push we both probably need. He asked me to talk to her, and for Jasper, I'd do just about anything. He's one of the reasons I even know what love feels like, so if he needs me to lay my soul bare for our girl, I'll bleed out right here and call it devotion.

"As tempting as that offer is," Zeke says, turning to graze his nose along Jasper's jaw, "I think we should make sure no one's in there wondering where that walking sack of shit disappeared to."

Zeke leaves Addie's side and steps in close, his scent wrapping around me before his hands even reach my face.

"You okay, big guy?" I nod, and he leans in, his lips brushing the shell of my ear. "I love you, and if you need us, you call."

He hands me the key to the cabin, and he and Jasper walk away, leaving me alone with Addison, who suddenly looks so vulnerable, it punches the air from my lungs. It makes me feel like a bastard for just watching her, but I wait her out. If she needs me to hold her, I'll know.

"Are you okay, princess?" She nods, but her eyes are distant. "I'm sorry."

Her brow furrows. "For what?"

"For what you've lost and the future I know you wanted."

Because I remember every piece of that dream and the way her eyes would light up when she talked about a boy and a girl with her golden hair and my smile. She used to say it was her favorite part of me because it meant I was happy, and she wanted a life built on that.

She swallows hard. "It doesn't matter. I can't change it."

"It matters, Addison," I tell her, stepping closer. Her eyes—those navy eyes I used to get lost in—finally meet mine, and they're empty in the worst way. She looks like she doesn't know what she's supposed to feel, only that she's feeling too much all at once. "You don't have to pretend this doesn't hurt. You've lost something, and you're allowed to be fucking angry at the world for it."

"Other people have suffered worse."

"That doesn't make your pain any less real." I rake a hand through my hair, chest burning, fighting to reach her. "You know I've seen some shit. I've lived through hell and convinced myself I didn't have the right to fall apart because someone else always had it harder. But Jasper and Zeke… they tore that bullshit right out of me. They made me feel it, every fucking bit of it. And they taught me it's okay to let it hurt sometimes."

She nods, but her hands won't stop fidgeting, twisting together like she's trying to wring the nerves out of her skin.

"Addie," I whisper, trying to pull her back to me. "Talk to me."

She just shakes her head, chewing her lip raw, and when I step toward her, she flinches back.

Actually fucking flinches.

"Addie?"

My eyes narrow because now she won't let me near her, and for the first time, I have no fucking clue why.

"Can I please have the key? I need... I just need space... I can't breathe in here."

I brush past her, jerking my chin toward the door. "Then let's go."

"You don't need to come with me."

"Like hell I don't. You really think I'm letting you walk out there alone with Mikey still slinking around with his dick in his hand? Not fucking happening."

"Roman!" she snaps, but I don't budge.

I step up to her, my jaw clenched so hard it aches. "Addie. Move."

She glares at me but doesn't argue this time. She shoves past, heels stabbing into the snow as she steps outside.

The walk is quiet, but not the kind of quiet that soothes. It's the kind that vibrates with everything unsaid. Every step is thick with tension, with questions that haven't been asked and answers we're too scared to say out loud.

We're ticking.

We're on the edge of something explosive, and when it hits, we'll either burn each other to the ground or burn together, holding on like we don't know how to let go.

Maybe I'm too late.

I unlock the door and step aside to let her pass. She doesn't even glance at me. She storms straight for the guest room—a hell of a statement, considering she's been in our bed for the past few nights.

"You should go back to Jasper and Zeke," she says, kicking off her heels. They go flying across the room, slamming against the wall with a crack that mirrors the one splitting down the middle of us.

She plants her hands on her hips and starts pacing like she's about to tear a hole in the floor. I shrug off my jacket, letting it drop over the back of a chair. I unbutton my cuffs and start rolling up my sleeves, watching her the whole time.

"I'm serious," she snaps, whipping around to face me, but I don't move.

"I'm not leaving you."

"Why?" she demands.

"Because you need someone, and right now, that's me, whether you like it or not."

"Well, if that's all it is, Roman, just obligation, then go get Jasper or Zeke. Or fuck it, get both. Then you don't have to be here."

"Is that what you want?" I bite back. "Just them?"

"No, Roman, that's what *you* want. Because it sure as hell isn't me anymore, and you've been really fucking clear on that."

Say it. Tell her.

"Addie, please." I exhale, and whatever anger she had left just drains right out of her as she puts as much distance between us as the room allows.

All that's left now is heartbreak—raw, brutal, and fucking devastating heartbreak.

"You know, I thought I could do this. I thought I could have them and still have you, even if it was from a distance. But every time you don't touch me, every time I see you loving them—and god, Roman, you love so hard—I remember what that felt like. I've missed it since the day I lost it, and now I have to watch it up close, right in front of me, but never *for* me."

She's sobbing, her whole body shaking, and her head is buried in her hands. I move around the bed, every instinct screaming at me to hold her, fix it, do something, but the second I get close, she recoils, like having me near is just another kind of pain.

"Don't—don't do that. Don't be my friend right now. I don't want that from you. It's not enough."

"Addie—"

My chest splits down the middle, her pain echoing all the shit I went through years ago. There's no satisfaction in seeing her like this. If anything, it fucking kills me.

"Don't say my name like that. Don't look at me like I still matter, because if I did, you wouldn't keep shutting me out the way you are."

"That's not fair."

"It's the truth," she chokes out, her breath hitching. "I went from meaning everything to you to meaning nothing."

"You think you're the only one hurting? You think this doesn't gut me every second of every day? Being around you, wanting you, and not touching you—I hate it. But I had to put up walls, Addie. You ripped my heart out, and I barely survived it. Yeah, Zeke and Jasper patched me up, but don't you dare think you ever left me. Don't you dare think I ever stopped—"

"Yes, you did."

She doesn't see how much I still carry her with me.

"I miss you, Roman. I miss you so much that it physically hurts. I need you. I need every beautiful, infuriating part of you. I want the man who used to love me so hard it felt like I was the center of the fucking universe, but I know you'll never give him to me again. So please don't touch me. Don't comfort me. Don't make this harder for me."

That's it.

That's the breaking point.

"Fuck that."

I close the space between us and press my mouth to hers. I drink down her cries as her hands fly up around my neck, and I lose myself in her—her taste, her touch, the way her tongue slides against mine. Every piece of me that ever broke starts healing right here in her arms.

"I love you, Roman. I'm so in love with you, and I'm sorry. I'm so sorry."

"No, I'm sorry... I'm sorry I didn't do this the second I saw you again."

I lift her, one arm tight around her waist, the other gripping her thigh as her dress rides high, and she locks her legs around my hips. I don't stop kissing her, not when I carry her to the bed, not even when we crash down together. It's like we never stopped. Our bodies just remember, as if we've been doing this every day. There's nothing to relearn, nothing to fix. We just fit. And fuck, I knew it. I knew it back then, and I know it now—we were always supposed to be this.

I lay her back on the bed, grinding against her so she feels just how badly I still want her. Her sobs have faded, but the tears still fall, and I kiss them away one by one while her hands fumble with my shirt, desperate to get to my skin. I shove her dress higher, exposing that perfect pussy, and this time I'm taking what I've been dying for every time I watched Zeke or Jasper touch her.

I sit up, yank my shirt off, and she drags her nails down my chest, just like she used to. My eyes slam shut, and my whole body shudders under her touch.

"Addie... I've never stopped loving you. Not once." I toss my shirt across the room and slide back down, cradling her head in my hands as my lips ghost over hers. "Tell me this is forever, baby. Please. Because I can't lose you again—I won't. I need you all in. If we do this and you walk away..." I swallow hard, my forehead pressed to hers, my heart hammering out every last piece of pride I have left.

"I won't," she whispers. "I'll never leave. My heart's been all in since day one, Roman. I just got a little lost along the way." She lifts her hips, grinding against the front of my pants. "I want you. Jasper. Zeke," she breathes out. "I want a life with you in Boston. I want us."

My whole body freezes. "What?"

"I need to be where you are." I kiss her because now that I've tasted her again, I'm never stopping. She pulls back, lips kiss-bruised, and her blue eyes burn like the heart of a flame. "Now will you please touch me because I've been pretending it's easy not having you, but it's killing me, Roman. It's killing me, and I—"

"I'll never stop touching you again," I promise, crushing my mouth to hers.

We fumble her out of her skintight dress, ripping it off her while she tugs at my belt until I shove my pants down, and we're finally bare—chest to chest, her nipples dragging across my skin, while my cock grinds against her soaked pussy.

I can't stop kissing her. I can't get enough of those needy little whimpers that spill out every time our lips meet.

"Roman... please." She lifts her hips, searching for friction.

"I forgot how fucking needy you get when you want my cock." I run my tongue along her jaw before sinking my teeth into her neck just hard enough to make her gasp. "You remember what that does to me, don't you? The way you'd moan, beg, and fucking demand it from me." I press into her, needing her closer. "I've got all night to pull every last orgasm out of you, so let me have this. Just let me touch you for a minute.

I lower my head to her chest, kissing the curve of her breasts, before taking her nipple into my mouth. My hands are everywhere —palming her tits, gripping her hips and thighs. I rut against her, my cock grinding against her slick, aching pussy.

"Holy shit, Roman... Keep going," she gasps out, breathless and begging.

I greedily suck in as much of her breast as I can while I tug and twist her other nipple. She meets me for every roll of my hips, and I feel it the second her orgasm rips through her. Nipple play always got her off, and fuck if it doesn't make me wild that I get to be the one to do it again.

I trail my hand down between her legs, soaking my fingers in her arousal before smearing it across her lips. I thrust my tongue into her mouth, desperate to taste how wet I make her, kissing her again and again, and getting off on the way she melts beneath me.

"You feel how much I want you?" she asks, arching into my hand as I slide a finger inside her.

God, she's still the softest thing I've ever had.

"You want another, Addie?"

"Stop teasing me."

I push in another finger, then a third, curling them deep as I grind my palm into her clit. I keep my eyes on her, memorizing every gasp that tells me she's seconds from breaking. She's come for me a hundred times before, but this is different. We're different.

I don't look away from her as I move down and lower my mouth, lashing her clit with my tongue.

Fuck, I've missed this pussy—missed the taste of her.

"Remember when you couldn't sleep without me eating you first?" I remind her, spitting on her clit before sucking it hard. "You still mine like that, baby?"

"Roman," she whimpers.

"Let it go. Come for me like you used to."

Her orgasm tears through her, body tensing so hard she arches off the bed. When I pull my fingers out, they're dripping with her, and I smear it down my cock, groaning at how wet she is for me. She's still trembling, but I don't give her a second to breathe.

I don't want her to come down.

I want to fuck her a thousand different ways, but right now, I just need to be buried so deep she forgets we were ever apart. And when I finally push into her, it's like every second I lived without her just burns away.

I drop my mouth to her ear, nipping her skin before dragging my lips across her throat. "Do you know how fucking wild you looked grinding on my cock like you'd forgotten how it used to feel? I bet you'd beg if I made you."

I pull out to the tip, then slam back into her, hard enough to make the bed rattle.

"Baby, I'd do anything you wanted," she whispers, "as long as you never stop moving inside me."

We're not just fucking.

We're taking back everything we lost.

We're locked together—eyes, bodies, and souls—uniting in a way we haven't in so long and moving like we were made to.

"Roman..."

"I know, baby. I'm right there with you."

This is everything.

This is home.

I catch her wrist, slam it above her head, and lace our fingers together. I drive into her harder, deeper, until the room is nothing but the sound of her moans. Sweat beads across her chest, running down that dip in her throat, and I lower my mouth to her skin, licking up the salt and heat as I fuck her into the mattress.

I want her to feel this for days.

I want every muscle in her body to remember me and ache for me tomorrow.

"You're almost there, baby," I murmur, brushing my mouth over hers. "Let me feel you break."

My name tears out of her throat as she tightens around my cock. She's falling apart for me—so completely, so fucking beautifully. It's everything I've missed, everything I swore I was done needing, and I'm already lost in it.

"Fuck, Addie," I choke out as my orgasm slams into me. I bury myself to the base, feeling her clench and pulse around me while I spill inside her.

Chest to chest, breath to breath, I look down at the girl I've loved every day, even when she wasn't mine, to find her staring up at me like I carved the constellations just to guide her home to us.

My fingers thread through her hair as she drags her nails gently over my back. We don't talk. We just breathe each other in and let the weight of what this is settle into our bones.

When I finally pull out, she lets out a soft gasp. I spread her legs wider, looking down and watching my cum leak out of her, and with two fingers, I push it back in.

"This is still mine, baby."

"It never stopped being yours. Not in here," she says, tapping her temple.

I kiss her forehead and linger there for a moment, my body exhausted but my heart wide open. When I roll to my back, I tug her against me, and her head finds my chest while soft, delicate fingers trace my ribs.

"Did you mean what you said? About coming to Boston?" I ask, my thumb brushing slow lines up her spine.

She lifts her head, resting her chin on my chest. "Of course I meant it. I can't come with you tomorrow, but I'll take care of things here and be with you as soon as I can."

I hate that. I hate the idea of leaving Addie here, even for a day. She knows that too. She knows patience has never been my strong suit when it comes to anyone I love.

"How long?"

"I don't know," she answers honestly. "But I refuse to spend another Christmas without you."

CHAPTER TWENTY-TWO
ZEKE

Pretty sure Jasper and I have never moved this fast in our lives, but when the girl you love video calls you with the guy you love eating her out, you haul ass back to them as quickly as possible.

"Are you hard?" Jasper pants, breath fogging in the freezing air as we power walk through the snow, and I can't help the laugh that rips out of me. "Fuck, I'm so fucking hard."

We don't even make it inside before I've got him slammed against the door, hips rutting against him with zero shame. "Yeah, baby. I'm hard."

"If I wasn't so obsessed with seeing Roman and Addie together, I'd already be on my knees with your cock down my throat." He grabs at my shirt like he's two seconds from tearing it off.

I drag my thumb across his bottom lip, watching his pupils blow wide. "You have no idea how much I want to ruin that mouth," I mutter before crashing my lips against his in a kiss that's all tongue and hunger. I pull back, grab his hand, and drag him toward the bedroom.

The second I see Addie and Roman together on the bed, I don't just want in—I need in.

"Holy shit," Jasper whispers, watching Addie writhe beneath Roman, her hands fisted in his hair while he lies bare, ass raised, with his arms wrapped tight around her thighs.

Neither of us speaks. We just start stripping—shirts hitting the floor, pants kicked away—-until we're both naked and fisting our cocks as Roman brings Addie to the edge over and over again.

"Roman, please... please," she begs, her voice breaking as he kisses the inside of her thighs.

"Roman and his fucking edging," I mutter, because I've been on the wrong end of that more times than I can count.

He glances up, lips glossy from our girl. "You fucking love it," he growls, then buries his face between her legs again, tongue ruthless as he licks her apart.

Jasper crawls forward, sliding up behind Roman, bending low until his chest brushes Roman's back. "You trust me, Captain?"

Roman's head snaps up once again, his eyes burning as they meet Jasper's blazing dark gaze. "You know I trust you."

I run my fingers through Roman's hair, watching the scene unfold before me. Addie's sweat-slick skin and overstimulated body are about to blow, and Roman's tongue is buried deep like he's trying to make up for every second he's ever spent away from her.

When I glance at Jasper, I catch him dragging his lips across Roman's solid, tattooed back, pressing slow kisses down his spine before he lowers behind him. His hands roam over Roman's ass, guiding his lips to follow, spreading his cheeks wide before his tongue slides between them. Roman's body tenses, and the sound that leaves him is so raw and vulnerable. It's pleasure and surrender wrapped into one deep exhale as he gives Jasper a piece of himself he's never given anyone before.

"You good, Rome?" I check in, my hand still resting in his hair.

"Don't let him stop," he grits out, reaching behind him, his hand finding Jasper's head. There's no force, just a silent plea to keep going.

Jasper hums, smug and hungry, his mouth working faster now.

My attention shifts to the beauty writhing on the bed. Roman's been edging her so long that she practically explodes the second I suck her nipple into my mouth.

"Breathe, beautiful," I whisper in her ear as her body jolts with aftershocks while Roman's tongue still lazily laps her up like he's drunk on it.

"Zeke... get down here," Jasper calls, and I slide in behind Roman. I run my tongue across his lower back, tasting sweat and skin before slipping between his cheeks.

Our wild boy's been desperate to claim Roman since day one, and now with my tongue buried deep in his ass and the way he's grinding against the bed, I'm pretty sure that day's coming sooner than any of us thought.

He's a top.

Undeniably.

Unapologetically.

Always in control.

But right now he's rolling his hips like he's chasing something he's ready to admit he needs.

I push myself up, and Jasper's got Roman by the jaw, kissing him while Addie watches, her fingers teasing slow circles over her nipples.

I trail kisses up Roman's spine, savoring the flex of muscle beneath my lips, before dropping my mouth to his ear. "I wanna watch you inside our girl," I murmur, locking eyes with Addie's sapphire gaze. "We need to see you two together, *really* together."

Roman leans back against the headboard, legs spread, cock in hand, holding it steady as Addie sinks down on him. His fingers clamp around her waist the second she takes him, halting her and keeping her still. He doesn't move, he doesn't thrust, he just holds her there.

The connection between them is undeniable.

It's not just sex—it's history.

It's love, pain, something raw and bone-deep, and watching it makes my chest ache and my dick throb in equal measure.

I circle the bed, and the moment I reach Jasper, my hand drops down to grip both our cocks.

He kisses me again and again and again. Each kiss is deeper, hungrier, and more desperate than the last, and I give myself over to it completely.

Addie and Roman's groans blend with mine and Jasper's. It's a symphony of want and surrender, of four people bleeding into each other with no beginning or end.

"Look at them, Addie. They're fucking everything." Roman's voice cuts through my Jasper-induced haze.

We break apart, foreheads pressed together, panting like wild animals. We both turn to watch Addie as she moves on Roman, her hips grinding in slow circles. Jasper's hand drops between us now, fingers wrapping around us again, his jaw clenched like he's barely holding it together.

"Get in her ass," Jasper growls.

Addie turns her head, looking over her shoulder at me.

She doesn't need to say a word.

She wants this.

She wants me.

She wants all of us.

Jasper curses under his breath, his hand falling away after one last slow stroke, and I crawl across the bed.

"You want me to stretch your tight little ass?"

"Please," she begs as Roman shifts beneath her.

"Here," Jasper says, tossing me the lube.

I catch it midair and slide behind her, slotting myself between Roman's spread thighs. Addie's already shaking, and I can see Roman's cock disappearing inside her with every roll of her hips.

"Press your chest to Rome's, angel. Push that pretty ass out for Zeke." She obeys, folding over Roman and moaning as she offers herself up to me. "Fuck, look at you, such a good fucking girl."

When I look closer, I see Roman feeding on her—hands gripping her tits, lips sucking on her nipples. I slick my fingers with lube and squirt a line down the crack of her ass, trailing one finger through it and circling her tight little hole. Roman keeps her stimulated, his cock buried to the hilt as he gently fucks into her.

I push my finger into her, feeling her clench around me, and when I lower my face, I drag my tongue along the seam of Roman's balls before sucking one into my mouth. He groans against her skin, and Jesus, it's perfect. Her moaning, his trembling, both of them completely undone beneath me.

"You're going to have to breathe for me now, Addie." I line myself up and press the thick head of my cock inside her. She tenses so tight it's like her body's trying to fight it. "Let me in, beautiful. You can take me, I promise."

I go slow, but when I finally bottom out, Roman grunts beneath her. "Fuck, Zeke, I can feel you."

"Tight, right?" I chuckle, the pressure making my eyes roll back. My fingers lace with his, resting on Addie's waist as we hold her in place.

"God, you three are so fucking hot, and every one of you is mine," Jasper murmurs, fist wrapped tight around his dick.

"Hey..." Roman says. "Get over here."

Jasper doesn't need telling twice. He drops to his knees on the bed, grabs a fistful of Roman's hair, and slides his cock past those full lips. Watching Roman suck dick like this—mouth full and under someone else's control—is one of my favorite things.

"Fuck," I breathe out, watching Roman work Jasper and Addie at the same time.

"Holy shit, you both feel so good."

"I've had them both inside me too, angel. They feel fucking unreal together, don't they?"

"Uh-huh. I'm so full."

Roman and I pick up the pace, and she cries out between us, Jasper capturing the sound in a kiss as they melt into each other.

"Roman..." I moan, my voice catching when I feel his cock rubbing against mine through the thin wall of her body. His piercing drags with every stroke, sending a sharp jolt of pressure and pleasure straight through me.

This goes beyond sex.

This is four bodies moving as one, all of us chasing the same edge, blurring the lines between who's giving and who's taking, desperate to fall together.

"I can't wait for the day you give that ass up to me," Jasper growls, eyes locked on Roman. "You'll be on all fours taking me like the good boy I know you wanna be, and you're gonna feel how much I fucking love you."

"Fuck, Jasper." I groan, my hips slamming forward as Addie lets out a moan beneath us.

"Keep talking," Roman grits out. "She's close... I can feel it. She just tightened up around me."

"Our dirty girl gets off on hearing how I'm gonna wreck our captain, huh?"

"I wanna see it," Addie whimpers. "Please, I need to watch."

Yeah, with all of them like this—moaning, begging, fucking—I'm hanging by a thread.

"You wanna know what else I want, Zeke?" I lift my head, and the second my eyes meet Jasper's, it's like the rest of the world disappears. "I want you inside me... while I'm inside him."

His words hit like a match to gasoline.

"Fuck, fuck, fuck!" My hips keep pounding deep into Addie's ass as I come, setting off a chain reaction that ripples through all of us.

"Oh my god..."

"Fuck, Addie, come on, baby, come for us," Roman growls, and then I feel it—the snap—her body clenches tight as her climax crashes over her, and she squeezes us both. Roman groans, losing himself right after, head falling back as Jasper catches his mouth in a kiss that steals the sound right from his throat.

"Jasper..." She pants, breathless. "I want you."

He inches forward, and the second her lips close around him, his fingers fist in her hair. He calls out her name as he lets go, and she swallows every drop. When it's over, Jasper folds in on himself, his breath ragged, one hand gripping my shoulder tight as he tries to pull himself back together.

"Now I've got all three of you inside me," Addie says with a wicked little smile.

We pull out slowly, one by one, from every hole we've used, and collapse together across the bed. The sheets are a mess—damp, twisted, and clinging to my skin—and the whole room is thick with the smell of sex.

I glance at Addie, lying between us. I know we could've been happy without her. Jesus, we were happy without her. But some part of us would've always missed her. She lit the match we didn't know we needed and burned down everything we thought we were until all that was left was this and every memory we haven't made yet.

We were whole together.

But with her, we're complete.

We're a mess of limbs, heat, and everything we're about to lose, and I'm really trying to take this in for what it is.

All we've got left are these few remaining hours.

We're leaving, and we're leaving without Addison.

None of us are happy about it. Least of all Jasper, who, the moment he found out she was ready to move to us, started googling moving companies. He had tabs open for *"How to pack up your life in twenty-four hours,"* *"Small-town escape plans,"* and my personal favorite, *"Professional email templates for quitting your entire life without sounding completely unhinged."*

"I'll write it for her," he said, furiously tapping away on his phone. "Dear whoever, I'm leaving and won't be returning. EVER. I've been claimed by three annoyingly hot men with questionable morals and excellent stamina. Please forward all mail to our shared bed."

He's going to hate being without her—we all will, but I know the wait will be worth it.

"Can I ask you something?" Addie's voice cuts through the quiet, all of us still wrapped up in the perfect mess we've made.

"What is it, beautiful?" I ask, my hand absentmindedly stroking Jasper's hair where he's curled up with his head in my lap.

"Do your families know? About you guys?"

She means Jasper and me. Roman didn't grow up with the kind of family where that question would've made sense. He didn't grow up with warm dinners or loud Sunday mornings or anyone waiting up just to know he got home safe. His childhood was built on silence, not support. But both my mom and Jasper's parents treat Roman like he's one of their own. My mom checks in on him more than she checks in on me sometimes—just to make sure he's eating, sleeping, and breathing. It's not biology, but it's chosen love, and for a guy like Roman, who spent years convincing himself he didn't need anyone, that kind of love hits different.

I glance down at Jasper, and he meets my eyes with a soft smile before closing them again, sinking deeper into the comfort of us. "Yeah, they've known for a long time. Why do you ask?"

"I just wonder what they'll think now that I'm part of this. It's been the three of you for so long. I wouldn't blame them if they had doubts."

Roman lifts her chin, forcing her to look up at him. "Are you planning on going anywhere?"

"No. Not unless you all do, and then I'm going with you."

"Then you don't have anything to worry about." Roman holds her tighter, savoring the closeness.

"It's everyone else that's going to be the problem," Jasper whispers, and I stop my fingers, hearing the vulnerability in his voice and hating it because I know he's right, and I hate that I can't shield him from it.

"I can't wait to get home. You know why?" Jasper tilts his face up, and my fingers brush along his jaw. "Because I get to kiss you. I get to kiss Rome and Addie whenever the hell I want. I get to hold your hand and let the whole world know I'm in love with you without giving a shit what anyone thinks—not the team, not Coach, not the media. Let them talk. It doesn't take a thing from us. And if we decide to say fuck it and disappear somewhere quiet and live off all the money we've made, then so be it. If it all ends tomorrow, I'll walk away without a second thought because I'll have you, all of you, and that's all that's ever really mattered."

"I know it's not gonna be easy—"

"It's going to be really easy, Jasper, because whatever this is between us, I've never felt anything like it. I've never been this happy."

She means every word. I can feel it deep in my chest.

"The easiest fucking thing in the world, baby," Roman agrees, and even though he can't reach Jasper right now, I know the second he can, his hands will be on him, grounding him, and loving him the way Roman does.

"Can you please hurry and get your shit together here, angel? Roman's gonna be climbing the walls waiting for you."

"Do you guys have a spare room for me?"

"Yeah, not happening, Addison," I shoot back, raising a brow as she smirks like the beautiful little menace she is.

"I meant for my things," she says, all faux innocence. "I had no doubt I'd be sleeping in your bed... assuming I fit."

"You're tiny," I say, brushing my fingers along her calf, "and the bed's huge. We don't sleep apart. Not ever. And that includes you now."

CHAPTER TWENTY-THREE
ADDISON

I used my lipstick to leave the boys a note on the bathroom mirror before slipping out at sunrise. It wasn't long, just a single line: *I can't say goodbye, so think of this as my see-you-soon. I love you.*

I knew I couldn't stand there and watch them leave. And honestly, I think it would've been just as difficult for them—especially Roman. After everything that happened between us, after falling back into him so easily, so completely... being in his arms again felt like coming home. I felt like I'd finally returned to where I was always meant to be.

I believe I was always meant to be theirs.

Nothing and no one is going to make me feel ashamed of that. Not the past or the distance. Not even the disapproval I know is coming from my parents. I'm done pretending, I'm done hiding, and I'm going to own what I feel because this time, I'm not letting it go.

The minute I stepped through my front door this morning, I opened my laptop and fired off an email to a lawyer. I need this divorce more than I need air. It doesn't matter where I am; I just need this marriage to stop trailing behind me like a storm cloud.

Next on my list is the bookstore.

God, my bookstore.

Eternal Chapter has been my sanctuary for years now. The smell of pages, the warmth of worn leather chairs, and the quiet shuffle of readers moving through the aisles searching for their next book boyfriend. I especially love being here around the holidays. I string fairy lights across the windows and set out cinnamon sticks by the register, hoping the scent might coax a smile from the regulars. It's saved me more times than I care to admit. My chest tightens as everything I've worked for threatens to slip through my fingers. But if I had to choose—if the universe forced my hand—I'd sacrifice it all for them.

Jasper, with his wild, unapologetic love—the kind that borders on obsession and possession. He loves me like I'm it for him, like there's no version of his future that doesn't include me, and he makes damn sure I know it. It's unfiltered, intense, all-consuming —the kind of love that grabs you by the throat and doesn't let go. And it terrifies me how much I crave it.

Zeke is the stillness after the storm. The calm in the chaos. He sees everything, feels everything, and always knows exactly what I need before I even ask. His love is quiet but absolute. He doesn't ask for anything but my peace, and with him, I always find it.

Then there's Roman. He's never stopped knowing me, not really. Not when I tried to pull away, not when life tried to wedge space between us. He's the one who reminds me, without ever saying it out loud, that I'm his world. He'd rip the stars from the sky if I so much as asked, because with him, it's not just love—it's always and everything.

My phone is a mess of reminders right now. Pack boxes. Call the utilities. Meet with the realtor. Sign the papers. Cancel the auto debits. Every task checked off gets me one step closer to them, and if I can get everything in order and tie up every last string, I'll finally be able to walk away from this town and run straight into the life waiting for me on the other side.

It's been a full, jam-packed, emotional roller coaster of a day—the kind where you're constantly swinging between exhaustion and excitement. Now, I'm sitting in my parents' living room, surrounded by decades of memories and twinkling Christmas lights, staring at the stockings hung along the mantel.

I'm just waiting for Willow to arrive.

My sister knows about the divorce and about my men. What she doesn't know is that I'm leaving, and I know that's going to hurt her.

Ten minutes later, she walks through the front door, calling out a quick hello as she shrugs off her coat. Thankfully, she's alone. I'm guessing Warren has their kids until tomorrow.

She steps into the living room, eyes bouncing between all of us. "Well, you three look weird," she says, raising an eyebrow.

"Thanks," I say with a nervous laugh, trying to play it off even as my palms start to sweat.

"Addison's got something to talk to us about," my mom chimes in quickly, but it's my dad who reaches for my hand, and suddenly my heart is thudding in my chest.

Willow narrows her gaze, tilting her head. "Wait... has this got anything to do with..."

"Yeah," I say softly, nodding.

She lets out a low whistle, then leans in and whispers, "Dad knows you're with them."

"Traitor," I murmur back, but there's no real bite in it. Not when I glance at my dad and see it written all over his face that he's okay with this. There's no anger or confusion, only support.

"Can somebody please tell me what's going on?" my mom says again, sounding more anxious as the seconds pass.

"Yeah... I, uh..." I swallow. "I'm leaving."

"Wait, what?" Willow blurts, her eyes going wide with shock. My dad just smiles and rises from his seat, still holding my hand. "Where are you going?"

"She's leaving for Boston," he says, answering before I can. "And it's about damn time."

CHAPTER TWENTY-FOUR
JASPER

It's been two days since Addie left us, and I swear, the second I get my hands on that girl, I'm bending her over and spanking that pretty little ass. That little lipstick note on the bathroom mirror? Cute. Thoughtful. But it wasn't even close to enough. Not when I wanted *my goodbye*—my hands on her body, my lips on her pussy, and my name on her tongue. I wanted to fuck the goodbye into her and make her feel it for days. Instead, she robbed me of all of it.

Right now, though, we've got bigger problems. Coach is currently eyeballing us with that stone-cold face he saves for when he's really pissed, and I'm doing my best not to care. Mostly, I don't, but I care about Zeke and Roman and what all this means for them. There's this gnawing guilt, too, because my little outburst might've forced them to open our secret before they were ready.

My guys have done everything they can to reassure me—loving words, rough hands, more orgasms than I can count—but no matter how many times they tell me it's okay, I still can't shake the worry that I've screwed things up for them here.

Coach's eyes are as sharp as knives as he looks between me, Zeke, and Roman. "You wanna run that by me again?"

Roman's teeth are clenched tight. "Do I need to?"

I know that tone. One wrong word and Roman will lose it. He doesn't tolerate disrespect, especially not toward us. So I step in because if anyone's going to lose it here, it's not going to be him.

"Look, Coach, it's not some big dramatic thing. We've been together for years. We've kept it professional, we've kept our heads down, but we're done hiding. We won't be on the ice forever, and we're done pretending."

Coach lifts his chin slightly. "Hiding what, exactly?"

I blow out a breath, run a hand through my hair, and meet Coach's stare dead-on. "That we're fucking boyfriends, the three of us, Jesus. We live together, we sleep together, we love each other... Is that enough for you, or should I break out a fucking diagram?"

Yeah... now I'm the one who's snapped, and honestly, it feels pretty good.

Zeke's voice cuts through, unshakable and calm as ever. "Coach, it's not a big deal. It only turns into one if people let it—us included, which we don't want. We're still the same players. Same work ethic and loyalty. Nothing's changing for the team. We're still us."

Coach leans back in his chair, arms crossed tight over his chest. "You know this is going to draw heat."

"Heat? You mean like when Bradley got blackout drunk and trashed a fucking hotel lobby? Or when your PR genius hired that influencer who gave head to our backup goalie on the rink during a sponsored shoot, and it went viral? That kind of heat?" Roman lets out a bitter laugh, and this time, I let him go. "At least we're giving you a heads-up so you can handle it before the press does."

Coach sighs, tapping his pen against his desk. "You can't control how this plays out. Once it's out there, it's going to be everywhere, whether you want it to be or not, and people are gonna talk louder than they ever did about a damn sex tape."

"So because people are bigoted pieces of shit, we're supposed to stay silent?" I snap.

He lets out a slow, heavy breath and finally looks up at the three of us—not as players or a liability—but as men sitting before him.

"What I think doesn't change the world, but I know this team, and if you've got each other's backs on the ice the way you clearly do off it, I'd be an idiot to stand in your way." There's a beat of silence before he adds, "I don't think the guys will give a damn—maybe just toss a little shit your way in the showers. The real heat will come from the media, the fans, and possibly the sponsors. There's always going to be someone who won't get it. Hell, I don't even get it. I've been with the same woman since I was nineteen. But I know you three, and if your happiness is with each other, then so be it. I'll do everything I can to make sure this isn't some kind of ultimatum for you guys."

Roman doesn't even flinch. "If it ever comes down to that, we'll walk. No decision to make." And damn, I want to kiss the hell out of him for that, but Coach would probably keel over, and considering I barely passed the CPR course they made us take, that would be a whole new mess to clean up.

"Let's not allow it to get to that point, yeah?" Coach says, pinching the bridge of his nose. "Just keep your personal shit tidy. That's all I'm asking."

Zeke raises a brow. "Have we ever not?"

I clear my throat. "We should probably mention we have a girlfriend too."

Roman and Zeke whip their heads toward me, eyes wide, and I shrug back at them. "What? May as well get it all out now."

Coach stares at us for a long second before groaning and

rubbing his temples. "Jesus Christ, you kids... I can't keep up. Whatever. You've got your boyfriend thing, your girlfriend thing, whatever-the-fuck thing. Just be ready for the press to chew you up and spit you out, and for the love of God, stay offline." He stands up and waves us out like we're bad dreams that he just wants gone.

We take the cue and leave his office. There are no more words, just the quiet understanding between us that whatever the hell comes next, we'll face it together.

By the time we head down to the lockers to get ready for practice, I finally let out a breath I've been holding for years. No, really —since the night I caught Zeke staring at my mouth as we walked home from Audrey Nicholls's party. I didn't give him a chance to overthink it. I grabbed him and kissed him, and that was that. No regrets, no looking back.

Most of the guys are already half dressed and itching to hit the ice. I know it's now or never—scratch that, it's now or now. Roman steps up like he owns the place, his voice cutting through the chatter.

"Hey, assholes, listen up." The room shuts up instantly, every head turning toward our captain. "We've just had a meeting with Coach this morning, and before this shit hits the media, we wanted you to hear it from us."

I glance around the room, watching faces shift from confusion to curiosity. This is it. Thirty seconds from now, everything is going to change for good.

Chambers leans back on the bench, frowning. "Everything alright, Cap?"

"Yeah, we just need to get this out there so you're not blindsided," he says, then pauses, taking a breath. "We're together, the three of us—me, Zeke, and Jasper. Have been since college. Living together, loving each other, all of it."

For half a second, there's dead silence, and I swear, you could hear a pin drop, and it'd sound like a gunshot.

And then the place fucking explodes.

Laughter. Cheering. Fists slamming lockers. Someone lets out a whistle that lasts way too long, a couple of guys start clapping, and a few shout things I'm pretty sure would get us all fined if anyone outside this room heard. Suddenly, the room feels like a post-win locker room, not the middle of some life-altering confession.

I glance at Roman—the smug bastard looks like he expected this. Zeke is smiling, seeming relaxed in a way I haven't seen before, while I'm just trying to process the fact that we didn't just set the place on fire—we lit it up, and the team is dancing in the flames right beside us.

"What the hell is happening?" I mutter, but Zeke just grins like he always knew it'd go down this way.

"No fucking clue," he says, clearly amused.

"Alright, alright—calm your tits," Roman calls out, trying to cut through the noise, but no one is calming anything, and they're still grinning like a bunch of idiots.

"Fucking finally, Captain," Lincoln says, clapping his hands together like it's Christmas morning. "You really think none of us knew? Come on."

I blink, convinced I've slipped into an alternate universe. "Wait, what?"

"Jasper's always been the giveaway," someone else pipes up from the back.

"Me? What the hell does that mean?"

"Dude, you look at them like you'd murder anyone who even breathes wrong around them. Only an idiot wouldn't have figured it out."

Zeke and Roman are both smiling, and my heart pounds like a

drum in my chest from this overwhelming rush of love I never stop feeling for them.

"Why didn't anyone say anything?" Zeke asks, shaking his head. "None of you went to Coach?"

"Hell no." Lincoln shrugs. "It wasn't our business. We figured you'd say something when you were ready. You've always had our respect, and nothing about this changes that."

It's strange how a moment you think might break everything wide open turns out to be the one that stitches you back together. There's no fallout, no disaster, just the strength of men who know what it means to bleed for each other.

Brotherhood has always been the backbone of this team, and today, it holds steady, just like it always does. I look around the room, at faces I've battled beside, and at the two men standing next to me who carry my heart in their hands, and I know we made the right call.

There's no more hiding, and whatever noise the outside world makes, whatever bullshit is thrown our way, we'll face it head-on. Because we're not just out, we're free.

CHAPTER TWENTY-FIVE
ROMAN

It's game day.

Zeke, Jasper, and I are already out on the ice—it's barely five in the morning, but none of us could sleep. This is our first game since we went public with our relationship, and the world found out that the three of us are more than just linemates.

According to Coach, it's all anyone's talking about—sports networks, blogs, the league, sponsors. Some fans are rooting for us louder than ever. Some... not so much. We're bracing for whatever's coming but secretly hoping it's not as bad as we fear. That's why we're here so early, skating laps and passing the puck.

Tonight, we play our rivals.

We'll walk into that stadium with our heads high, with our team behind us, and maybe with the weight of the world on our backs, but we'll carry it together.

I'm on edge, and I can feel it in every part of me. I miss my woman. We all do. It's been a week since we returned to Boston, and every second without her feels like a punishment. I'm skating hard, pushing myself to the edge just to burn off the need clawing beneath my skin, but it doesn't help.

Not when all I see is Addie.

Last night, we fucked our fists while she touched herself. Her fingers were buried between her thighs, her mouth parted, and her eyes half lidded and locked on us through a screen. That call should've taken the edge off, but it didn't. It just made the distance worse.

We're not built for separation. We're built for touch, for skin-on-skin, and the kind of love that demands blood and bone and everything in between.

"Rome," Jasper says, snapping me out of my spiral. "What's up?"

"Nothing," I call back, a little too loud.

"You're all over the place," he says, and he's right.

My brain's a fucking minefield, and every thought is way too loud. I'm trying to figure out how to protect Zeke and Jasper when that puck drops and thousands of strangers are watching, attempting to dissect something they'll never understand. They don't know our hearts, and they don't see how fiercely we love or how deep it runs between us. And Addie... fuck. I don't even know when she's getting here, and that uncertainty is chewing me up from the inside.

Suddenly, both of them are at my side, skates scraping the ice. I lean back against the boards, my helmet clattering against the wall.

"What's going on, big guy?" Zeke asks, searching my face for answers.

"I don't know... I'm just—"

"She'll be here soon," Jasper says softly.

"It's not just Addie. It's everything about tonight too."

Zeke cups the back of my neck, and the second his skin touches mine, it's like the chaos quiets. "We've got this."

"I know the team's got our backs, but I keep thinking about

what happens when we hit the ice and the arena's packed. When the crowd starts in on us, I just—" I stop, my breath feeling tight in my chest. "I want to keep you both safe. I just want us to be okay."

"We'll be fine. I swear to you," Jasper promises. "Yeah, the judgment's gonna come, Roman, because there's always one asshole with too much to say, but it doesn't fucking matter."

"It matters to me." My breath punches out of me, and I blow out a "*Fuck*" as I turn toward the tunnel, my emotions boiling over and burning me alive from the inside.

"Hey, don't fucking do that," Jasper snaps, ripping off his helmet just as I yank mine free. Zeke's already standing there, helmet in hand, his eyes fixed on me. "Since when do you walk away?"

"Since I realized I can't protect you from this," I shoot back, my chest heaving as I fight to keep my shit together.

"What about you, huh?" Zeke says, moving close and pressing his side to mine while Jasper stands tall before me. "Who's looking out for Roman in all of this?"

"That's not how this works."

"The hell it isn't," Zeke fires back, not angry or yelling, just that solid certainty he always has. "This only works because we take care of each other. You don't always have to carry it all. You have to trust us, Rome."

"I do," I rasp, the words rough in my throat. "You know I do."

Jasper presses his forehead to mine like he's trying to fuse us together. His hand fits around the back of my neck, and I drag in a breath just as Zeke runs his tongue along my jaw. Jasper's hands slide down, fingers finding the laces on my hockey pants, and he tugs them loose.

"Let us get you out of your head, just for a minute," Jasper murmurs.

Zeke steps behind me, his chest pressed to my back. I melt into him, sinking into that comfort, letting his arms lock me in place while Jasper captures my mouth. His tongue slides against mine, slow and intimate, the kind of kiss that says *mine* without ever needing to speak it. He drops to his knees in front of me, and I feel his hands on the waistband of my gear. He tugs everything down, knuckles brushing my thighs, and then he looks up at me like I'm the altar and he's about to pray.

"Look at our wild boy on his knees for you," Zeke growls, his voice rough against my ear as he runs his tongue along my lobe. "You know he'd live down there if we told him to. He wouldn't care who was watching—he'd suck your cock in front of the whole damn world if it meant proving he's ours."

I curse under my breath, hand wrapped tight around the base of my cock as I stare down at Jasper—our beautiful fucking mess. His brown hair, which is always a shade darker when the cold settles in, is sticking up in every direction from my fingers. His lips are parted, breath coming fast, and his pupils are blown so wide there's barely any color left.

"Open that mouth for me, baby. Tongue out. Let me see it." Jasper obeys, offering himself up like he was made for this. I slap the head of my cock against his tongue once, twice, watching him when he presses a kiss to the tip before teasing my piercing.

"Now show Roman just how good you suck his cock. Show us that nothing out there touches what we've got right here."

Jasper wraps his hand around me, spits on my length, and then seals his lips over my head. He sucks slow and deep, stroking what he can't take with a twist of his wrist that has me biting down a moan.

"Fuck... Jesus, Jasper," I hiss through clenched teeth, my head falling back as my hips snap forward.

Behind me, Zeke's hands trail down my spine, nails scratching hard, like he wants to mark me up just for the hell of it.

"I love watching him touch you." I look down at Jasper, his lips swollen, cheeks hollowed around my cock, and I swear I could come just from the sight of him. "I love the way you love each other."

"And you..." I whisper.

"Yeah? You love me, big guy?"

"You know I do," I grit out. "I couldn't live without any of you."

"You'll never have to," Zeke whispers against my skin, then holds out his hand to Jasper. "Spit."

Jasper releases my cock and spits right into Zeke's waiting fingers. His hand disappears down the back of my pants, dragging his finger up the crease of my ass.

"Now I know Jasper gets this ass first, and I know you're ready to give it up to him, but how about you let me play a little now, yeah?" He's asking, not taking. But that's Zeke. He could wreck me if he wanted, and we both know it, but he's never careless with the things he loves.

Beneath me, Jasper groans like he's unraveling just from watching us. His hand glides up my thigh, fingers digging into my skin. His mouth hovers just over the head of my cock, his lips slick, and his breath is hot enough to burn.

"Fuck, Zeke," he pants out, eyes glazed over with hunger. "You're gonna make him come so hard."

Zeke smirks, glancing over my shoulder at Jasper. "And you get to swallow every drop, baby."

Jasper grins like the fucking devil and sinks his mouth back down onto me. He moans low in his throat, and I feel it everywhere. I turn, grabbing Zeke by the shirt, and crash my mouth into his, kissing him and begging without words for more, giving him all the permission he needs to *take me, ruin me, just fucking own me.*

Zeke's slick finger finds my hole, tracing slow, firm circles, while his cock presses hard against my thigh.

"Take a breath for me," he murmurs, and I do, one hand buried in Jasper's sweat-damp hair, gripping tight as Zeke starts working me open. "That's it, that's our good boy. Relax your body and let me in." Jasper's hand disappears beneath me, and from the way his throat vibrates around my cock, I know he's touching Zeke right where his finger is moving inside me. "I think Jasper likes knowing I'm touching you here. He's got his fingers right where I'm fucking you open. He can feel what you're giving me."

"Give me more," I choke out because the stretch is nothing like I expected.

Jasper lets my cock slip from his mouth. "Keep going," he rasps. "He fucking loves it. I can taste how much he loves it."

Yeah, no shit, I'm precumming like I've been strung out for hours, and all they've done is tease the edge of what they really want from me.

"God, I can't wait to fuck you," Zeke growls, grinding against me, his cock rutting against my thigh. The lucky fucker doesn't even need to touch himself to come.

Jasper strokes a hand up my stomach. "You're taking it so well. Our perfect fucking boy, begging for more."

"You're gonna love having Jasper fuck you. I already know how good he's gonna make you feel. He knows what your body needs, and he likes it rough, just like you do. When you come with him buried deep inside you, and you can't think straight, it wrecks him. It breaks him in the best fucking way. Watching you lose it because of him drives him wild."

Zeke grinds harder against my thigh, his breath coming in ragged bursts as his fingers probe deeper, dragging me closer to the edge.

"Jasper's gonna be buried inside you, fucking you while I'm

driving into him and pushing him harder, just to feel the way it makes you moan. And you?" He exhales, his mouth brushing my jaw. "You'll have our girl straddling your face, grinding that perfect pussy against your tongue, soaking you in her cum while you're stuffed so full of Jasper's cock you won't know where one of us ends and the next begins. But I swear to you, I'm next, and when I finally get this perfect ass to myself, you better believe I'm gonna take my time. I want to feel it tighten around my cock. I want to watch you fall apart knowing you're mine."

"I fucking love eating her pussy," Jasper growls, right before he sucks me down hard enough to make my hips jerk.

"Holy shit, you're getting me so fucking close."

"Imagine how much fun we would've had if you'd let us play with you sooner," Zeke taunts.

"Fuck, I need to touch myself." Jasper pants around my cock. "You two are killing me, and I'm about to fuck the damn floor." He doesn't wait for permission. One hand keeps working my cock, and the other unlaces his pants and wraps around himself, fisting his own dick hard and fast.

"Show Roman how much you fucking ache to please him." Zeke's voice is a low growl beside my ear. "Show him how much you love choking on his cock while your own dick's dripping."

Jasper groans, mouth sealing back around me, fucking whining around my cock.

Zeke grips my jaw, tilting my face toward his. "Look at him, baby. Look how far gone he is for you. That's what you do to him. That's how bad he needs you."

Jasper rips himself away, rising to his feet before crashing his mouth against mine, tongue-fucking me with a hunger that borders on savage. He's mid-orgasm when his cum spills over my cock, his groan so loud it bounces off the walls.

Zeke's fingers thrust deeper until I'm practically shaking.

"Keep fucking me," I choke out, barely able to breathe. "Baby, get your mouth on me again, I need it."

Jasper drops without a word, like he's been waiting for the command.

Zeke's hand clamps around my throat, tipping my head back until his lips are right against my ear. "We've got you, baby. We've always had you. Now fucking come, Roman."

My body seizes, convulsing hard as the orgasm rips through me. Jasper takes every inch, nose pressed flush to my skin, my piercing hitting the back of his throat as I unload.

"Fuck, fuck, fuck—" I gasp, shaking, as I keep coming.

Zeke ruts against my thigh, his breath hot against my ear, "Good. Fucking. Boy."

His fingers still inside me, and his cock jerks in his pants as he finishes just after me.

Jasper finally releases my cock, pulling back with a ragged breath. I glance down just in time to see him wipe his mouth with the back of his hand, lips swollen, and his brown eyes wild. He stands, and we're on each other instantly. We kiss like we fuck—rough, greedy, and possessive. Grabbing at each other, like we don't care who's who as long as we're all together, and soon... she'll be here with us.

I've been dreading this moment.

Yeah, my boys made me feel better. They pulled me back from the edge like they always do, but it doesn't change what's waiting outside this bubble we've built.

I tried to reach Addison earlier; I just needed to hear her voice, but she didn't pick up. Now here we are, lined up in the tunnel, shoulder to shoulder with the other team, the smell of the rink already in our lungs. Only this time, the tension isn't just in the air—it's aimed straight at us, and they're not hiding it.

They're staring, smirking, and whispering loud enough to make sure we hear every word. "So where are they? The ones who decided blowing each other equals good team morale?"

Zeke shifts beside me, not because he's offended, but because he's watching me. Like he's ready to grab my jersey if I lose my shit. But I don't need to because Lincoln's already stepping forward, all swagger and zero fucks.

"Right here, sweet cheeks. Want me to show you how it's done?" He blows the opposing goalie a slow, exaggerated kiss, and some of our guys snicker.

I can't help it—I laugh. It's not just amusement. It's relief and gratitude knowing the team's actually with us.

"That's if we can even find your cock with all that tiny-dick energy you're throwing around," Lincoln adds.

"Come on," the left winger calls out, voice echoing in the tunnel as we wait to hit the ice. "You have to admit, it's fucking hilarious that three guys on one team are all banging each other's brains out. Is that your new strategy? Suck, fuck, and win?"

I meet his stare head-on, refusing to flinch. He falters, just a fraction, and it's enough—I know the smug little bastard didn't expect me to lean in, let alone own it.

"What's even funnier is that they both got me off only a few hours ago, right where you're standing." I step close enough that he has to tilt his head to keep eye contact. "You never know, it might bring you some luck. Though judging by how you played last game, I'm not sure anything could help that limp-dick performance."

Jasper cackles behind me, while Zeke rests a hand on my back, and Lincoln winks at us. We're not just teammates. We're a unit. A fuck-you to every locker room whisper and closed-door insult, and the second that puck drops, I'm making damn sure the Red Wings regret ever opening their mouths.

Jasper grins, flashing a wicked smile at the guy's scowl. "It was fucking beautiful, man," he says, smug as hell. "Guess you had to be there."

He smacks my ass, hard enough to make me jerk. I shoot him a glare, but it's useless—he knows it's all bravado. And when I finally crack a grin, Zeke's low chuckle joins mine. With that, the three of us skate out onto the ice, shoulders squared, hearts pounding, ready to show everyone exactly who we are.

For the next forty minutes, we throw everything we have at their net, but nothing gets past those assholes. It's not that we're off our game, but the puck just won't go in. During the time-out, I pull the team together and give them the kind of pep talk that comes from the gut because nobody, and I mean nobody, comes into our rink, runs their mouth, and walks out with a win.

But when play starts again, it's like they've found another gear. They start flying—tight, fast, and clean—and then it happens. One mistake. One shot and they bury it.

I catch Jasper's eye across the ice just as he throws his arms up in frustration, his stick slamming against the boards on his way back to the bench. Zeke skates past the crease, his jaw locked, rage in every stride, and I already know what's coming next: If we lose this, the media will eat us alive. They won't care about the effort or the stats. They'll spin it all into our fault—mine, Zeke's, and Jasper's.

Fucking parasites.

The whistle blows, and play stops. My chest's still heaving, and my gloves are clenched, but I find myself looking to the stands for any sign that the crowd's as disappointed as we are. I know it's dumb—I know they're probably just as gutted as we feel.

But then, in the blur of faces, I spot a flash of blonde hair rising from a seat a few rows up. My heart stutters, and the world narrows.

Addison.

Just the sight of her makes everything else fall away. I forget the game, the noise, the pressure, and every headline trying to tear us apart—none of it matters. Because when the ice melts and the lights go out, we're the ones who get to take our girl home.

Addison lifts her hand and points one finger in the air—our code: *I love you. You're the one.*

A grin breaks across my face, uncontainable, and I lift two fingers: *I love you too.*

Jasper and Zeke are at my sides, following my gaze until they see her, and then they smile too. She's laughing now, already moving down the steps in a full sprint, her hair bouncing and cheeks flushed, like she can't wait another second. We skate to the wall, as close to her as we can get, all of us aching to touch, kiss, and hold her—ten more minutes and she's ours.

She doesn't wait for quiet; instead, she cups her hands around her mouth and calls out, loud enough for half the rink to hear, "Get your asses moving! They pick up on the left side, but you can outskate them there, Zeke. Jasper, you're the best defenseman I've ever seen—get a handle on that puck and get it to Roman. He'll finish the job. You've all got this... Now go win, or I swear I'll put my underwear back on and keep it there till tomorrow!"

People are definitely listening, and maybe there are a few raised eyebrows, but none of us care—not one bit—and we hit the ice like the world's on fire.

We destroyed the Red Wings, dominating every play from the moment she called out. Maybe it was adrenaline. Maybe it was pride. Or maybe it was just the fact that our girl showed up exactly when we needed her most.

CHAPTER
TWENTY-SIX
ADDISON

"Merry Christmas, baby." Roman's voice is thick with sleep as he presses slow, lazy kisses along the curve of my neck, pulling me tighter into his arms until there's no space left between us. We're tangled together in the bed I've been sharing with my three men every night since I landed in Boston, and honestly, moving here is the best decision I've ever made.

They can't keep their hands off me, or each other, and it feels like we're trying to make up for all the time we lost—not just the time they've been back in Boston without me, but all those years we spent apart, wanting and waiting and never quite letting ourselves have this.

Ever since that night when Roman and I finally stopped pretending the tension between us was anything less than love, it's like all that old pain just vanished. Every kiss, every possessive graze of his fingers, is as intense and raw as what he gives Jasper and Zeke. I get the same hungry, desperate affection that leaves my skin buzzing and makes me feel more wanted than I ever thought possible.

"Merry Christmas," I mutter against Roman's jaw, my lips dragging over the stubble on his skin before I catch his mouth in a sleepy kiss. I roll over to face Zeke, grazing my mouth over his, teasing him awake. He starts to stir beneath me, lips parting, his tongue lazy as it licks into my mouth.

Jasper's arm reaches across Roman's chest, where he spent the night glued to his back, and I slip my fingers between his, squeezing tight.

"Can we get up and do gifts? I've been itching my ass off to give Addie hers."

"What is it?" I ask, and the second Jasper opens his mouth, Roman's already twisting and pinning him to the mattress with one arm braced beside his head and his knee pressed between his legs.

"Do I need to keep your mouth busy just to keep it shut?"

"Are you threatening me or making a promise, Captain?" Jasper fires back, cocky as ever, and Roman shuts him up with a kiss.

Zeke slides his arms around me, pulling me tight against his chest. "Ready for your gift, beautiful?"

I laugh, brushing his messy dark hair back from his face. "Pretty sure nothing will beat waking up between you three."

"Oh, this is going to make you so fucking needy for us, angel," Jasper says, still laughing as Roman climbs off him and drags him out of bed by the wrist.

Zeke flips me on top of him, his big hands grabbing my ass as he pulls me down for a kiss.

"Love you," I whisper against his mouth.

He flashes that devastating grin, then rises to his feet, hauling me up with my legs still cinched around his waist. He carries me from the bedroom, one arm under my ass, the other wrapped securely around my back, holding me tight against his chest.

The living room is glowing with warm, twinkling lights. They waited for me to get here before decorating their place—well, our place now, since they refuse to let me call it anything else. Every time I slip and say "your apartment" or "your couch," they're quick to correct me. And god, did they romance me. Christmas music was playing, champagne was poured, and the three of them pulled me into the middle of their world while Zeke and I hung ornaments side by side, laughing while Jasper and Roman watched. It ended the only way it could with us—me wrapped up in a mess of Christmas lights, wrists bound and body on offer, while each of them took turns teasing, playing, and worshipping me. Their hands were on my thighs, while their mouths were between them, using me in the most devastatingly delicious way.

Like I said, best decision ever.

Zeke lowers me into Jasper's arms when we reach the tree, settling me into his lap. He wraps his arms around my waist, and his chin hooks over my shoulder like he has no intention of letting me go. At the same time, Zeke moves behind Roman, curling himself around him and pressing gentle kisses along his shoulder.

We pass around gifts like we've been doing this forever, and somehow, it's effortless. My gifts are a mix of everything I love—books I've been dying to read, impossibly soft lingerie of all different colors, and a pair of delicate, angel wing earrings.

Roman leans forward and places one last box in my lap. It's smaller than the rest, wrapped in plain black paper and tied with a strip of red velvet, and I know the second I touch it, whatever this is, it matters.

"Before you open this, baby, I need you to know that whatever you feel, or any reaction you have, it's absolutely okay," Roman says.

"That's... honestly a little terrifying," I admit, glancing at him before I start on the ribbon. When I look up, three sets of eyes are locked on me. "Are you all okay?"

"You're killing me, baby. Just open it!" Jasper blurts, practically bouncing in place beside me now. I lift the lid and see a set of keys nestled inside. Not keys to this place—they already gave me those the second we walked out of the rink after their game.

"What are these for?" I ask, turning the keys over in my hand.

"They're for a building," Roman answers, watching me closely.

"A building?"

"Your building," Jasper cuts in, grinning so wide it nearly splits his face in half. "It's yours to do whatever the hell you want with."

"We know how much you loved your bookstore and how hard it was to give it up to be with us. So if you want to recreate it here, you can. If you want to do something completely different with it, then do that. And if you're not ready and don't want to do anything with it right now, it'll sit there until you know. We just want you to be happy and to have the life you always dreamed of." My throat tightens at Zeke's words, and my eyes fill with tears.

Jasper leans in and gently swipes his thumb under my eye, catching the tear as it falls. "Are these happy tears, angel?" I nod, then throw myself into all three of them, arms around shoulders and necks, buried into what has to be the best hug on earth.

"I don't know how to thank you. I never... I could never have expected this." My voice cracks as I shake my head, still in disbelief, and my boys hold me tighter. "Thank you so much."

Roman grabs his phone and pulls up photos of the building, the location, and even a list of designers he's already saved for me so I can have the best of everything when I'm ready. I have no idea what I did to deserve this kind of love, but I know I'll never let it go.

"Who wants breakfast?" Jasper asks, but before anyone can answer, Zeke tugs me into his lap, lips brushing my ear.

"Watch," he murmurs, nodding toward the two of them just as Roman stands and grabs a present from under the tree.

"Jasper," Roman calls, tossing the box across the room. Jasper catches it easily, grinning at him. "Merry Christmas, baby."

Jasper rips open the box, and inside sits the biggest bottle of lube I think I've ever seen. I can't help it—I snort, clapping a hand over my mouth as Zeke chuckles behind me.

"You better not be fucking with me, Captain. This had better mean that you're giving me that ass."

"It's all yours, baby." Jasper launches himself at Roman, slamming into him with a kiss so intense it borders on violent.

"Fuck breakfast," Jasper growls against Roman's mouth.

Roman grabs him by the jaw, forcing Jasper to look at him. "Tell me what you want. Say it again. Let me hear how bad you need it."

"I want to fuck you so deep they'll hear the way you beg for me from the next state," Jasper murmurs, already sliding his hand inside Roman's underwear. "God, I'm gonna fucking ruin you."

Roman catches Jasper by the waist and guides him backward toward the bedroom, their kisses so messy it's a miracle they don't take down the Christmas tree.

"Ready to watch them get everything they want?" Zeke murmurs, his hand sliding into mine.

"Absolutely," I whisper, letting him pull me to my feet.

By the time we reach the bedroom, clothes are already scattered across the floor. Jasper's straddling Roman, hips grinding down, kissing him like nothing else in the world matters.

"Look at them, baby." Zeke's hand slips into my underwear, and he presses his mouth to my neck as his skilled fingers find my clit. "I love how much watching them like this turns you on."

"I've come so many times just thinking about the way you touch each other."

I reach behind, tugging his cock free from his boxer briefs, and wrap my hand around him, pumping slowly as he buries his face in my shoulder.

"Get your asses over here," Roman demands.

Zeke yanks my T-shirt over my head and tosses it aside before pulling me down onto the bed with him. His mouth is everywhere—licking down Roman's chest, biting, sucking, dragging his tongue lower until Roman's practically trembling beneath him. Meanwhile, Jasper's lips are wrapped around my nipple.

He's obsessed—ever since Roman told him how crazy nipple play makes me, it's all he wants. I thread my fingers through his hair, keeping him pressed right where I want him, my breath coming faster as he sucks. Then Roman's hand slips down between my thighs, and I gasp as he pushes my red lace panties aside and sinks a finger into me.

"Holy shit... fuck, I'm gonna come if you two don't stop." My eyes flutter shut as Zeke drags his mouth up to my neck, his tongue hot against my skin.

"Be our good girl and scream for us. Give us what we want before Roman gets fucked."

Jasper's still latched onto me, sucking like he's trying to drink my orgasm straight from my skin while Roman's finger crooks just right, and I shatter into a thousand pieces, crying out as my orgasm rips through me. Roman keeps fucking me with his fingers, Zeke licks a path up my neck, and Jasper growls against my breast, sucking harder as I break.

"Okay, as good as that felt, that was fast." Roman pulls me in and crushes his mouth to mine in a kiss that tells me exactly all I need to know: *we're not done, not even close.*

His hand slides along Jasper's thigh, fingers climbing higher. "You gonna get my ass ready, or what?"

The way Roman's ready to give himself over makes my whole body light up.

"Zeke asked for the first taste," Jasper's voice drops lower. "Now spread those legs for me, Addie, and let me get my fill of that tight little cunt."

I drop down beside Roman, propped up on my elbows because I need to see everything, and Jasper settles between my thighs, spreading me open with his thumbs.

"Such a pretty pussy," he mutters, then slowly drags his tongue up my slit.

My head tips back on instinct as pleasure burns through me, but Roman's low grunt pulls my attention. Zeke's got his face buried between his thighs, hands gripping hard at his hips to keep him open while Roman strokes himself, eyes half-shut and his lips parted.

"Fuck, Zeke... your tongue."

Jasper pauses, glances over at Zeke, and lets out a quiet *"Fuck"* before wrapping his lips around my clit. I clutch Jasper's hair, holding him close as he eats me like he's ravenous, and my body turns to liquid. Roman turns his face toward me, hair plastered to his forehead, and I find his mouth, kissing him deep and messy while we both fall apart under our boys' hands and tongues.

Jasper pulls away from my pussy, my whole body shivering from the loss of his mouth, and pins me beneath him. He kisses me hard, his tongue slick with my arousal, and god, I love it. I love the way I can taste myself on his lips.

"You have no idea how badly I wanna be the one to finish you off, angel, but Roman is gonna need you to sit on his face now."

CHAPTER TWENTY-SEVEN
JASPER

I'VE SPENT SO LONG IMAGINING WHAT IT WOULD FEEL LIKE TO FINALLY be inside Roman—to have every inch of him and claim the part he's always kept just out of reach. He took pieces of me without even trying, shared them easily with Zeke, and then pressed some into Addie's waiting hands like they were gifts. And now I get the last piece of him—the one I knew was mine, even if he didn't.

In my head, I've played this moment out a thousand ways—bending him over, fucking him into the mattress until the only thing he remembers is my name and the way I make him feel. I want to take his breath, steal his thoughts, and own every sound that spills from his mouth.

But the other half of me needs to give him so much more than a release. It isn't enough to fuck him until he's shaking—though I want that too.

I want that deep, soul-binding kind of lovemaking that leaves you wondering if you'll ever be the same again.

I want every second to be so devastatingly perfect that he begs for more the second it ends.

I want him to crave me, just like I crave him.

I watch him reach for Addie, and I kneel between his thighs. Roman hooks his fingers in Addie's thong and yanks it down her legs, fisting the lace in his hand. He drags her onto his face, making her straddle him with her back to me, and locks his arms around her like a vice, hauling her down until she's smothering him in pussy.

Lucky bastard.

Zeke remains beside me, close enough that his breath ghosts over my neck. His lips find my ear, voice low and meant only for me.

"You and Roman... you need this more than anyone. I know what this means to you." His fingers ghost down my spine, leaving fire in their wake, and I feel it all the way to my knees. "I'm gonna fuck our girl the way she needs. But you and him... This moment belongs to you, so touch him the way you've dreamed about, and make him feel it, baby."

My eyes are on Roman's cock as Zeke lazily circles his thumb around his rim, like he's teasing himself with the idea of fucking him too.

"But once I've made Addie come, I'm burying myself inside your ass because I need to feel you."

"You fucking better," I growl, grabbing him by the jaw to catch his mouth in a bruising kiss.

I reach for the lube, slick up my fingers, and slowly slide one into Roman. His abs tighten at the intrusion, and a deep groan rumbles from his chest as he eats Addie's pussy like she's his last meal.

I slide in deeper, then add a second finger and stretch him open. Addie starts to rock her hips, fucking herself on Roman's tongue, and I thrust my fingers faster, twisting and scissoring, loving every grunt and gasp he lets out. His cock stays rock hard, thick, and perfect, every muscle in his body pulled tight.

"Keep riding his face, angel. Fuck his mouth until you come all over his tongue." I urge her, and fuck, does she deliver.

Her whole body locks up, hips jerking forward one last time when her orgasm hits. She's gasping and panting, and her fingers twist in Roman's hair like she's trying to hold on to what's left of herself.

"My turn," Zeke says as he lifts her effortlessly off Roman and pulls her into his lap. "You wanna ride my cock, beautiful?"

She doesn't say anything, but she doesn't need to. She just lifts herself and sinks down, and the second he's inside her, her mouth falls open with a broken gasp.

We all know that sound. That sound means Zeke's buried deep. Because Zeke doesn't just fuck, he fills, and he owns, and that first push steals your breath every single time.

Her nails dig into his shoulders, and Zeke groans into her neck, already rolling his hips.

"That's it," he whispers against her skin. "You feel how full you are?"

"Uh-huh," she breathes out, lost in it, and I turn my focus back to Roman.

My fingers are still buried inside him when I lower myself on top of him, my chest brushing his, our noses almost touching. He grips my wrist, halting me—not pulling away, just holding me there. He gives me a single nod, and that's all I need. I slide my fingers free, grab the lube with hands that won't stop shaking—because I want him so goddamn bad I can barely see straight—and coat my cock from base to tip. I brace one hand beside his head, the other still wrapped around my length, and line myself up.

My heart starts pounding in my throat as I begin to push, and fuck, it's overwhelming—the heat, the tightness, the raw, hungry way his body takes me. It's erotic in a way that makes my head spin.

"Roman," I rasp as I push in deeper, my eyes squeezed shut from the sheer intensity of it. "Are you okay?"

Zeke and Addie's soft moans begin to fade into the background.

"I can stop," I whisper, my hips barely moving, just enough for him to feel me. "I swear to you, Roman, I'd rather never use my dick again than do this without you being fully with me."

"I've never been more with you. Keep going, you feel... Jesus, it's different, but it's you, and I need you to keep going."

I press my forehead to his, both of us breathless, my heart jackhammering against his chest. He lifts his legs a little more, giving me that last inch of space, and I ease in until I bottom out inside him.

"I've got you," I whisper. "When you're ready, I'll move, okay?" He nods, and the second his lust-drunk eyes meet mine, everything else falls away.

I start to thrust, slow at first, barely rocking back before rolling my hips forward again. I keep it easy, fighting every urge to rush because I want him to feel every second of this.

Little by little, I feel his body gradually unfurl as he trusts the stretch and opens for me.

"Look at them, Addie," Zeke murmurs from beside us, but I don't even blink.

I can't tear my eyes from Roman—not when he's giving himself to me like this, and not when it feels this fucking good. It's too much and somehow still not enough. It's better than anything I ever let myself dream about.

"Feel good?" I groan, but I'm not even sure I get the words out right. I'm dick-deep and ready to sell my soul to the nearest demon if it means Roman keeps gripping me like this and losing himself in the way I fuck him.

"So good. You can give me more." I slide my hand up his chest, and crash my mouth to his. I want to crawl deeper. I want to fuck him so full of me he never forgets what this feels like.

I start to move harder, my lips still brushing his, never letting go of that point of contact. "I love you," I choke out, the words burning against his lips. My chest is flush with his, our hearts beating wild between us, and I need him to feel what he does to me.

"I love you too. I'm sorry I made you wait."

"Baby, no," I whisper. "You were worth every second I spent aching to have you like this."

I kiss him, open-mouthed and hungry, my tongue sliding against his, desperate to taste his release before it even happens.

"You're beautiful like this," I whisper, lightly dragging my teeth along his jaw. "My perfect boy." His hand slips between us, and I feel his knuckles brush against my stomach as he strokes himself. "You gonna come for me, baby? I want to feel it. I want every second of your pleasure to belong to me... Say it. Tell me it's mine."

"Fuck, Jasper... It's yours. I'm yours."

"Give it to me, Rome." He spills with a shudder, and I stay right there with him, watching the man I love fall apart for me.

When I know I've wrung the last of his pleasure out of him, I dip down and lick him clean before letting his cock slip into my mouth. I hold him there, breathing around him, my tongue cradling him while I try to catch my breath and keep myself together.

Just having him still swollen, still pulsing against my tongue... yeah, I'm here for that.

I don't want to move.

I don't want to let go.

I just want to stay here in this exact moment.

A little wrecked.

A lot in love.

And utterly his.

His hands are in my hair, massaging my scalp, and when I finally release him, I keep teasing him with soft, shallow thrusts.

I lift my gaze to Zeke and Addie. Zeke's watching us with eyes full of fire and devotion, while Addie's barely breathing. She's holding herself still, as if she moves too fast she might miss the magic surrounding us.

"Ride him, Addie," Roman growls, holding his hand out to her. "Get yourself off on his cock."

She slips her hand into his, and Zeke's palms are already on her hips, lifting her just enough to line her up before slamming into her from below. He fucks her hard, and from where I'm kneeling, I can see every bounce of her tits and twitch of her thighs.

"Holy shit, Zeke... Don't stop," she whimpers, already losing herself.

"Come on, baby," I growl, rolling my hips slow and deep into Roman, who's clenching around me like he needs this as much as she does.

She cries out, her head thrown back as she rides the line between pain and bliss. I reach for her and grab a fistful of her hair.

"Look at you," I murmur. "You love this, don't you? Being our beautiful little fuck toy. Ours to use. Ours to love."

She moans, broken and breathless, and yeah—she fucking lives for this the way we do.

"I'm coming... oh my god," she screams, her whole body shaking.

Zeke holds her there, fucked open and spent, until the last

ripple runs through her and her legs finally go slack around his waist.

When he lifts his face, the heat burning in his eyes makes it feel like he's already inside me.

"Think I can borrow Zeke? I want him to fuck me the way he just fucked you."

Addie climbs off Zeke, still catching her breath, and he moves around the bed. He goes to Roman first, cups his face, and brushes their mouths together, grounding them both in that unspoken *You good?* Roman nods, and Zeke moves behind me. His hand grips my jaw, and he kisses me. I melt into it, hearing the sound of lube being pumped.

"Fuck, that feels good," I manage, my mouth falling open the second his finger slips inside me.

Zeke chuckles, and I feel his warm breath on the back of my neck. "That's because I know exactly how you like to be played with."

I look up, and Roman and Addie are kissing. She's stroking his cock, teasing him while he moans into her mouth.

"You ready for me, wild boy?"

"Hell yes." I gasp, and the second he replaces his fingers with his cock, my eyes roll so far back I might see God—or the devil, not that I care because if this is hell, then chain me up. "Fuuuck—"

Roman's tight around me, every muscle clenching, while I fuck into him. Zeke's trying to rearrange my entire existence, and it's working because I'm pretty sure my soul's about to leave my body. And then there's Addison—she's a masterpiece—naked, spread, wet, and gorgeous, put on display for us like the filthy dream she is. She watches all of us with her pouty lips slightly open and eyes wide, like this is the best day of her life.

But she's not just watching us; she's feeling us.

Every kiss she gives Roman.

Every time she strokes him.

Every sound that leaves my mouth when Zeke nails that spot that makes me almost black out.

It's overwhelming in the best possible way. Filling Rome. Getting fucked by Zeke. Watching our girl melt between us. Yeah, this is it. I've peaked. I've fucking ascended. If I died right now, face down and fucked stupid, between the people I love, so be it.

Best death, best life, no question.

Zeke and I find a rhythm, and Jesus Christ, I'm not gonna last. I'm already holding on by a thread, and it's fraying fast.

Addie's dragging her tongue along the ink on Roman's chest while she pumps his cock in her fist, but he's watching me now—his eyes dark, and when he nods once, that's it.

That's him handing everything over.

That's him telling me not to hold back.

I start to thrust roughly, pounding into him. Zeke's behind me, railing me like he owns me. His hands dig into my shoulders so hard they'll bruise, and he's grunting like an animal right against my spine.

"Jesus, baby, suck me into that pretty little mouth..." Roman begs, and watching the way Addie fucks her mouth down on him, and the way his cock disappears between her lips while I'm balls deep in him, has me on the verge of losing it.

"I'm close... Fuck, I can't..." I pant.

"Don't you fucking dare," Zeke growls from behind me. "You hold it."

Roman's hands are in Addie's hair, guiding her. His face is etched in pleasure—lips parted, brows drawn tight, eyes hooded—and I can't look away.

"Zeke," I moan, "Fuck—you're fucking me so good. Don't stop. Don't fucking stop." Zeke slams into me roughly, his hips slapping against my ass with enough force to knock the breath from my lungs. It punches me forward and makes me fuck Roman even harder.

"Addie, baby—" Roman gasps, his breath breaking.

She groans around his cock, and I feel the exact second he starts to come down her throat. His ass clenches around me like a damn vice, and that's it—that's my undoing. Pleasure rips through me like lightning, and I go rigid, roaring my release into Roman's body. I'm coming inside him for the first time, and fuck...

"Fuck, I can feel you," he chokes out.

Yeah, you fucking can.

"God—this ass. So tight. So perfect," Zeke hisses behind me, and then he's gone—thrusting into me one last time, his hips stuttering as he fills me up.

None of us move, not for a long time. We're breathing heavily, our bodies are shaking, and we're all skin stuck to skin.

"I think I'm dead. Am I dead? Is this heaven? Because I swear I just had a spiritual experience." Zeke just chuckles, kissing his way up my neck, whispering, "I love you," under his breath before finally pulling out of me. I slide out of Roman, but hell if I don't keep his legs spread, just to watch myself leak out of his ass. "That's so fucking hot... You know you're mine now, right? My cum's dripping out of your ass. I've marked you."

Roman just groans, limp and utterly spent, his head turned against the pillow with a blissed-out smirk playing at the corner of his mouth.

Zeke sprawls out beside us and kisses each of us in turn. "Until later, when it's my cum filling your ass instead."

Addie collapses next to me, her hand draped lazily across my chest. "Can I just watch that?"

I pull her closer, brushing her golden hair out of her face.

"How about you sit in my lap and we both watch Zeke fuck him while I play with you."

She hums in agreement, and her lips find mine.

"Not yet, please. I've been thoroughly fucked, and for someone new to this, I think I need a little recovery time." He laughs, and we all end up a naked heap on the bed.

I glance around the room, taking in the Christmas decorations—tinsel hanging a little crooked, lights blinking, and the scent of pine lingering beneath the unmistakable smell of sex. Michael Bublé's voice drifts from the forgotten playlist in the background, which is a little too cheerful considering we all just got fucked into next year. But somehow... it fits.

I'm curled up between the three people who are, without question, my everything. My body's sore in all the best ways, the sheets are damp, and despite the chaos, or maybe because of it, I've never felt more whole.

This love isn't fragile. It's fierce. It's honest, and it's loud. It's built from bruised lips and whispered words of adoration, along with the kind of trust that only comes from being fully seen and chosen anyway.

We'll fight, tease, and keep each other on edge, but we'll also keep choosing this over and over again every Christmas morning and every day in between.

Because this is ours, this is home, and this is our forever.

EPILOGUE
ROMAN

It's been two years, and sitting around eating breakfast with my three people still makes me have to take a minute sometimes—just pause, fork halfway to my mouth, and remind myself this is real, that they're mine. That I get to have this every single day for the rest of my life.

An hour ago, I had my palms pressed flat against the shower wall, Zeke's mouth hot at my ear—telling me how tight I was, how good I felt around his cock, and calling me his good boy like he fucking owned me. Addie was pinned between the tiles and Jasper's chest, her legs locked around his waist as he rocked into her, his thrusts turning her feral. We were close enough that I could feel her breath on my neck, tilt my head, and drag my mouth along her shoulder while Jasper reached blindly for my hand and laced our fingers together.

There's something so beautiful about giving yourself over and trusting someone else to guide your body until the rest of the world disappears. I'll still pin them down and fuck them raw until there's no question who they belong to, but handing myself over and letting them claim me... it's everything I never knew I was starving for.

Zeke's phone starts to ring, and he stretches across the kitchen island to grab it, his brows drawing together before answering with a cautious "Hello?"

I've got one hand on Addie's thigh and the other wrapped around a fork, scooping up another bite of the scrambled eggs she made for us this morning. She's in my lap, wearing nothing but one of my T-shirts, and her skin's still warm from the shower we dragged her into before breakfast.

"Damn, angel, this is so good."

She laughs softly, her head resting against my shoulder. "It's literally the same thing I made yesterday."

"And yesterday's eggs were perfect too," Jasper adds from across the island, smirking as he lifts his coffee to his lips.

"Well, I won't be making them tomorrow because I've got a bunch of indie books arriving first thing in the morning, so I'll be at the store early."

"Are you serious?" Zeke's voice punches through the room. He shoots up from his stool, slowly backing away from the counter. The phone's still to his ear, but his other hand moves to his hair, pushing through it roughly. His bare chest rises and falls too fast, and something cold snakes down my spine.

My fork hits the plate.

Addie sits up straighter.

Jasper stops chewing mid-bite.

Someone's hurt.

Something's wrong.

When he ends the call, he just stands there, clutching his phone. I ease Addie from my lap, ready to go to him and hold him up if he needs it.

"What is it?" Jasper asks, worry etched across his face.

But Zeke's face breaks into the biggest smile I've ever seen, and now I'm just fucking confused.

"You're scaring me," Addie says, her brows pinching as she steps closer to him.

"That was..." He blows out a shaky breath while the three of us stare at him. "That was Victoria."

"Victoria from the agency?" I ask.

My heart's going a mile a minute like it already knows, and Zeke gives the smallest nod, his lips parting as if he can't believe it himself.

"What did she say?"

"She called because... we've been matched."

Addie's hands fly to her mouth, and Jasper bolts up and steps forward, both hands buried in his hair as he looks between all of us in shock.

"Wait, wait—matched? Like, matched matched?" he asks.

Zeke nods again, and his voice cracks when he says, "With twin boys."

"You're serious?" Addie asks, and Zeke nods, pulling her into his body.

"They're just over a month old," he murmurs, his lips brushing hers, "and they're ours."

Addie cries into his neck, and Jasper crashes into me, grabbing my face and kissing me hard before pulling back and pressing his forehead to mine.

"We're gonna be dads, Rome."

With his chest pressed against mine, I let myself feel everything—the hope that's been quietly building inside me for months, ever since we first talked about growing our family. The fear that's always been there too, whispering that maybe this would never happen for us. But beneath it all is the overwhelming, all-consuming love I have for Zeke, Addie, and Jasper.

"This is really happening," he says, and his voice cracks just enough to make my throat burn.

"Yeah, it is." I close my eyes and breathe him in before I pull back and turn to Addie.

I wrap her up from behind and press my lips to the top of her head before leaning in and catching Zeke's jaw with my lips.

"You're going to be the most amazing mom," I whisper in her ear, feeling her melt into us.

Jasper's wiping at his eyes, Zeke still has his arms locked around Addie like he'll never let go, and I'm just standing here in awe of the life we've built.

"How long until we can bring them home?" I ask.

"A month, maybe two," Zeke answers, and the four of us just stand there, wrapped up in each other, as the full weight of it settles in—*our whole world is about to change.*

"God, I'm going to be even more outnumbered." Addie sniffles, laughing through her tears. "I can't wait to see them in their little jerseys when I bring them to your games."

Two sons cheering us on with their beautiful mom—yeah, I can definitely get used to that picture. Tiny hands clapping from the stands, Addie pointing us out on the ice and teaching them which numbers to look for as we skate by. The thought of it makes my chest tight with something I can't even name, but I want every second of it.

I look at the three people I'd walk through fire for, and I still can't believe we're about to add to this love, making space for two tiny heartbeats that already belong to us.

Not born of our blood but meant for us all the same.

Five hearts.

DECKED, WRECKED AND PUCKED

Five pieces of my soul.

And every single one owns me in a way I never want back.

THE END

AFTERWORD

If you enjoyed this book, it would mean the world to me if you considered leaving a review.

Reviews are such an important part of helping indie authors like me reach new readers, and every single one makes a difference. Whether it's on Amazon, Goodreads, or even just a few words on social media (whatever you feel comfortable with), I'm endlessly grateful for your support.

ALSO BY LEA ROSE

Rosewood Falls

Where We Burn

The Broken Devotion Duet

Velvet Thorns

Poison Petals - Coming March 1st 2026

Breaking the Rules

Until We Meet Again

After All This Time

Standalones

His For Christmas

ACKNOWLEDGMENTS

Thank you so much for reading Decked, Wrecked and Pucked. Honestly, without you picking up my books and taking a chance on me, I wouldn't get to live this little indie author life, and I'm so grateful for it.

This one was spicyyy, right? I fell hard for those boys and ugh, the way they loved... *swoon*. It was my first why choose, and I had the best time writing it.

To my little family, who were worried about me before this release as I drove myself straight into exhaustion—thank you for letting me power through, and for allowing Mama to rest the second it was done.

To Marie and Holly, who fell for these men right alongside me —I'm sorry you've had to share them now. I know you were protective, but thank you for loving them with me.

To my street team, you already know how much I love you. I genuinely wouldn't know what to do without any of you.

And to every reader and ARC reader who keeps showing up, trusting me, and shouting about my books, thank you. I'm so grateful for you.

ABOUT THE AUTHOR

Lea Rose is a contemporary romance author who writes about strong women and men who'd drop to their knees for them. She loves a good slow burn with a twist of angst or a fast burn that explodes with chemistry—either way, readers can always expect a guaranteed happy ever after.

Lea lives in a small village in the UK with her husband and four children, and when she's not lost in her writing, you can find her curled up with a cup of tea, powering through her never-ending TBR pile.

Connect with Lea on Instagram: @authorlearose
Website: learoseauthor.co.uk

Printed in Dunstable, United Kingdom